D0733446

THE FORMER ASSASSIN

by
Nikki Stern

Ruthenia
Press

445 Sayre Drive
Princeton, NJ 08540
rutheniapress@gmail.com

ISBN: 978-0-9995487-0-7
LCCN: 2017916735

Library of Congress Cataloging-in-Publication Data is on file with the Library of Congress.

Acknowledgements

Heartfelt appreciation to the talented Diana Ani Stokely for design services above and beyond.

Shout-out to the talented writers in my Facebook hive mind, whose input and support means so much: Lezlie, Amy, Anne, Joan, Diana, Becky, Drema, and Connie.

Thanks to the fine people at the Association of Independent Authors, whose collective wisdom and indomitable spirit lift up authors everywhere.

As always, infinite gratitude to sister Deborah for her unwavering confidence in my ability to tell a tale and spin a story. Her invaluable input makes this book possible.

PART ONE

Chapter One

Today is not a good day to die.

No day is, not really. We humans are hard-wired to survive. By most standards, though, this morning is exceptional. The weather is balmy, even for May. The fierce winds that often pound the Welsh coastline have remained offshore. Purple heather blankets the emerald cliffs that encircle Bristol Bay. Small breakers gently lap the shoreline and wash the sand clean of debris. The water sparkles in the sunlight. Shades of azure and aquamarine yield to cyan and lapis further out. In the distance, the sea meets a cerulean sky just where the earth curves. No slate clouds gather at the horizon. All is calm.

Nothing suggested that today I would find myself on a bench in one of the most breathtaking spots in the world with a gun to my head, held by a predator who speaks just two words: "Don't move."

Not that the sea would have volunteered a warning. When it comes to human concerns, it can be a withholding bitch. That's what Brian would have said. A sea-going man, he described the ocean as a kind of temptress: a teasing, unpredictable, mysterious, sexy, seductive sort, all surges and curves and hidden treasures. I've never looked at nature that way. To me, neither earth, sky, nor water are particularly interested in either our needs or our fears.

I sigh.

"I said, don't move."

To add emphasis to his orders, the demanding speaker pushes the barrel more firmly against my ear. No, two barrels, which tells me he's holding an AF2011a1. I'm impressed. The pistol is new. The first double-barreled .45

ever made, it was released at the beginning of 2011, just a few months ago. As a deterrent, it's overkill. Still, it's an effective way to make a point. I should feel flattered my assailant thinks me worthy of such a weapon. Then again, the man he works for is prone to flamboyant gestures.

My eyes wander to my hands. Despite careful grooming, they look worn. These hands have stroked a loved one's cheek, held a newborn, signed contracts, dug in the dirt, and caused the deaths of more people than I care to remember. That last thought makes me flinch. This in turn triggers a movement near my shoulder. I hold my breath, waiting for a reaction. Nothing. I exhale.

My gunman (I'm already feeling possessive) stands just out of my sightline. He's alone; that much I can tell. The acrid smell of his sweat mixes with the salt air. I cut my eyes hard to the right and catch a glimpse of him. He's young, perhaps twenty-two, average height but well-muscled. He's outfitted in the typical mercenary uniform of tight black leather jacket, worn jeans, and thick-soled shoes. He speaks with a heavy dialect, most likely Slavic. I can make myself understood in several Eastern European languages. I can't tell if he speaks more than a few words of English. Not that we'll be having a conversation.

It's impossible to know how long we'll be here. We seem to be waiting for something. I'm not going to be able to hold still for much longer. The gun barrel is giving me a headache. Something somewhere on my body itches. In order to even shift my weight, I'll need to establish some sort of rapport with the triggerman. What simple gesture could I make, some small sign to communicate that, yes, we're on the same page? A nod of the head or a thumb and forefinger pressed together (got it) might reassure him. A simple "okay" could convince him I know who's calling the shots, so to speak.

I'm making jokes. That's a good thing, isn't it? Humor in time of peril?

I settle for palms forward, the universal sign for "stop" or "I surrender." Apparently, this doesn't get the message across. The man with the gun thumps the side of my head.

"What did I tell you?"

Don't move, I answer silently. I get it.

I project calm, although I am anything but. It takes everything I have not to curse him and his boss and, while I'm at it, my own past indiscretions. Everyone makes choices, and choices have consequences. Dwelling in the past is chancy, though. Regret makes you sloppy. There's no room for error when life is at stake. I remind myself I've been in dire situations many times before.

The gunman comes to stand in front of me, blocking my view. His right hand lightly roams my body, searching for weapons he knows I don't have. He's already done this. I suspect he takes a perverse pleasure in reminding me I'm apparently defenseless. Or maybe he's received his own set of instructions; he seems to be wearing an ear bud. I hold my tongue. He knows I'm unarmed. I know he's left-handed, a useful piece of information I file near the front of my brain.

He concludes his search and looks me up and down as if I were past my expiration date. "So, you are Susan Smith," he says with a faint note of wonderment. "The former assassin." Perhaps he expected something other than a slender, blonde-haired, blue-eyed woman of a certain age dressed in Wellies and a shawl. I appear to be the wife of a prosperous country squire, not a notorious ex-employee.

Suzanne, I want to scream, my name is really Suzanne. And not Smith, either. It was all a charade, a subterfuge, a misunderstanding. What's the use, though? I've lived so many lies wrapped inside other lies, I doubt I even know who I am anymore.

"You are very important to Mr. Kemp," he continues with a shrug. "I wonder why that is. No matter." He makes no attempt to disguise his disdain, yet his interest is palpable.

What would I tell him? "I am important to Victor Kemp. He forced me to work for him for decades. Then I went against his orders, and he decided to have my family murdered. I left, but not without taking back something he'd tried to steal from me. That didn't sit well with him, and here we are."

I might also add that although I blame Victor Kemp for many of my life's heartaches, I bear some responsibility. One impulsive decision and he owned me. Until the day I quit, I answered only to him. I worked only for him. I killed only for him.

I doubt my guard would be shocked at the notion of a female assassin, even a former one. Women nowadays fly drones, drop bombs, hack into intelligence programs, and pummel assailants twice their size and half their age. We have more opportunities than ever to prove we can be as amoral as men, assuming we want to quibble about the morality of killing.

After all these years, I wonder how I managed. I must have murdered more than a hundred people over twenty-five years. I suppose I compartmentalized, just as any CIA operative or drone operator might. When it comes to thinking about either the person who hired you or the person you've been hired to kill, you don't. You employ a kind of tunnel vision. You just do the job. I recognize that as being the transparent excuse of brutal enforcers everywhere. It's not personal; it's professional.

One of Brian's friends, Bill Poplar, was a profiler for the FBI. He described contract killers as high functioning, analytical types, capable of the most elaborate sort of pigeonholing. They're likely to be living a socially acceptable life complete with homes, partners, pets, and even children. Overall, they're pretty much indistinguishable from the rest of the population, except they're of above-average intelligence. That, and they kill for a living.

Bill especially wanted me to understand most contract killers aren't responding to a need to murder. "They aren't necessarily narcissists," he insisted. "Nor are they crazy. They're efficient workers. What most people don't realize is that killers for hire view themselves as people with tasks to do. Morality doesn't factor into their performance."

"So, contract killers aren't really immoral?" I asked.

"You might say they're amoral, although contemporary thinking doesn't see it quite that way. We tend to throw around the word "psychopath" quite a bit. Professional killers likely live by their own version of a moral code. We know they can still function as loving parents or loyal spouses. They might even view lying as unacceptable or cheating as unconscionable."

"They must be hard to profile," I suggested.

"They are." He looked at me, his eyes assessing. "Did you know that a number of profilers now suspect more women might be working as assassins than previously thought? Many psychologists tell us the fairer sex is calmer in stressful situations and steadier under pressure. Unfortunately, there's little in the way of substantive data to support that particular theory."

"Really?" I murmured. "Fascinating."

Calm. Unflinching. Less prone to stress. These are the characteristics profilers and psychologists have ascribed to people like me or the version of me I used to be. It's easy to imagine I'm exactly as cold and unfeeling as those words imply, nothing more than an emotional cypher. Victor might have believed as much. For all I know, the gunman believes it as well.

I sigh again.

"Don't worry," says my captor with ill-concealed pleasure. "It will be over soon enough." I expect him to remind me once again to stay still, but he doesn't bother. And where would I go? I'm pressed into this bench, held down by the weight of the choices I made and the choices that were never mine to make.

I suspect my gunman is bored, but he remains alert. I doubt he expects me to try anything. He nonetheless keeps the gun trained on my right temple, perhaps in deference to my reputation. I admire his discipline.

"Tell me," I begin. "How long have you been working for Victor Kemp?"

"Shut up," he replies, not unkindly. He doesn't seem invested in making conversation as a way to pass the time. He could study his phone, apart from stealing furtive glances, but that would mean he has to take his eyes off me. Something must be telling him it's not a good idea.

"Three years," he says suddenly. "You?"

I answer without moving my head, "I was in his employ for twenty-five years."

"Long time," he says.

That seems to be the end of it. Too bad. I was ready to tell him how Victor and I crossed paths. Serendipity, one might say. I was at the time newly out of the Army, a twenty-two-year-old engineering major at Vanderbilt. I was having a good time, having survived negligent Haight-Ashbury parents and my own brief time on the streets.

THE FORMER ASSASSIN

Would my story impress the young gunman? Probably not. These Eastern Europeans are a hard lot.

Curiosity gets the best of my captor. "How did you meet Mr. Kemp?"

"I shot someone who worked for him."

He moves just within my line of sight, eyebrows raised. I've impressed him.

Chapter Two

Victor Kemp had already created a substantial empire in 1978. Nominally CEO of an energy company, he oversaw an international underworld conglomerate with tentacles in high-stakes gambling, arms trading, sex trafficking, money laundering, bio-weaponry, genetic engineering, cyber-terrorism, and the buying and selling of information. The man could have procured an army, sabotaged a fail-safe system, or overthrown a government. Any number of formidable men were in his pocket or in his debt.

A cosmopolitan man, Kemp retained apartments in New York and Paris, along with a house complete with wife and daughter in London. He kept company with a very attractive Brazilian woman, an international real estate broker by whom he fathered two sons. He was wealthy, but wealth was never more than a means to an end for Victor Kemp. He used it the same way he used intimidation: to accrue power, including the power to purchase people to do his bidding.

I didn't know any of this. I was focused on my studies, content for the first time. I loved university life. A few years older than my classmates, I remained apart from most of them, save for a few carefully chosen liaisons.

While in the service, I'd discovered a talent for marksmanship, but I never expected to make use of it after I discharged. Then a vindictive drug dealer named Rico beat my roommate Greta nearly to death over a missed payment. Maybe if he and his associates hadn't deposited her, bloodied and barely breathing, back in the room we shared, I would have let the authorities handle it. I didn't know her attackers, but I had to assume they knew me. I must have determined they constituted a threat to my well-being. I don't remember my thought process or even if I spent time thinking, which I realize is a little too convenient.

Kemp, on the other hand, never forgot and he never forgave.

What I can say with certainty is that on October 30, two weeks after Greta's beating, I pulled my Remington M-700, a gift from an army buddy, out of my storage locker and headed to Nashville.

According to the news reports, four people in the middle of a thick crowd of patrons outside Tootsie's Orchid Lounge were conducting a drug deal around midnight when the shots were fired. The dealer and his companion went down, one bullet each. The buyers, two college students, ended up traumatized but otherwise unscathed. Precision shooting, the police said. An experienced sniper.

Someone reported spotting a slender figure dressed in a fatigue jacket and carrying a duffle bag. The empty second floor storefront had been swept clean. The detectives had little to go on and even less incentive to focus on the crime. A bad man and his crony were taken off the street; they considered it a blessing in disguise.

The cocaine Rico sold came from a supply line that extended from Nashville to Biloxi to the Bahamas and all the way back to Colombia. By any measure and regardless of what intermediaries stood between, he ultimately worked for the Medellín cartel. His companion, I later learned, had been dispatched by Kemp as a favor to a Southern congressman with ties to the Dixie Mafia. That man's role was to observe and negotiate, if necessary, in order to guarantee no one encroached on anyone else's territory.

A bad man, but not a man who had anything to do with Greta's beating.

It took Kemp four months to find me. No one assumed a female shooter, but Victor Kemp always thought outside the box. Given what I've since learned about him, I'm not surprised he located me in the days before computers, cameras, or digitized data. The search likely required patience, persistence, personnel, and plenty of money. He had all of those.

He didn't send men to threaten me. He simply called one evening and invited me to dinner. When I demurred, he pointed out that a woman with the ability to hit not one but two targets in a crowd at night must be much sought after—or soon would be.

We met in Nashville on a warm and windy March evening. I wore a black stretch sheath, the only dress I owned, added a cheap locket, and pulled a comb through my hair. I can't recall where we ate. Perhaps on the same block where I fired the shots that defined my future. That would have appealed to Kemp's sensibilities. I remember two men standing at the door with not so subtle bulges under their boxy jackets.

The food might have been delicious; I know it was expensive. My appetite failed me. I would never learn to enjoy a meal with Victor Kemp, and I would have occasion to endure many of those.

When he stood to greet me, I saw a short but powerfully built man in his late thirties, his wrestler's body encased in a well-tailored suit. Pale blue shirt, relatively subdued tie for the times. Wide soft hand with blunt fingers tempered by manicured nails. He wore his sable hair fashionably long. His face was broad and flat below thick brows and a much-broken nose. He would always bear the trace of a shadow, though he was nominally clean-shaven and fastidious about grooming.

His most arresting feature was a pair of eyes the color of a Siberian lake in winter.

He wasn't conventionally handsome, although he radiated a feral sort of masculinity. I suspect any number of women and even some men found him appealing. I was never one of them. To me, he came across as a barely tamed monster in a suit.

We made small talk about the advantages of a higher education, especially at a prestigious university like Vanderbilt. He knew I was a few years older than my classmates, that my scholarship came courtesy of the Army, that I'd spent two years stationed in Berlin. He seemed to know a lot about me.

He smiled at one point, if you can call what he offered a smile. It was more a display of large bright teeth that looked as if they'd been sharpened.

"Miss Smith. May I call you Susan?"

I raised my shoulders. It was the name I'd adopted after I'd been put out on the street by my mother when I was fifteen.

"Susan Smith." He spoke like a purring cat. "What an interesting name. Very plain yet very American."

"Blame Mom," I said. And instantly regretted those words.

"Of course, your mother. Although normally the father would bear some responsibility as well. Where did you say you grew up?"

"I didn't say." I pulled my cheap shawl tightly around my shoulders. It felt as if the temperature had dropped several degrees. I cleared my throat. "Mr. Kemp, what can I do for you?"

"A no-nonsense woman of business. Very well, then." His smile evaporated.

"You killed an employee of mine, Miss Smith. I don't care about your foolish roommate with the bad habit or the dealer who had her beaten nearly to death. I don't even care about my man, who had unrelated business with the dealer and who died because some college girl with a rifle decided to become a vigilante."

I had an argument ready. I opened my mouth to speak, but he held up his hand. It was a gesture I would come to know well.

"You will let me finish," he said. "I hold all the cards here."

He made his proposal, which amounted to a blueprint for how I would live going forward. Immediately upon graduation, he informed me, I would start work in his New York office. My title would be corporate security manager. My primary task would be to keep his various subsidiaries safe from espionage. Since I was already up to speed on threat assessment, thanks to my Army training, he had every confidence in me. He could guarantee substantial bonuses. The company would provide me with a rent-free apartment in a nice neighborhood right in Manhattan.

"Perfect for a single woman." He winked.

In addition to my legitimate job, he told me, I would moonlight as his assassin. I'd eliminate, remove, or discharge ("use any euphemism you like") those individuals he and his associates deemed a hazard to their business ventures or alliances. My assignments would be sprinkled throughout the calendar year, dovetailing whenever possible with legitimate meetings I took with clients. Every target would be outside the city, often abroad. My skills as a long-distance marksman would almost always suffice. Almost always. Occasionally, close-up work would be required. I would be trained so as to fill in any gaps. I would learn to overcome any inhibitions I had.

"You don't seem to have a problem with killing at a distance. That will be your primary task, although you won't always have that option, I'm sorry to say."

I sat in stunned silence.

"I understand you learned Russian as well as a smattering of German. Excellent. We'll add another language. Probably Farsi or Arabic. Later on, perhaps Chinese. I have a highly qualified instructor in mind."

He cast his frost-colored eyes over my shabby outfit and shook his head.

"You'll require a complete makeover to appear as a successful business person. Really, what woman wouldn't welcome that?"

Kemp paused to take several hearty bites while I pushed my food around my plate. He took a long draught of his Margaux.

"So, Miss Smith, tell me. Do you accept my offer?"

I swallowed. "Do I have a choice?"

He dabbed almost daintily at the corner of his mouth. Then he fixed me with his arctic stare.

"You really don't."

Nine months later, I graduated mid-year. In January of 1980, I began my new life.

My position near upper management would have appeared quite an accomplishment for a woman in the 1980s and '90s. I built on what I already knew about secrets and risks and created protocols that impressed my coworkers. Once or twice a month, I handled the "other" work. I went where I was told and did what I was designed by training and temperament to do. At least that's what I convinced myself.

I had no supervisor. I reported directly to Victor. If anyone within the legitimate organization found this odd, they never said. I must have been the only mid-level manager with direct access to the boss. In twenty-five years, I never received a promotion, never became a senior officer or even a director.

As a long-range assassin, I still faced risk. I planned every detail, reviewed every action, and tried to account for every potential glitch with the help of specialists Victor assigned to me. There were never any guarantees. I nearly got caught a couple of times. Usually I managed to extricate myself without causing further harm. Usually, but not always.

I hated the rare close-up assignments; Victor knew it. No doubt he had other resources, other contractors better equipped and less squeamish. He was willing nonetheless to risk his high-value specialist. I think it was his way of exerting control over me.

As for whom I murdered, I must have decided they were bad people. Who else would populate that world? Let's be honest, though. Most people would conclude my actions were immoral. I deprived someone of a father, a son, a lover, or a friend. My observations as to their fitness to live are irrelevant. If anything, they may reflect my shortcomings as a human being.

I did refuse a job once. Something in my research led me to doubt the victim's guilt even in Victor's morally relative universe. I said nothing about my reservations; I simply invented some physical issue. If my boss privately questioned my action, he never told me. Perhaps he believed I'd never willfully take such a chance.

Did the intended victim die? I'm certain he did. Not by my hand, though.

THE FORMER ASSASSIN

As promised, the company paid for both my apartment and wardrobe. The one-bedroom, located in a doorman building on the East Side, came fully furnished and tastefully, if impersonally, decorated. Kemp also sent me to a stylist named Dmitri. The man shopped for me and even custom-designed a few outfits. He helped me with hair and makeup. We got along well. We never discussed my work.

Dressing up helped me feel as if I were playing a part, and that may have shielded me from sinking into the moral abyss. I let myself believe I was simply a career-oriented single woman. Other times I pictured myself as the fictional heroine of a spy novel. Or I pretended to be an employee of the CIA, something I'd actually considered as a career choice. At the same time, I learned to become the other characters I occasionally needed to impersonate.

When the reality of my double life began to intrude, I willed my mind to go blank. I tried meditation, although I never became good at it. I perfected *ujjayi*, a yoga technique that teaches the practitioner to slow her breathing. At first, I intended it as an exercise designed to banish my pervasive anxiety. Instead, I perfected an ancient practice popular among peace-loving yogis to prepare for a kill shot.

I never slept with Victor Kemp. The very thought makes my skin crawl. Fortunately, he didn't believe in mixing business and pleasure. I dated appropriate and eligible men he always prescreened and sometimes preselected. I even became engaged to one of them, which amused my employer no end. He had instructed me to live my life as a modern woman, someone who could juggle my work and social lives. Love was not to enter into it. On that point, he and I agreed. Until we didn't.

I can't say whether I had a choice in what happened next. The heart always seems to have a mind of its own. I let my heart persuade me that love and marriage and even a family were all possible. That despite my unresolved past and encumbered present, I might have a normal life.

I should have known better. Assassins don't get happy endings, even retired ones.

Chapter Three

I've stopped talking. Or maybe I've stopped thinking. At any rate, my throat closes. The pain of loss is like a physical blow, but I don't move.

The gunman has shifted his position. He's lost interest in my sad tale.

I stare out at the water, willing myself to breathe as long as I'm still able. For five years, I've lived on this remote coastline. Despite the constant threat of discovery, I've known moments of peace and even joy. Today might have been one of those occasions. Except for this gunman and his employer, the man who tried and failed to control my life.

All because I fell in love.

~

Brian Foster. Who could have seen it coming? Not my mother, who probably believed me incapable of any feelings. Not Victor, whose comprehension of passion's power has always been incomplete. He knows how to manipulate human emotion in order to prey upon his subordinates' weaknesses or vanquish his enemies. I doubt his ability extends to recognizing love in all its raw glory.

And not me, for whom such feelings have always carried too much risk.

Had I been younger, I might have understood how I could develop a crush on my teacher. As an adult, I considered myself immune to any such adolescent impulses. When I first encountered the language teacher Kemp hired for me, I was nearly twenty-eight. I'd been working for Kemp for four years. I was a jaded woman of the world, or so I thought.

If I expected a fussy sort in a bowtie, I was in for a surprise. A tall, broad-shouldered man awaited me in the conference room. He looked like the type who worked outdoors. I noticed his tousled red hair, bright green eyes, and big hands. A lopsided grin kept him from being model-perfect. It didn't matter. He combined masculinity with an appealing boyish quality.

I tried to ignore the heat that rose in my body, ascribing it to a weird hormonal surge. Slow breathing didn't work and neither did thinking of the luckless man who'd been recruited to be my latest boyfriend. I can guarantee Arabic studies weren't on my mind. I'm amazed I ever managed to learn enough to carry on a conversation.

Belgian-born and Cambridge-educated, Brian Matthew Foster left a career in the Navy to start a consulting business after his father was killed in a car accident. He was fluent in seven languages and conversant in eight others. His talents as both instructor and meeting facilitator were much in demand; he marketed exclusively to high-end international corporations. His widowed mother resided in Bruges; his sister Juliette lived in Brussels with her banker husband and twin boys.

Brian maintained an apartment in London, although he was on the road most of the year. In his mid-thirties, he'd never married. He had little trouble attracting beautiful women, I soon learned.

Or so Victor Kemp told me. No surprise my employer knew so much about his language consultant. Any hire would be subject to his stringent vetting process. It did occur to me to wonder why he chose to fill me in about a short-term instructor. One never asked, though. Kemp had his own reasons and kept them close.

He couldn't have known how Brian would affect me, akin to lust at first sight. I'd never experienced anything comparable. The only thing that kept me from fleeing the room in embarrassment was that Brian looked as if he'd been hit by lightning. Mutual attraction. We could have powered a mid-sized city with the charge that ran between us.

Even after we'd been together awhile, I denied ever being pulled to him so forcefully.

"You might have sparked a bit of interest. You're tolerably good-looking. I was mostly attracted to your mind, however. And your wit."

He laughed, something he did with ease and frequency.

"Really? I don't know whether to be flattered or insulted. You must be either blinded by love or in denial. Or both. I'm much more than tolerably good-looking, as my mother will tell you. Although I'm not in the least surprised that you recognize how truly clever I am. I've my Irish great-grandmother to thank for that."

We went to bed. The physical pull couldn't be ignored. I told myself it would be a one-time-only experience and knew I couldn't keep that promise. At first, I put it down to lust. The need went beyond that, though. Brian reached into me. His desire filled me, suffusing parts of my being that had been dormant for years. To my surprise, something about me answered a longing on his part as well.

Our affair went on for more than half a year. We arranged to meet in odd little corners of the city far from work. We even met abroad from time to time. My job performance didn't seem to suffer. In retrospect, however, I wasn't as alert as I might have been. For instance, I refused to ask myself how Brian found it so easy to get to Munich, Madrid, or wherever I happened to be.

My biggest fear was that the man I worked for would find out about the man I loved, would sniff out our connection like an animal on the hunt. Every encounter mixed anticipation with apprehension. I often felt physically ill. Simply passing Brian in the corridor set off a tidal wave of emotion. Even in those pre-cellphone days, before the ubiquity of cameras on street corners and buildings, I felt exposed. What did Kemp suspect? What did he know? Brian couldn't have understood how truly vulnerable I felt. He might not have understood how devious my employer could be. Not the way I did.

I shouldn't have been surprised to discover what Kemp really expected of me. Yet he caught me off-guard.

"How are you feeling, Susan? You're looking a little thin."

We sat in his office one afternoon drinking the strong tea he favored. It was a ritual I could not avoid when he was in New York. At that point, I'd been studying with Brian for nine months and sleeping with him for five.

Victor Kemp's concern for my well-being didn't fool me. He wanted something.

"I'm fine. Working hard."

"You've been studying hard as well. Tell me, what do you think of your teacher?"

"He's a good instructor."

Kemp raised an eyebrow. "Really?"

"What do you want me to say, Victor? He's good-looking and sort of charismatic if you like that type." I couldn't meet his eyes, so I preoccupied myself with my tea.

"I want you to get close to him."

I choked and flushed at the same time.

"Hot. The tea." I cleared my throat. "What exactly do you mean by close?"

"Physically and emotionally close, Susan. Get under his skin. Get into his bed. Get into his heart. I don't care how you do it."

I didn't bother to hide my surprise. "Victor, I'm not a prude, but that does seem to be above and beyond the call of duty."

He waved away my comment as if it were an annoying gnat.

I tried again.

"My lessons must be coming to an end soon. It's been nearly a year. What would I use as an excuse to see him?" As if I needed one, I thought, and wondered if my face had reddened again.

"We'll find some pretense to continue the lessons. Perhaps we'll add another language."

"I'm still confused. What exactly am I looking for?"

Victor tilted his head, a gesture more Gaelic than Russian.

"I think the professor is something more than a talented teacher who charges his international clientele an arm and a leg. He's hiding something. Maybe it's personal; maybe it's professional. I want to find out what our friend is keeping from us."

He grinned, revealing those frightening teeth.

"I should say, I want you to find out. Perhaps he's a corporate spy. Perhaps he's something more. It should be easy for you to discover. So. You will get to know him, and you will tell me what he tells you. I will decide what is valuable and how I wish to proceed."

What did Victor know? What wasn't he telling me? I started to object. Victor's grin disappeared.

"You will do this, Susan. Is that clear?"
I knew I was in no position to refuse.

Chapter Four

I move; I can't help it. The gunman is almost relieved. He's got another excuse to scold or yell or take some sort of action. Anything to relieve the tedium.

We're both brought up by an insistent roar. The sound of a boat has reached us, shattering the calm like a fist through a window. Its engine is enhanced for speed and power. The boat moves aggressively, bow thrust out of the water. There's nothing restrained about the vehicle. Whoever chose it wants to make his presence known.

My companion grins and points.

"There's Mr. Kemp now. He's eager to do this in person."

I don't need to ask what "this" is. Discovery is not Kemp's endgame, only death.

Minutes pass. I'm not sure how many. Three? Five? The henchman tracks the speedboat, shading his eyes even though he's wearing those stupid mirrored sunglasses favored by muscled hitmen everywhere. He might be dreaming of a rich payday or an end to this nonsense that requires him to hold a gun to the head of a harmless-looking older woman. Maybe he's a sadist (Kemp has no shortage of those in his employ), and he's looking forward to a grisly show, one in which he might even get to participate.

I can make out five separate figures on the boat, including one who is both shorter and broader than the others. His improbably brown hair barely moves in the breeze. Kemp must be seventy by now, but he appears unchanged even at this distance.

Unchanged, unrepentant, and always one step ahead. He knew how ill-advised my choice of lover would prove to be long before I ever learned the truth.

~

Bad enough I was expected to spy on Brian. My employer's veiled suggestions now caused me to doubt my lover. Was he keeping something from me? How would I know? Could I learn his truth without his ever learning mine?

Several weeks into my newly complicated life, I was sent to Bombay. Brian arranged to work with a corporate client at the same time, a situation I might at one time have considered lucky but now found to be suspicious. The stifling July heat couldn't mask the jittery unease that enveloped the city. Not a month earlier, Air India Flight 192 had exploded on a transatlantic journey from Delhi to Montreal via London. Intelligence pointed to Sikh militants. Three hundred of the dead passengers were Canadian, prompting official protests from that country. While we were in India, a bomb intended for another Air India flight went off at Tokyo's Narita International Airport. The Indian government was in an uproar, the country on edge.

As usual, I had two tasks to perform. My scheduled meeting was a cover for my real business. Kemp's people had been using the services of a lower-level district administrator in order to get inside information on board members Kemp intended to blackmail. They discovered the man had also accepted money from a local criminal organization for the same purpose. His dossier hinted at other perversions. None of those warranted action. No, the singular sin in my employer's mind was disloyalty. While

Kemp had no intention of taking on the crooks that caused the conflict of interest, he wanted to send a message. My target was the greedy man playing both sides against the middle.

Brian and I booked adjoining rooms at the Taj Mahal Palace, a grand old establishment with a world-class collection of artifacts amassed over more than half a century. They were connected by a door he arranged to leave open. The space was obscenely luxurious. Its magic was lost on me. I was struggling under the weight of too many secrets.

I'd been given one of those close-up assignments I both feared and detested. It seemed the sheer number of people filling the streets of Bombay made a long-distance kill too difficult. I'd have to do a hit and run. I think Kemp gave me these jobs just to see how I'd do. No, that's not it; he knew I'd succeed. He assigned them to me because he knew they made me unhappy. He wanted to remind me he ran every aspect of my life. I wasn't simply an assassin; I was his assassin.

I argued forcefully against using a knife. I was given a syringe. I didn't ask what it contained. On the appointed day, I walked head down in front of a government building at lunchtime. I'd dressed in a traditional sari and veil and held the hypodermic hidden in one hand. I'd practiced the routine in my head for hours. Brush past the target as he reaches the sidewalk. Pretend to stumble into him. Push the needle straight into his heart. Empty the syringe before pulling it out. Get away quickly.

It didn't quite work as planned. Instead of clutching his chest, the victim surprised me by grabbing my wrist. Before I had a chance to yank my arm back, he fell to his knees and then backwards, nearly pulling me on top of him. The scrum of office workers should have provided adequate cover, assuming I wouldn't end up straddling a dying man.

I spoke in Hindi. "Please help this gentleman!" The bureaucrats, businessmen, and passersby moved back. Not the reaction I wanted. I tried again in English. "He needs assistance!"

A young man in business attire stepped in and others followed suit, creating a tight circle. I pulled myself free of the man's death grip and scurried away, back hunched and knees bent. I didn't dare stand up straight until I'd put some distance between us. I looked back once to see a well-dressed middle-aged man with a black bag rush over. He issued commands in three languages.

"Excuse me. Step aside. I'm a doctor. Let me through."

Eyes lowered, I continued to walk as slowly as I dared to the hotel. I'd had close calls before. None had affected me quite like this one. I splashed water on my face, checked myself for blood (there was none), and hurriedly changed. Back on the street again, I disposed of my disguise and went to the meeting I'd arranged with an executive management team. How I got through the afternoon without fainting I can't imagine. I remember clasping my hands together so no one would notice they were shaking.

As far as the home office was concerned, the trip had been productive. The message waiting for me at the Taj's front desk read, "Well done. Victor."

At the hotel bar, I knocked back two Scotches, neat. Then I sat with a glass of tonic water in one of the lounge chairs with a view to the entrance. Brian arrived a little later without seeing me. I waited until he picked up the keys and headed upstairs, allowed several minutes to pass, and followed.

I heard the shower running when I came in. Kicking off my shoes, I threw myself on the bed with an arm flung across my face. Though I'd tried to slip in unnoticed, nothing got past Brian. The water stopped. He called through the door to inquire about my day. We swapped our short stories about horrific clients. Apparently satisfied, he went back to his business while I questioned my ability to neatly pack away this latest incident.

A couple of minutes later, he walked out of the bathroom, a towel at his waist. He regarded me with sympathy.

"You had a particularly rough time, didn't you?"

I sat up and pasted on a smile. "You know how it goes in my world . . ." I let the words float away. Maybe Brian would take the hint.

"It must be hard to work for Victor Kemp."

It wasn't what he said. He knew I worked for Kemp; he'd been hired by the man, for heaven's sake. It was how he said it that set off the flashing red lights and the whooping alarm sounds in my head. Warning: get out now! I pretended a nonchalance I didn't feel.

"It's not always easy."

"Maybe it's time we talked about a few things. Let me dry off and get into some clothes. Stay right where you are."

Brian turned back into the bathroom without closing the door. Steam filled the bedroom. I fell back, pinned to the bed like the heroine in a horror movie. Something was coming, something very bad, and I couldn't do anything to stop it.

When my lover emerged with his pants on, his blue chambray shirt half buttoned, I hadn't shifted so much as a muscle. After a couple of seconds of awkward silence, he walked over, took me by the arms, and pulled me to a sitting position. Then he stepped all the way across the room and began talking.

As my employer suspected, Brian had indeed been hiding something—the fact that he worked for MI6, Britain's Secret Intelligence Service. He'd been on loan for years to an Interpol task force assigned specifically to bring down one of the largest global criminal enterprises the agency had ever encountered, the one run by none other than Victor Kemp. My employer's activities made him a high-value target. His connections with so many well-placed people made him a difficult one on which to hang any charges. Brian became a roving inside man. He contracted with Kemp's partners, allies, and subsidiaries, collecting what insight and information he could before moving on. This latest assignment had put him directly into Kemp's headquarters and into my life.

Somewhere in the middle of his revealing speech, it occurred to me that I was safe. No one at SIS, including Brian, apparently suspected me of anything. I was simply another well-placed lead, someone who might be persuaded to help identify suspicious activities behind the legitimate-looking ventures. Brian was supposed to add extra incentive by being his charmingly persuasive self.

"I couldn't tell you before now. I didn't want to frighten you." Brian walked back to the bed and looked down at me. "I didn't want to fall in love with you, either. Ah, well. No turning back now, is there?"

I stood up too quickly and felt lightheaded. Brian reached for me. I folded my arms across my chest and looked down. My mind went into overdrive trying to sort out the truths from the lies. I thought I might sink into the floor or explode like one of those inflatable dolls. He watched me silently, waiting for me to look up. I did. In his eyes, I saw compassion and yes, love. Then, to his surprise and mine, I burst into tears.

I can't remember ever crying. Not as a baby or a young girl, not when I was hurt, not when my father was in the midst of a drug-fueled rant or when I learned he died, not when I was molested and then kicked out of the house. Not even when Victor Kemp took control of my life. Now I wept as if to make up for a decades-old drought. I gulped, gasped, bawled, and yelped like a wounded animal.

To Brian's great credit, he said nothing. He took me in his arms and rocked me.

When the worst of my outburst had passed, I took a deep breath and said, "My turn."

Brian had already heard quite a bit about my lonely childhood. He knew I was the daughter of self-involved parents stranded between the Beat and Flower Power generations. I'd told him my birth name was Suzanne Brooks and that my parents, Mo and Lisette, had never married. I'd even shared a few of the more horrifying examples of their monumental neglect, which I tried to spin as amusing life lessons.

Now I filled him in on the rest of it. He learned how and when I went from university student to security manager and Victor Kemp's handpicked on-call killer. That last bit of information was harder for me to put on the table than all the fictions I'd invented up to that point.

"So," Brian said when I'd finished. "Victor Kemp's assassin."

As emotionally drained as I was, I couldn't protest or come up with a phrase that would turn my profession into a kinder, gentler version of itself.

He pulled back and looked me in the face, his green eyes full. "Suzanne," he said, "this may be hard to believe, but what you've told me doesn't change how I feel about you."

In that moment, I became his, always and forever.

We left Bombay a half-day early. We made a stop in Brussels and traveled to Bruges. There we were married in a tiny chapel in front of his mother, his sister, her husband, and their two small boys. We spent much of our twelve-hour honeymoon trying to figure out how we would beat Victor Kemp.

I still had one more surprise to share with Brian: I was three-and-a-half months pregnant.

Chapter Five

If there was no possible way to hide my pregnancy, neither could I take the chance Kemp might discover the identity of the father. I told him the baby was the parting gift of someone who broke up with me because I wouldn't abort. Though he seemed surprised, he didn't argue with my decision to keep the child.

"Odd. I never thought of you as a mother. Oh, well. I imagine we'll have to keep you more or less out of harm's way until you deliver." Initially, his concern surprised me, until I realized he was simply being practical. Between physical and emotional changes, he didn't want to take any chances.

He didn't refer to my condition again.

Brian took the opportunity to bow out as my instructor. He explained to Kemp he had other clients and prior commitments. He even noted I seemed too occupied to focus on my studies, a ploy I found breathtaking in its audaciousness. I'm glad I didn't hear their exchange. I would have been seized by a fit of hysterical laughing.

During my pregnancy, I continued to work for both sides of the business. I developed security plans. I traveled as required to meet clients. Sometimes I served as a courier, carrying papers or other small items on behalf of Kemp's underworld interests. I didn't have to refuse any elimination work; I wasn't given any.

I still hoped to be on the road as close to my due date as possible, have the baby abroad, report it stillborn, and send the child to live with Brian's mother for a year. The separation would be hard on all of us, but I'd be occupied.

I'd have my work and my new assignment on behalf of Brian's Interpol team.

Brian, my husband! The thought sent shivers up and down my spine.

All that preparation ended up wasted. I nearly had the baby in the back of a taxicab on Christmas Eve after a particularly grueling trip. It was a false labor, but I stayed home after that. The holidays provided a convenient excuse. Brian, who had arranged for me to deliver at a private hospital, got in just after Christmas. On December 31, 1985, a healthy baby boy we named Michael arrived just about on time. The doctor joked about our little tax deduction. Would that our lives had been that simple.

In the absence of GPS, Kemp couldn't easily track me. He wouldn't know whether I was suffering through a pregnancy gone wrong or delivering my firstborn son not fifteen blocks from the office. He had spies, of course. So did we, which is how we knew he was in London at the time. He likely relied on local underlings who weren't expending much effort monitoring the activities of a pregnant security manager, even if they suspected I worked in another capacity.

We left the hospital after three days and moved to my apartment. There we lived as a family for another week and a half. Brian took care of everything. Someone brought food. Someone else kept a lookout and collected my mail, mostly sympathy cards from coworkers who couldn't have known how happy I was. My husband occasionally slipped out. I stayed where I was with the new man in my life.

My employer called once and left a message on my answering machine absolving me of any need to phone him back. At the end of the ten-day period, Brian took little Michael out of my arms and across the Atlantic to his grandmother while I went back to work and tried to push motherhood into its own hidden compartment. The feeling was nothing short of awful. My body ached. My heart ached.

A year passed, an entire year, in which I lived my multiple lives as corporate consultant on security issues, paid assassin, spy for Interpol, and secret wife and mother. Brian had already decided he would tell only one person at M16 what I really did for Victor Kemp. Even that presented a risk.

Brian's decision brought up another problem I faced, exacerbated no doubt by fluctuating hormones and my new role as a mother. I was panicked at the thought of resuming my work as Kemp's killer.

"What if one of my targets turns out to be a double agent or someone working undercover for Interpol?"

I'd never allowed myself to think in those terms, never considered that the mark wasn't in some way responsible for being in my sightlines. It was a way of maintaining my equilibrium; blame the victim. Moral deficiency or survival technique, it didn't used to matter. Now it did.

"It's very unlikely that would happen, darling. Besides, you're only going to be at this another year or so. Then we'll pull you out and go somewhere as far away from Victor Kemp as possible."

My employer inquired solicitously about my health immediately upon my return, then went back to being his usual brusque self. If he suspected something was different about me, he never let on. Perhaps he assumed any changes were temporary, owing to typical female challenges. Not that he possessed anything remotely resembling empathy. I was simply a prized asset, and he wanted me working at capacity.

He gave me another three weeks of deskwork and sent me to a meeting in Zurich. My sorrow trailed me everywhere like a shadow.

"She lost her child," I heard colleagues whispering. Indeed, I had.

Everything returned to normal, meaning I went back to playing the leading role in a production whose ending I couldn't foresee. I worked diligently and kept social interactions to a minimum. Brian and Michael commanded my emotional reserves, even in absentia. At that, I had to keep thoughts about them in their own inviolate space if we hoped to survive.

In early March of 1987, I made my way from London, where I'd gone on business, to Brussels for a belated birthday celebration for Michael. Under the watchful eyes of a few family friends, a group of one-year-olds frolicked in late-winter sun, along with Michael's two older cousins. I couldn't take my eyes off my petit chou or sweetheart, as his grandmère called him. He looked just like his father, except his hair was more umber than red. He had my mother's blue eyes. Like Brian, he laughed easily and displayed endless curiosity about the world around him. He appeared fearless. I wanted him to stay that way.

Brian took me aside during the birthday party. "I need to move *Mamà* and Michael. They're not safe here."

It was as if a hand—five blunt fingers topped by beautifully manicured nails—had reached inside my chest to squeeze my heart.

"Victor knows." I stated this as fact. Brian's curt nod made me catch my breath.

"I don't care what it takes to keep them safe—to keep you safe. Do it."

He promised to call me in exactly two weeks. When the date came and went and I didn't hear from him, I willed myself to remain calm. I could do calm, I reasoned. Two more days passed. I called Brian. A recorded message politely informed me the number was no longer in service.

Five more days went by. Nothing.

One week after the call that didn't take place, Kemp invited me out to lunch. It was a lovely New York day, just a hint of spring in the air. Over yet another expensive meal I could neither smell nor taste, he chatted about inconsequential nothings. His wife had decided to redecorate the flat; his daughter adored her school in Switzerland.

"Family is so important, isn't it?" he continued. "Speaking of which, did you hear about your former teacher, Brian?" Kemp flicked his brittle glance in my direction before returning to his steak Diane.

I grasped my knife so hard my knuckles turned white. I didn't think I could answer, so I shook my head and moved my hand under the table.

"He became a family man, married with an infant son. Imagine that! They lived somewhere in Belgium. Which was his birthplace, as I recall." Kemp's attention was on his food, yet I felt myself being watched.

"Imagine that." I wouldn't meet his eyes.

"Well, we just received news of a horrifying event." He paused, studying the carved platinum ring he wore on his right hand. I'd always wondered about it. Wedding band? Friendship ring? Visual reminder of a blood oath taken by a band of fellow evildoers?

"It seems there was an accident. I believe he was with his young son and the boy's grandmother when their vehicle crashed near the Belgian/French border. The car went off the side of the road, down an embankment, and burst into flames. Just like that. No one survived." He shook his large head. "Such a tragedy. I don't know how they made any identification at all. Apparently, the wife wasn't with them. I can't guess how it must feel to have one's entire family suddenly wiped out like that."

He cut a tiny piece of meat and inserted it surgically into his mouth.

"To love so deeply is to risk so much heartache. Don't you agree?"

He'd been looking at his plate. Now he brought his icy eyes up to mine to see if I would react. I struggled to keep my face a blank. I didn't even blink. Beneath the tablecloth, my hand held the knife as if it were a sword.

"I wouldn't know," I managed to say.

We locked onto each other, his wintry gaze challenging the flame he must have seen in mine. Time passed: a thousand years or a few seconds. Then he smiled, all teeth and no warmth.

"My goodness, death and grief are not really appropriate topics for lunch, are they? I sometimes forget myself. Hazards of the profession, I'm afraid. You should eat your food before it gets cold."

My searing fury disappeared, replaced by a cold resolve as powerful as anything I'd ever experienced. I threw my anger into one of my many compartments, hidden but not forgotten, and I allowed myself to become as hard as my antagonist. If I ever had a soul, it shriveled in that moment. My heart closed. I assessed my odds of success should I jump across the table and thrust the knife into his chest. Not good. Kemp undoubtedly had guards posted at the restaurant perimeters. I couldn't turn my cutlery against myself, either. Too dramatic. I'd never give him the satisfaction.

I think I muttered something about how sad the world could be, and we moved on.

For the rest of the interminably long luncheon, I pretended to eat. I listened, I responded; I behaved as if I was with a decent human being, not the beast who'd ordered the death of my loved ones.

When we got back to the office, I ducked into the ladies' room and threw up. I went back to my desk, finished the workday, and went home. In my apartment that night, the explosion or collapse I expected didn't take place. No howling like a banshee, no punching the walls until my fists bled. I didn't pick up a rifle and head for a high place so I could randomly shoot people. I slept without dreaming for a few hours. The next day I went to work. And the next and the next, for nearly two more decades.

I should have gone insane. I almost did on several occasions. I wanted to leave him. Actually, I wanted to kill him or hurt him as terribly as he had hurt me.

I did none of those things. I contended with my pain and my rage. I had no choice. He watched me like a hawk, at once secure in his power yet wary I might turn on him. My strength came from not doing what he expected. If I'd really thought about how long it might take to get free of him, I might not have made it. I didn't think about it. I focused on the tasks in front of me. Tunnel vision.

Chapter Six

I quit Victor Kemp five years ago. When I ultimately made the decision, I did everything right. I finished my assignments, gave notice, and handed in my paperwork. Admittedly, I failed to give him two weeks. It didn't seem prudent. I packed up, cleared my desk and walked into Kemp's office with a resignation letter I placed on his desk on his desk.

"I'm leaving."

His reaction was typical of him. A chuckle, as if he found me amusing. A sigh, as if I were a disappointing child. And not far below the surface, a simmering fury.

"What is this?" Victor pretended to read the letter, then pushed it aside. His small pale eyes bored into me. "Early retirement? It hardly seems your style. I expected you to continue to work until you were an old woman."

Old woman. I fought not to flinch.

"I've been doing this a long time, Victor. I'm tired. I've earned my rest, and I'm taking it."

I turned away and opened the door to his office to leave. My soon-to-be former employer stopped me, his voice like ice. "You're still an asset, Ms. Smith. Improbably or not, you still retain skills I find valuable. I shouldn't need to remind you that my assets don't leave until I've fully realized my investment."

"As of now, you have." I walked out and closed the door without looking back.

He didn't try to stop me. I didn't expect him to, not then. After all, he'd hired me as his personal killer, exacted his punishment when I strayed, eliminated all possibility for happiness, and held onto me for decades. How much more was he going to get out of a woman he'd wounded so grievously? All I wanted to do was disappear. He should have been glad to be rid of me.

No one walks away from Victor Kemp, though. Especially not someone who sets in motion an act of defiance too big for him to ignore. Deep in my heart, I knew that. I knew that if and when he discovered what I'd done, he'd come for me. Which was why, when he finally did, I was ready.

~

My gunman is on the phone. He's muttering in Russian. I can follow the bare outlines of his conversation: "yes . . . no, no trouble . . . easy . . . old woman."

Old woman? I grit my teeth.

He doesn't notice the presence of a second speck on the horizon, so faint as to be mistaken for an indolent insect. I see it, though. I know both its purpose and its target. I run some calculations in my head. How long? How fast? How far? Timing is everything.

The boat my companion has yet to register as such is moving rapidly toward the first vessel. I gauge its distance as too great to factor into my strategy. My companion speaks, his voice heavy with pleasure

"Not long now."

I'll show you an old woman, I imagine telling him. Instead, I gasp and clutch at my chest.

"My heart."

If the situation weren't so grim, his expression would be laughable. Irritation and panic fight for primacy on his face. He's plainly torn. On one hand, I may be sick or even dying. His job is to deliver me alive. It's not just the money: this is Victor Kemp we're talking about. On the other hand, he doesn't want to deal with this new development. He doesn't know what kind of help I might need, or what might be required of him.

How will he justify his inaction? It's nothing. She'll be okay. Anyway, I've done what I was asked to do. Or maybe: she's not worth worrying about. I can see it in his body language as he begins to relax.

The gunman has made a mistake common to many who deal with older people (that is, anyone over fifty). He's decided I'm exactly as inconsequential as he wants me to be. He's not surprised I'm ill or weak; it's not his problem. He looks away.

The second he does, I fall onto my left shoulder and reach under the bench where my 9mm is taped. The move is awkward because I'm right-handed, but I've practiced. Roll over, reach under, roll back, and shoot while sitting up. Years of working out guarantee I have reliably strong abdominal muscles.

The side of his head erupts in a spray of bright red and dull beige. We stare at each other in disbelief, both with the same question: what just happened? I'm also wondering who fired the shot. It wasn't me; I'm close enough that my bullet would have produced a small hole in the man's forehead. As his lifeless body drops, I jump off the bench, searching frantically in front and behind. A rangy young man with reddish-brown hair lopes towards me. In one hand, he holds a smoking shotgun. Before I have a chance to do or say anything, he points to the water. "Look," he yells.

Not thirty seconds later, the boat that surely carried my death explodes. A giant fireball extends straight up with a roar that echoes off the cliffs. I watch with my mouth open, as if at a fireworks display. The second boat I spotted earlier approaches the burning wreckage tentatively and circles before reversing course and coming around from the other direction. The driver repeats the maneuver. After a time, I stop counting the sweeps. It will take as long as it takes. The occupants of the other craft are being cautious, as they should be.

The young man is by my side, out of breath. I turn to deliver a fierce hug, then stand back, holding him at arms' length. My slightly stern expression dims his triumphant look.

"I had a clear shot, Michael."

"So did I." He's gone serious. "I didn't want you to be the one to kill him. Former assassin, right?"

"But—"

"It's done. Besides," he can't resist a small smile, "it was a bloody good shot."

My son looks so much like Brian, I'm afraid my heart will burst. I thank whatever gods I fitfully acknowledge that Victor Kemp was never able to take from me what I most love. "You're my hero," I tell him.

"Hope your mother doesn't mind spreading the hero worship around a bit. Unless she thinks that boat blew itself up."

The voice is a more mature version of Michael's and as comfortably familiar as the shawl I've wrapped around myself to ward off the chill. The speaker stands at the bow of the boat like a heroic Celtic figure. Copper and silver strands of hair catch the sunlight above a pair of emerald eyes. The man jumps like a boy into the water.

"You did a fine job, son. Couldn't have managed without your help. As for you—" He plows out of the shallows, reaches for me with both arms and envelops me in a bear hug. "I'm just glad you're all right."

I sink into the warmth of my husband's chest, suddenly shaky. I ignore the sea, the sky, the fire, my son, and the body of the hapless lackey who chose to work for Victor Kemp and ended up dead on a beach in Wales.

"Are they gone, Brian? All of them? Even Kemp?"

"Every one of them, Suzie. I saw five people board a chartered boat in Bristol, Kemp included. No one else got on or off in the interim. The gunman Michael neatly dispatched was hired strictly for this job. Only a few confederates even knew about this operation. Kemp kept his interest in your whereabouts hidden from many of his most trusted advisors, you know. He was afraid to appear foolish or impaired by poor judgment. Nothing brings out the jackals like a leader weakened by a personal vendetta."

A personal vendetta. To end me. I shudder.

Two more men jump out and wade to shore. One of them is Charlie Campbell, MI6's favorite chameleon. To call him a colleague of Brian's does their relationship a disservice. Charlie has known Brian for thirty-five years. He's been savior and protector of my family for decades, even as the two of them tried to push through the investigations into Victor Kemp's various criminal endeavors. Kemp's band of lawyers successfully derailed every effort to bring him to justice.

I'm still galled that his attempts to kill an agent of Her Majesty's Government didn't prod the authorities to issue an arrest warrant. Supposedly, there was never enough evidence to act. Even in the world of spies and secrets, bureaucracy moves slowly, if at all.

I give Charlie a hug that nearly crushes him. He leans back, his ruddy face wreathed in smiles.

"You're strong for such a small thing." Charlie's brogue is thick as a Scottish mist at dawn. "Nice work, by the way. You too, Michael."

He claps Brian on the shoulder and they embrace, two old friends who have always had each other's backs. Michael comes over and hugs the master spy whom he loves like an uncle. The man who's accompanied Charlie hangs back until he is waved over. More backslapping.

I stand back to observe the timeless ritual of male bonding. I also marvel at the loyalty on display, loyalty that has saved us all once again.

"Okay," Charlie says. "If you'll excuse us, we've got a bit of work to do here. Let's at it, Fred."

He and the other man pick up the body on the beach and roll it in a tarp before depositing it in the boat. He promises to return at dusk. I invite them for supper. All very civilized, considering recent events.

The three of us climb the ancient steps to an old stone cottage, past a small gravestone. We laid Brian's mother to rest there last year. When we reach the back patio, he goes inside to make a few calls. My son pulls out a cell phone and telephones someone, probably his girlfriend, Kate.

I take a moment to study his face and glance back at the fire that sends black plumes skyward. The flames are smaller, more contained. The authorities will have received reports. I expect to hear a helicopter before long.

For now, all is silent, save for the soft sighing of the waves that lap the shore.

I turn back to the cottage just as Brian exits. He looks tired. What a toll this ordeal has taken on my little family. How utterly resilient they all are. We all are, I tell myself.

Michael disconnects and we embrace, a group hug that lasts nearly a minute.

It's over, I think. I note the uncertainty in that thought and will it away. Brian feels it and pulls me to him.

I glance over his shoulder at the waters as they push the blackened shell of the boat this way and that. Bits of the mast have broken off; a portion of the hull collapses into the water as if exhausted. A tiny piece of what appears to be debris breaks off from the wreckage. The movement seems almost deliberate, as if the fragment is self-propelled. I shake my head to free it from its nightmare. "It's over," I say aloud. Then the three of us walk arm in arm back to our home.

PART TWO

Chapter Seven

How long is eighteen months? A year and a half cycled through six seasons. For a baby, a micro-lifetime during which vision, awareness, mobility, and speech are acquired. For someone who grieves, it's no time at all. For someone who waits, it's forever. Wounds heal in eighteen months. Lives change. Some end.

Since Victor Kemp died in a fiery explosion off the coast of Wales, I've been learning to live unencumbered by fear. I'm free to shop, daydream, take a yoga class, or attend a concert, all without seeking permission or weighing the consequences. I still don't trust most people, not yet. I'm still watchful. Nonetheless, I feel as if a great weight has been lifted off my chest. Freed prisoners must feel this way or those reprieved from death row.

I continue to be plagued by restless dreams and the chronic anxiety that burns in me like a pilot light, always ready to ignite. Sometimes when sleep proves elusive, I stand on the balcony of our tidy Mayfair flat. I clear my mind and allow memories to come to me. Buried in the pain and seclusion that have governed so much of my existence are little gems worth holding up to the light. No life is all bad or all good.

In the pre-dawn, London lies under a blanket of fog. I stand outside, wrapped in a wool throw, and feel tiny pinpricks of moisture cling to my face. This time of year, the sun that might burn away the mist arrives late and leaves early. Dampness lives in the air and is absorbed into our way of life. While coastal dwellers get used to it, fog is for many people unsettling. It presents a hazard for airline pilots, sea captains, and truck drivers. It surrounds and confounds, distorts and disorients. Within its impenetrable folds, one can more easily hide misdeeds or obscure truths.

On the other hand, fog reminds me of my San Francisco childhood. Though I had a difficult upbringing, I knew small pleasures: the smell of the sea, the taste of salt breezes, the crying of gulls muffled by the mist. I often awoke to low-hanging clouds pushing against the windows of our apartment. I'd run outside, hoping to wrap my arms around the gray bundles of moisture. In the swirling vapors, I saw possibility. Out of the fog, a boat, a stairway, or a knight in shining armor might one day emerge. Anything would do. I wanted to believe that behind the dense blanket that confronted me, hope lay in wait.

One foggy morning—I must have been seven—we took a family trip. This turned out to be an extraordinarily rare occurrence. Before I left for good, I only got out of the neighborhood twice more, once on a school trip to visit a museum, another time with a friend's family to Chinatown. The opportunity to escape the confines of my limited life thrilled me. Not that I told my parents. I worried it might irritate them, especially my father. Especially when he called for his absent muse by indulging in his penchant for narcotics.

The night before our outing, he managed to get into a reading at San Francisco's iconic City Lights Bookstore. Lisette already worked there as a bookseller. Mo, far more educated and far less disciplined, had lost his job as cashier. He announced it was for the best; the job had distracted him from his art. In truth, he so resented his employers' easy-going tolerance that he pushed their patience to the limit by showing up as infrequently as possible. All things considered, they let him down gently.

The bookstore's cofounder, Laurence Ferlinghetti, attended the soirée. For Mo, this was akin to performing in front of the president. I was there because my parents didn't know what else to do with me. I'm not sure the audience liked Mo's work, but at least no one booed.

We returned to our pocket-sized apartment, my father ecstatic. He believed he'd knocked it out of the park. Mo predicted he'd be included in the bookstore's Pocket Poets series, a respected anthology that included such mid-century Beat stars as Alan Ginsberg and William Burroughs. Mo Greenbaum would never be published by anyone, but he didn't know that at the time. All I knew was he was in a good mood, fueled by what seemed like gallons of cheap wine and other, less visible means.

Lisette woke me at 6:30 a.m. the next morning to announce we were going on an outing. I wasn't sure what to expect. I don't think either of my parents had slept. They looked rumpled and gave off a faintly vinegary odor. Nevertheless, they seemed energized, and I couldn't help but be mesmerized by their mood and by my inclusion in their plans.

We walked a few blocks to pick up a car from someone Mo knew, a 1957 Plymouth Fury. I wondered why a car would have such an angry name. He left us outside, shivering in the early morning mist, while he went inside to argue, cajole, barter, and promise who knows what. Ten minutes later, he emerged victorious with the car keys and a mug of coffee he'd wrangled out of his friend. My father could be charming when he chose to be. He simply chose not to be most of the time.

We walked around the corner. There it was, an eggshell-colored convertible with a gold stripe and massive fins pointed skyward. As soon as we climbed in, Mo lowered the top even though the damp autumn chill made my teeth chatter. Lisette tied a scarf over her head and wrapped it around her neck. She looked like Jackie Kennedy.

Off we went, headed for a mysterious town called Sausalito.

Sausalito was an artists' colony, Lisette explained to me as we rode toward the Golden Gate Bridge. I didn't understand. We'd learned in school about ants living in colonies. I asked my mother if the place consisted of holes in the ground we crawled through.

"Nothing like that, Suzanne. It's the most beautiful place in the world, and it's always sunny. You'll see."

We crossed the Golden Gate Bridge and emerged from a cloudbank. Ahead of us, the chill had fled. The sun sparkled off the water. Small sailboats bounced off the docks. Sausalito was indeed a magical place. I could have remained forever.

Yet my parents found it wanting. For one thing, we arrived too early in the day. Absent the poets and writers who normally filled the cafes, the town seemed deserted. Mo felt let down. He'd been seeking an audience with which to share his City Lights victory. Lisette had hoped to mix with artists.

Bored within half an hour of our arrival, my father piled us into the car for the return journey. I surprised my parents by demanding they stop the car at the foot of the bridge. I hadn't had anything to eat or drink, which may have fueled my small act of rebellion. I jumped out, barely avoiding an early morning delivery truck, and ran part of the way onto the structure.

The far side of the Golden Gate Bridge offered a startling vantage point. San Francisco, barely visible beneath its gunmetal cape, gave off a mysterious air. I could almost mark the point at which the fog appeared. I stood for a moment, a little girl suspended between two worlds, one wrapped in shades of gray, the other bright and sunny. I knew which one I wanted to choose. I feared which one might choose me.

~

"Suzie, can you help me with this?"

Twelve hours after my early morning reverie, I'm sitting at my dressing table trying to attach a particularly stubborn earring. Brian emerges from the bathroom looking like a male model. He's all broad shoulders, tapered waist, and red hair silvered at the temples. His tux and starched shirt fit him beautifully. His shoes are shined to a fare-thee-well. Runway-ready, save for the untied bow, and even that lends him a rakish air.

He's wearing the diamond cufflinks I gave him last year. We'd been married twenty-eight years but had only spent six of them together. I pointed out we'd missed the simpler anniversaries altogether.

"Perhaps I should be giving you jewelry made of paper or wood."

"Or lead."

We actually laughed.

Now I eye my handsome husband with amused suspicion. This isn't his first time in a tux. He certainly knows how to handle a bowtie, though it's been several years. We had no need for formal clothes while we hid from Victor Kemp. Back then, we lived in fleece jackets, wool sweaters, slickers, and boots to keep out the cold and rain and protect against the mud. The raw and unforgiving weather suited our uneasy existence. While Brian and

Michael managed some interaction, I mostly kept to myself. I didn't mind being seen as standoffish. No one knew where we were from and no one in the village, as far as we could tell, ever learned about the obsessive man who wished us dead.

These days, Brian and I divide our time between London and the old stone farmhouse outside the Welsh village of Rhossili. I thought I'd have trouble going back after five years of exhausting vigilance. It turns out I like to be secluded from time to time, especially now that I no longer fear for my family.

Michael is in the city full time, pursuing an advanced degree in civil engineering. He also wants to be near his fiancée, Katherine Edgerton. Despite his nomadic early life, my son appears to be thriving. The strain has mostly left Brian as well. I can tell by the set of his shoulders.

There are some days I could swear I'm walking several inches above the ground. This must be what joy feels like. It doesn't last. I don't expect it to.

While we can scarcely be considered members of society, London has provided us with opportunities to step out. I've begun to donate to organizations whose work I support. We've even been honored at a couple of fundraisers. Brian received a lifetime achievement award from SIS last year, all very hush-hush but great fun nonetheless. He claimed at the time the honor simply made him feel old. I know he was proud and justifiably so.

The biggest boost to our social life comes from our soon-to-be in-laws. Michael's betrothed comes from a noble family, all tall, fair, and patrician-looking. Katherine's father is Lord Thomas William Edgerton, 1st Viscount Brackley. He serves in the House of Lords. The family is terribly casual about titles. Katherine goes by Kate ("You know; the other, non-pregnant one"). Her younger brother Edward has been called Widgy forever. Her father insists we call him Tommy. His wife prefers to be called Maggie. It fits her sunny disposition. Tommy calls her "my Mags."

Entrance to even the edges of their rarified circle brings other chances to dress up. Fortunately, I've collected a few outfits over the years that have managed to hold their fashion relevance. There are a few young London designers whose work I'm getting to know. I actually don't like to shop. I'd rather purchase just a few high-quality or unusual custom-designed pieces.

These days I'm most comfortable in tailored slacks or jeans. Brian insists I'm wearing the same pair I had in high school. I've changed some over the years and yet, in my mid-fifties, I look not unlike the girl I was back in San Francisco. Same blue eyes, dark-blonde hair with a few artfully added highlights, cautious smile, slender build, medium height. I've even reclaimed my first name, the one my mother presciently bestowed upon me during the early days of Flower Power.

"All right, you," I say to my husband. "Come over here so we can get this right."

Brian steps up to my outstretched fingers. As I reach for the tie, he slides his hands around me. My high-necked L'Wren Scott evening gown shows a bit of exposed skin at the back. I lean away and narrow my eyes, pretending to be shocked or surprised. I'm neither.

"You sneaky rascal. I thought you needed my help."

"I have ulterior motives. Hmm, not revealing too much, are we?"

His hands caress my bare skin, causing me to shudder with pleasure.

"I don't think so. I have a little jacket I can use to cover up. I might put it on right now, just so you can keep your hands to yourself."

I pretend to push him away. We both know I'd stay in the circle of his embrace for the rest of the evening. Forever, if I could freeze time.

Duty calls. We have tickets to the Royal Opera. Maggie, a patron and significant contributor, has secured box seats for the opening night production of Faust. Brian pretended to fuss when I told him. Nevertheless, I know he has a special place in his heart for the flawed hero. To tell the truth, I feel a bit queasy about meeting up with Méphistophélès. In the past, I've made a pact with my own version of the devil. Tommy has hinted at a possible royal visit. I'm only too happy to play the star-struck expat.

My task with the tie completed, I pat Brian lightly and turn to the dressing table for my bag. He heaves a dramatic sigh.

"Foiled again. I don't suppose we can be late."

He opens the door onto the dim hallway. The air is cool and slightly damp. I shiver again. This time the experience is less pleasant.

"Let's get your jacket on." My ever-helpful husband assists and rests his hands lightly on my shoulders. "You okay?"

"When we open the door, I always feel . . ." I searched for the words.

"Vulnerable. Defensive. Alone. I know."

We lock gazes.

"It'll pass, Brian."

"I know that, too." He takes my arm and leads me to the lift.

THE FORMER ASSASSIN

More than anyone, my husband understands that there are depths to me I haven't revealed, much less explored. He'd like to protect me from unpleasant discoveries. I don't know that he can. His love lifts me out of the darkness. The idea that I'm worthy of it elevates me.

Yet the mystery of who I am remains shrouded in a fog that both obscures and beckons.

Chapter Eight

East London's Wapping district used to be a thriving center of dockside commerce both legitimate and black market. Once a haven for smugglers, it's now home to financial types who don't mind paying for converted warehouses that fetch six million pounds or more. Some have suggested Wapping has replaced one kind of thieving scoundrel for another.

While the area took a hit during the 2008 economic meltdown, real estate prices recovered. The few remaining warehouses were immediately snapped up as investments. Two became luxury rentals. One became something else.

Set a bit back from the river but retaining a commanding view, the building offered a great deal of privacy. No closed-circuit cameras appeared in the immediate vicinity, save for those installed by the new owner. Access was via the front door only. Even regular tradesmen went through an elaborate security system. The parking garage underneath was off limits to all but three or four people. Invited guests—and there were almost none—left their vehicles at the front door or were dropped off by a private service hired by the man who lived inside.

The interior served as both workspace and residence. The lower level was minimally furnished with three desks, an assortment of utilitarian shelves, two white boards, and Wi-Fi. The lighting was topnotch, both functional and artistic. It would have worked perfectly in a gallery setting. Both freestanding and installed fixtures expertly masked a state-of-the-art security system. The upstairs penthouse, tastefully decorated in a classic modern style, commanded an unobstructed view of London's Tower Bridge. Not that the new owner noticed. He rarely used the space. Instead, he spent much of his time below.

Now Victor Kemp sat at one of the desks staring at his MacBook. An old-fashioned logbook lay open to his right. His large head swiveled back and forth between the screen and the pages of the book. He occasionally touched the keyboard with his left hand. The forefinger of his right hand, the only digit remaining, followed a column of numbers in the log. Reviewing the handwritten notations was tedious work, but he deemed it essential.

"Arkady. Get the hell over here. The computer entries don't match what I'm seeing in the log. Something's missing or perhaps it's been added. Wait a minute . . ." He leaned toward the computer screen, squinting. "Where are my goddamn glasses?"

A clean-shaven, heavily tattooed man in his early forties stood up from an adjacent desk and walked over. Despite thinning sandy hair, Arkady Dyukov came across as a much younger man. Not an ounce of fat rested on his impressively muscled body. His broad Slavic face with its square jaw and even features just missed being handsome.

"They're on your head, boss." Whereas the older man had used Russian, Dyukov spoke in accented English. "As for the mismatch, mind if I take a quick look? Yeah, I see how you missed this entry. The captain wrote it in the margin. I think he was using some kind of personal shorthand."

Kemp pulled off his glasses and slapped his good hand on the table.

"God damn it, Arkady." Kemp also spoke in English. "I don't need the man to be inventive; I need him to be attentive. Do you understand me? We have a system in place for a reason. If our employees aren't going to follow it, perhaps we should consider other employees."

Although Kemp didn't raise his voice, he weighted his words with an implicit threat. He pushed himself up from his chair and faced his employee.

He could see Dyukov resist the urge to flinch. His number two had worked for his share of difficult men. He'd grown up on the streets of Solntsevo, one of Moscow's roughest neighborhoods. He'd labored for the Brotherhood and had done a stretch inside Russia's infamous prison system. He'd even served for a time in the military, all before turning twenty-five.

Kemp had gone through worse, though. He was born at the height of World War II. Exactly when and where were unknown. Some said he came from a small town in Yugoslavia; others suggested he'd been born in the Ukraine. One story had it that he slid out of his dead widowed mother's womb without food, family, or friends and lived on the streets as soon as he could walk. What he encountered and what he had to do to survive became the stuff of legend. Kemp did nothing to discourage the stories.

In the 1950s, he worked in Moscow for a post-war version of a criminal element thriving in the era of deprivation. Soviet gangsters controlled the black and gray markets. They produced and distributed privately made goods and services with the tacit support of the corrupt government. Victor started as a runner, progressed to a sort of underground administrator, and caught the attention of a notorious gang leader named Sergei, who sent him to good schools, aiming to groom him as a successor.

Kemp had a different agenda. He eliminated every possible rival, including his protector, took as much money as possible, and left dreary Russia for more exciting opportunities in America. There he established parallel above and underground businesses and became successful beyond anyone's imagination—except his.

In his later years, he'd become more cunning and more careful. His only mistake, and one he intended to rectify, involved the former assassin.

He watched Dyukov carefully. For the past eighteen years, the younger man had been a key player in Kemp's worldwide criminal operations. A capable enforcer, he instilled fear when necessary. Though not formally educated, he had a head for figures, which earned him his employer's admiration. In return, Dyukov provided dependable loyalty and the appropriate amount of respect. He knew how ruthless his boss could be. Kemp understood it wasn't his mood that caused Dyukov to tread carefully. It was the older man's face.

"Gruesome" best described the injury. Scalding flames had caused a hideous burn that stretched from forehead to collarbone on Kemp's right side. A mass of pulp, still buckled and raw, covered the worst area. The cheek had collapsed into itself, so the outline of bone pushed against the blistered tissue. The wound was an angry, wet-looking red at its center and gray at the edges where the dead skin curled.

Despite several operations and repeated applications of various ointments, the injury refused to heal completely. When it did ("eventually," the doctors promised), Kemp could have reconstructive surgery, if he wanted it.

Otherwise, Victor Kemp seemed relatively unchanged. In his early seventies, his hair remained a rich brown, long and swept back from his low brow. His watchful, nearly colorless eyes turned up slightly at the corners. He radiated authority, power, and something else that only the most astute observer could see: inconsolable grief. That alone made him vastly different from the man he had been before.

"Maybe I'll head out and get us something to eat."

"Wait a minute." Kemp reached across and laid his left hand on his associate's forearm. "I'm sorry, Arkady." Kemp spoke quietly. "I suppose I am tired and perhaps hungry."

"S'okay, boss. Let me grab us some lunch; then we'll go over the figures together. Maybe we need a new system." Dyukov went back to his desk, picked up a set of keys, and headed for the door. He knew when to leave well enough alone.

As soon as the man left, Kemp sighed. Pain cut into his focus and caused his rigorous discipline to slip at times. He had to learn to control his mood, particularly with trusted underlings. There were few enough of those, and he needed every one.

The boat explosion that should have killed him instead severely maimed him. He was tossed from the boat and hit the water with such force he could have broken his neck. He didn't. That he had survived, hidden beneath a piece of burning debris, his face seared and his fingers gone, was a miracle he had no time to contemplate. Even the appearance hours later of a curious Welsh fisherman happy to accept money for safe passage caused him no joy. Kemp lost four men on the botched expedition.

The fisherman took him to Swansea, a port town large enough to have a decent clinic. He refused treatment until he could make a phone call. Dyukov, who waited in Bristol, covered the 128 kilometers in less than an hour. With his man in charge, Kemp finally lapsed into unconsciousness, overcome by pain. Dyukov arranged for his employer's transport to a private burn center in London. The fisherman never made it home, but his wife and daughter were well compensated for their loss by an anonymous donor.

Victor Kemp began his recuperation in the London apartment he'd shared with his now-dead wife. By his side were a well-paid nurse and his Brazilian mistress, Luisa Guzman.

Within weeks, it became clear Kemp had no intention of dying. His injuries were serious but not mortal. He refused to go through the process of skin grafts in the short term. His doctor warned him he might have a hideously scarred face. Victor compensated and dismissed him. He kept the nurse. When he became strong enough to move, he relocated to the new building in East London. At that point, fewer than half-dozen people knew he had survived. He was determined to keep that number small.

The shareholders and directors of his legitimate company learned about the terrible boating accident from local authorities. Kemp presumed his saboteurs put their own spin on the report. Five deaths were confirmed. The directors sent out a press release announcing the demise of the company leader and several others and arranged a memorial service.

Kemp observed the mourners on a closed-circuit camera. They included his daughter and her family. While watching his own funeral amused him, he briefly regretted any pain he might have caused his child. She appeared to be grieving, although that might have been a performance. He hadn't spent much time with her, and he'd only seen his young grandchildren twice. He still cared about them, after a fashion. At least the family received a substantial sum from the estate, even though the daughter's husband came from money.

At the next board meeting, the directors selected as CEO someone from within the corporate world Kemp knew to be malleable. Not that he needed the company to provide cover any longer. It would stand on its own. The board would make certain the organization grew. At some point, he might be able to influence a sale. He didn't need to share in any profits; he had more than enough money. He simply wanted to keep his options open.

As for his underworld connections, he pondered at length how he might continue to operate and on what level. He had no intention of retiring. It wasn't in his nature. He realized any move he made might set off alarms in certain quarters. At the same time, he would need to be in touch with old contacts. Kemp recognized the risk. He also relished the challenge.

In the end, he allowed a few trustworthy cohorts to know a version of the truth. He communicated with them using intermediaries or via private closed-circuit networks. Sometimes he sat in front of the camera with his left side forward; sometimes he turned his full face to the screen. Sometimes he covered his wound, often not. He used his injury the way he used everything, as a tactical advantage or as a cudgel.

He lived to play the game. He simply decided to play it differently, working on a smaller scale. No more buying, selling, or trading. He'd be a middleman, the best and most successful middleman possible. "I will be king of the sea," he told Dyukov.

Eighty to ninety percent of the world's trade occurred over water. Weak and poorly enforced maritime laws gave ship owners nearly free reign. Companies purchased boats in one country and registered them in a handful of nations that offered "flags of convenience" under which the ships could sail. A ship owned by a Greek company incorporated in Nigeria by an owner of uncertain origin might fly a Panamanian flag. The captain could be Moroccan, the crew a mix of a dozen or so nationalities. The more layers that were piled on, the more difficult it was to monitor how the ship was used or what it carried.

Four months after his near-fatality, Victor Kemp entered the shipping business with a vengeance. He began with a new identity as a reclusive Portuguese businessman named Francesco Guzman. Why not? He already spoke the language and using Luisa's surname made sense. During his convalescence, Kemp set up four companies, each in a different business-friendly sovereignty. Agents for these companies then purchased six ships apiece. They bought modern vessels in top condition. All displayed a variation of a peregrine native to Brazil. Kemp liked the symbolism. A bird of prey served as a warning to others who made a living at sea.

The ships were equipped with the latest weaponry, all legal and acquired ostensibly for protection. The proxies hired seasoned captains, first mates, and crews, each one carefully vetted. Everyone received decent wages and food to ensure loyalty. There was zero tolerance for indiscretion of any kind. No one stowed aboard Francesco Guzman's vessels; no one mutinied. Even pirates gave the ships wide berth.

For the first six months, the cargo onboard the two dozen vessels consisted exclusively of lawfully exported goods. In that half-year, Kemp's companies turned a modest profit and brought a measure of confidence to his insurers and his investors. When he finally approached his former black-market competitors, he brought an intriguing proposal. He would no longer buy or sell narcotics, weapons, or contraband of any kind, although he reserved the right to barter information. He would transport these things for his former rivals and for new customers.

Kemp didn't expect anyone in his underground circle to refuse his services and almost no one did. One-time competitors were happy to give business over to someone whose professional acumen they recognized. Few of them wanted to deal with the headache of how goods got from one place to another. Yet successful transportation was key to building and expanding any number of enterprises, criminal or otherwise.

Kemp/Guzman offered the kind of competent security that made for good business. Moreover, he continued to run his own organization with coldblooded efficiency. Even those who had never faced his ruthlessness firsthand knew that aligning with Victor Kemp was a matter of self-preservation. They learned from associates or, if they happened to deal with him directly, they saw it in the frozen eyes above the ruined face.

Throughout his recovery, Kemp remained disciplined and focused. He accepted his reduced circumstances with forbearance. On those few occasions when he left the building, he wore a custom-made bandage that covered nearly his entire face. People stared, naturally, but Kemp deployed a persona that deflected fear and revulsion. He adopted a passive body language. He spoke soothingly. He performed, though he hated doing so. He wanted to thrust his spoiled face into the public space, to hear adults gasp and see children run away screaming.

All things considered, Kemp managed his ordeal as well as could be expected. He avoided a business crisis and kept himself connected to and on an equal footing with powerful criminal elements. His name still evoked respect and terror in certain quarters. He had men and women who remained faithful to him, including his mistress.

At the same time, he employed the services of others, whom he rewarded and watched carefully for signs of disloyalty. He even obtained a measure of comfort in knowing his daughter had married well and become a mother. The grandchildren wanted for nothing. That meant everything to him.

Almost everything. More important than his progeny, more vital even than his empire-building, were his plans for retribution. Deep beneath his surface self-possession, Victor Kemp nurtured a bottomless rage over what had happened in Wales. His life had been upended. He'd had to fake his death, go into hiding, endure abiding agony, and risk his business. Worst of all, the four men who died on the boat included the single most important person in his life: his eldest son with Luisa. Paul. He intended a suitable punishment for the former assassin, one that would rob her of any possibility for happiness or peace. He hadn't yet worked out the details. In due time, he would.

67

Chapter Nine

Breathe. In, out, in, out. Find your rhythm. Slow your heartrate, narrow your focus. Don't anticipate.

I run through my mantra, just once. I know the routine. I'm on my stomach, flat against the hard ground, rifle pressed to my shoulder. My hands caress the stock of the L115. The bolt-action rifle is the weapon of choice for the British military and in-the-know private contractors this year. More accurate even than the M110 favored by the Americans, or so some insist. Past users have set world records with this rifle.

Most long-range shooters, particularly those with a single perfect shot to make, find the bolt-action rifle more reliable and more accurate. I do. It's also lighter and it breaks down more easily. To be honest, there's something wholly satisfying about the sound of an ejected cartridge.

The air is unusually clear and dry for November. The wind has receded; the temperature requires only a light jacket and jeans. I'm wearing noise-cancelling earphones, not that I need them. I line up my target through my Schmidt & Bender scope. I'm using the best equipment possible under the best conditions possible in order to make the best shot possible.

A small shudder of anticipation interrupts my concentration; it passes.

I briefly consider how much long-distance shooters need to know about physics, ballistics, and biology. Marksmanship is about discipline; it's also sensual at some level. The rifle becomes an extension of the body, its contours and heft as familiar as those of a long-time lover.

I banish the thought, all thoughts, in fact. Everything disappears as I enter an almost Zen state. I'm there; the feeling is as natural to me as breathing. I count down—three, two, one—and pull the trigger.

The target falls; the small electronic score card beside me lights up. I remove my earphones and realize I'm not alone.

"Holy shit, ma'am, pardon my French." The young corporal is staring at my score. I hastily reset the board to zero, but he's already seen the number.

"Just a lucky shot," I say with a smile and a shrug. He nods and moves away.

Brian has worked it out so I can practice at a range used by SIS operatives with military backgrounds, chiefly snipers and the like. We've concocted a reasonable cover story that fits nicely with my former service in the United States Armed Forces. I use British military equipment, which keeps me up to date on the latest available hardware.

Fortunately, the sight of a female military veteran at a rifle range is no longer unusual in 2012. I'm older than most, but that's not what might cause me to stand out. As I routinely hit targets at 1500 meters and beyond, I worry about raising eyebrows. Today's number was 1620, far above average for all but the most elite marksmen. I'm proud but also nervous about being noticed.

I never enjoyed killing. Never. I managed to go numb when human targets were involved. I knew I was proficient; otherwise, Victor Kemp would have disposed of me early on. I never thought about how accurately I shot or how far the bullet went, because I'd have to think about what damage it did to the person I killed.

I love to shoot, though. Skill or sport, recreation or release; it doesn't matter. I picked up my first long gun when

I joined the Army and felt as if I'd discovered a part of myself. Only later did I learn that my skills had a genetic component.

My maternal grandfather was an engineer. Not just any engineer: Sandor David Brooks made his fortune as the lead designer of a self-propelled artillery vehicle. The invention likely changed the course of history. Grandpa Sandy retired from the Army after his brief career as a decorated WWI sniper was cut short by a mishap at a shooting range. He went on to accrue money and enjoy life before being felled by an aneurism while playing tennis just before he turned sixty-five.

This is the tale Lisette told me when we returned from Wales. It may have been apocryphal. She harbored a deep resentment of the parents who disowned her after she moved to the city and took up with a failed poet. The story seems logical, though, or at least as possible as anything else.

I return the gun to the supply room. Normally, I might stay just to listen to the other shooters talk shop, as it were. The technology is changing so rapidly; I'm trying to catch up and keep up. One aspect of all this fancy new equipment is that even an amateur can make a reasonably accurate shot. I find that to be a disturbing concept.

Today, I decide to leave. I don't want to discuss my latest score with anyone. Yes, we're all professionals; we're all there to maintain our skills. Still, best to be circumspect.

I'm actually pursuing a long-time goal of mine: an 1800-meter shot. That's about 2000 yards or just over a mile. Only a handful of men have hit that distance. To my knowledge, no women have. Not that a trained female asset would be public about chasing world records. Neither will I.

THE FORMER ASSASSIN

I can't say why I've set this task for myself. I have no plans to shoot long-distance. I've considered competing but that's down the road.

The British may be vigilant about gun control, but they still take their sport shooting very seriously. Gallery, bench rest, multi-position, long range, field target, precision, action: all manner of competitive shooting is supported by hundreds of clubs that welcome adults and juniors. Britain shows well at Olympic competitions and at other contests around the world.

At Michael's urging, I've joined the Clay Pigeon Shooting Association. Application for membership has turned out to be less daunting than I feared. My son's recommendation goes a long way. It helps that he specializes in double trap shooting and has done quite well at the amateur level. Math and marksmanship: those skills run in the family.

The idea of aiming at clay objects with a 12-gauge shotgun initially flummoxed me. Otherwise, it's been a marvelous experience. I'm adept without being an expert. My former profession never once required me to shoot something out of the sky. The sensation is familiar, yet novel, like being a practiced water colorist who switches to oil painting.

Best of all, membership in any Home-office approved club qualifies the applicant under a blanket certificate. This means I don't need to make an individual application and draw unwanted attention to myself.

After just three visits, a young instructor is on me to compete. He's suggested I would "crush" the senior division. I can't decide whether to be flattered, amused, or alarmed. I propose I train as an instructor instead, then immediately wish I hadn't.

"Why not, Mum?" Michael asks. "You'd be brilliant at it." Easy for him to say. Moving into his late twenties, my son grows more handsome and self-assured with each passing day. He knows exactly what he wants to do: finish his graduate studies, marry Kate, and study further in the exciting new field of cyber-engineering.

My future daughter-in-law is also quite the academic. After a post-university architecture internship, she's back in school and nearly through a master's program. After that, she'll sit through a series of exams she's required to pass before she obtains her professional license. The UK sets the bar high for would-be architects.

Tommy and Maggie and Brian and I joke about having such intelligent and expensively educated children. The truth is, we're as proud as can be of both of them.

What most touches my heart about Kate is her combination of cheerful resolve and diplomatic skill. Michael tells me she handled some very difficult situations in Africa with grace and wit. I imagine more than a little danger was involved. No doubt she'll handle her future mother-in-law with the same assurance. I look forward to it. In fact, we're overdue for a girls' lunch.

The wedding is set for spring. If we were hardheaded, we parents would insist our two children wait. Why bother? These two smart young people are clearly suited to each other. They're also dedicated to their professional development. I don't see them letting anything slip by. Besides, I find myself suffused with joy at the prospect of a happy event in the not too distant future.

Tommy and Maggie aren't privy to all the details that led to our exile in Wales. They know we were in hiding from my former employer and that Interpol was watching him. They may suspect I got inadvertently caught up in criminal matters. They don't know I worked as an assassin. Keeping that bit from them is critical as long as Tommy is in the House of Lords.

Besides, I don't know how or when I could share that sort of information. Perhaps someday. They've become dear friends; we're likely to become closer. For now, they don't press. Tommy, whose brother committed suicide in 2002, insists life is to be lived in the present.

I must learn to do just that.

Now that I'm a bona fide member of a British shooting club, my son's new in-laws will see me using a rifle at some point. Even if I'm new at this sort of shooting, my abilities will show. I once asked Michael if that would cause a problem. He gave me a peculiar look.

"With whom? I mean, it's Great Britain. Sport shooting is as common as tea. Gun club members practice. Why wouldn't you be proficient? You're ex-Army. And let's not forget, people over here assume all you Yanks are handy with guns."

He cleared his throat. "Besides which, Kate is aware of your expertise with a rifle," he said.

I forced myself not to react. I always promised not to interfere, to let Michael fill in his fiancée as he sees fit. It isn't good to start off a life together with secrets. On the other hand, it's my secret, isn't it? Maybe not. Kate will be a member of our family soon. I'm not losing a son; I'm gaining a daughter.

I decided to look into becoming an instructor. To do so, I first had to qualify as a safety officer. I paid a £99 fee to attend a daylong course, passed a simple written exam, and demonstrated a working knowledge of firearms. I was older than my classmates but no one seemed to notice or care. I did meet a nice man in his forties who turned away from a middling career as an insurance agent in order to pursue a more interesting workaday. We both agreed mentoring young people and staying active are excellent reasons for becoming a teacher.

While he's gone on to become a Level 1 Instructor, I've hung back. It isn't the cost, although the £700 needed for the next step seems steep for the opportunity to keep busy. No, it's this: as a club member, I'm covered by the club's certification. Instructors, however, must obtain individual shotgun certificates. The idea of someone taking another run at my history gives me pause. I can't help it.

True, anything might be doctored these days. On the other hand, what can be hidden can also be found. Michael thinks I'm being paranoid. I promise to reconsider after the wedding. I've decided I'd make a good instructor.

Meanwhile, I relish both my practice sessions. At the military range, I improve upon well-developed skills in long-range marksmanship. At the club, I keep my reflexes sharp by responding to targets that might be thrown at any number of angles, speeds, elevations, and distances. Most of all, I enjoy shooting for the sport of it, quite apart from notions of offense, defense, rights, privileges, obligations, or threats.

Except, perhaps, the threat of being outed as a former assassin.

Chapter Ten

Few people knew Victor Kemp had not one but three children. His wife bore him a single daughter, Annabel. His mistress, Luisa Guzman, presented him with a son three years later, then another son five years after that. Kemp was beside himself over his good fortune. To have sons by a woman such as Luisa, with her dark beauty, her intelligence, and her independence, meant more to Kemp than he could say. He respected her business acumen; her connections proved invaluable on several occasions. He enjoyed her company in and out of bed. Most significantly, he trusted her. She knew about his two worlds and accepted them both. She never judged.

Luisa originally came from money, which her father Guillermo lost to bad investments and worse partners. Facing threats to his family and his life, he sought to marry off his eldest child at eighteen to a wealthy much-older suitor. Luisa refused. With her mother and brother's support, she defied him and the cultural expectations of a sexist Latin culture. She earned a business degree and became a well-regarded and wealthy real estate broker serving an international clientele. Failing to intimidate the women in his family, her father abruptly left. She took care of her mother until the old woman died.

Luisa met Kemp through one of her clients when she was just twenty-two. He never considered what attracted her to him. Not his wealth; she'd already begun to build her own bank account. Not his looks, either. Perhaps it was the aura of danger that traveled with him. Whatever the reasons, she immediately connected with him.

Her younger brother had the opposite reaction. He was repelled by her suitor. Fortunately for Kemp, Luisa ignored her sibling's advice on her love life. She nevertheless remained close to the brother, who became a doting uncle.

Luisa made her own choices, however. She chose Victor Kemp.

Kemp understood that Luisa lived her life more or less on her own terms. She invested herself in her children and her career. Her success required determination and even a particular strain of ruthlessness. Her resourcefulness impressed him. He also liked that she didn't need him but apparently wanted him.

Kemp's sons were unalike in every way possible. Paulo's soft blond hair and soulful blue eyes evoked his European ancestry. He seemed a gentle boy without his father's rough edges. Luisa thought of him as her little angel. A quiet, diligent student, he took up fencing and developed a passion for baseball. "Thinking man's sports," Kemp claimed.

The younger son, with his wavy dark-brown hair and limpid brown eyes, resembled his mother. The boy traded on his considerable charm from the time he was a toddler. Indifferent about school, he preferred spending time at the beach or on the soccer field. He played the sport aggressively, earning a spot as starting wingman. He took up surfing. As a teen, he'd go off to hot spots like Itacaré and hang with an older crowd. Luisa put up with his antics. Kemp accepted that a single mother and a career woman could only do so much. They both hoped he'd settled down.

Kemp traveled to Rio as often as he could. The visits amounted to perhaps six in a year, no more than four or five days at a time. The four of them even managed a few vacations together, to Miami, Nice, and Cancun. He hoped these brief interludes would suffice as family time. At least, he reasoned, the boys had Luisa's family around. If he functioned less as a father than as a wealthy European uncle with a soft spot for the two boys, so be it. Knowing so little about him, his sons never learned to fear him. They looked forward to his visits, expecting to be spoiled. They were rarely disappointed.

The two brothers attended excellent private schools in Rio. Paulo excelled at math and science. His parents thought he might pursue a career in medicine or research. He had other ideas. Despite infrequent contact, he formed an early and abiding attachment to Victor. At nine years of age and again at fourteen, he announced his intention to work with his father. Perhaps he hoped to make up for the man's absence. Maybe he yearned for international experience. In any event, he made up his mind and would not be dissuaded.

Kemp never anticipated either of his sons would join his business. He found himself unexpectedly touched. As he deferred to the boys' mother when it came to their upbringing, he broached the subject carefully.

"If you'd like, I can put a stop to this immediately."

"You can, but why even try? He has his mind made up. Young minds can change, though. Give it some time and let's see what happens. He must attend college first, yes?"

Kemp agreed. Children changed; they became independent and shifted allegiances. He couldn't help being delighted by the prospect of being in business with a blood relative. Paulo had found his way into his father's well-protected heart. Once there, he was impossible to dislodge.

The eldest son attended the London School of Economics and graduate school at Columbia University, where he enrolled as Paul Guzman. Just as he finished, his brother arrived in Manhattan to study real estate at New York University. He announced he would be using his middle name, Daniel. His parents acquiesced. Luisa even joked about it.

"We have two North American children now."

Daniel's decision pleased Kemp. He worried the younger son had inherited his maternal grandfather's unfortunate combination of avarice and weakness. The name change and the chosen major together suggested the boy might have a backbone after all.

Kemp suddenly saw more of his sons as young adults than he'd ever seen of them as children. He enjoyed his expanded role. Daniel obliged the older man by meeting for dinner every other week, where he shared amusing stories of college exploits. Otherwise, he lived his own life, which Kemp decided would be indulged only to a point.

Paul meanwhile went to work in the finance department of Kemp's legitimate corporate entity. Not long afterward, the son came to his father, troubled about a discrepancy he'd uncovered. The problem concerned a tiny import-export business, a client of the parent company.

"You see?" He spoke in English. "Some of the exported objects appear to be more valuable than reported, especially in countries where antiquities theft is a problem. I'm not saying we're doing anything wrong, only that in a few instances, the export data doesn't match the import data. I worry these are items that may have been stolen."

Many of Kemp's clients unknowingly or deliberately facilitated criminal activities. The particular company that attracted Paul's attention fronted a much larger operation involving the illicit buying and selling of high-value artifacts. That trade ranked behind only drugs and arms in terms of profitability. Dealers could get pieces out of object-rich countries like Greece, Egypt, and Iran with bribery and corruption. The irony was that even where exports were carefully monitored, for instance in tightly regulated Western nations, imports didn't receive the same level of scrutiny. Once illegal goods left the country of origin, they might not register as contraband when coming into high-demand markets like Great Britain or the United States.

Kemp and his confederates took precautions in all their business dealings. On those infrequent occasions when mistakes were made, he expected well-paid employees to look the other way. He should have known his son would prove to be the exception.

"Paul." Kemp got out only a single word before the younger man held up his hand, a gesture the father recognized as his own.

"Facts do not cease to exist because they are ignored."

"You're quoting Aldous Huxley to me?"

"I am. Now I will follow with a question: Do you trust me?"

"Why on earth would you ask me something like that?"

"Just answer me."

"You know I do."

"Okay. Then you should know I'm not interested in rendering moral judgments. I simply need all the facts in order to best do my job. My interest is in making sure you can be even more successful than you already are."

Kemp could not have loved his son more.

From then on, he kept nothing from Paul. He introduced his son to his intricate group of interconnected businesses, some related to the core business and some not, some legal, some not. He didn't seek to explain or justify. He didn't mention the lives he'd ruined or the deaths he'd caused. His son would ask, or he wouldn't.

Paul didn't ask. He began to suggest ways to streamline the various operations. He proposed jettisoning some activities and ramping up others. He drew up two organizational charts that tracked income and expenses as well as activities and personnel. They could be read independently; they also fit nicely one over the other to provide a comprehensive map of Kemp's enterprise. It was a thing of genius.

Kemp didn't hesitate; he made Paul his chief financial officer. The young man, who'd been at the firm only one year, was touted as an innovator. If the employees were startled by Paul's rapid ascension, they kept it to themselves. While some may have suspected a special bond between the head of the company and his new star, no one asked. Kemp had thrown a lavish wedding for his daughter five years earlier. She was pregnant with her second child. He didn't need to broadcast that he'd hired his illegitimate offspring.

His wife knew, of course. She chose to turn a blind eye, preferring the apartment in Knightsbridge and a handsome income to scandal and a divorce court. Kemp assumed his daughter remained oblivious. He wanted to keep it that way.

Father and son worked closely together for fifteen years. Paul consolidated or eliminated divisions, made recommendations to the board concerning certain opportunities, authorized (with Kemp's permission) personnel changes, and relentlessly focused on profitability. He treated the non-legit side in the same manner, ferreting out inefficiencies with an unforgiving precision that matched his father's. Paul suggested Kemp outsource more often. He endorsed selective investing in lucrative operations. Under his watch, profits rose.

While Victor Kemp wasn't given to placing a premium on emotions, he felt content for the first time in his life. He genuinely enjoyed working. He felt expansive toward all his progeny. True, his other son caused him some concern. Daniel appeared bent on living as a stereotypical wealthy playboy. He was headed for trouble; Kemp had no doubt. He was close to putting his foot down. Luisa was sure to welcome the intervention.

Kemp's one disappointment concerned the departure in 2006 of his favorite asset, the talented if stubbornly reluctant assassin. She'd deceived him once, despite knowing how he felt about treachery. He'd dealt with her, harshly perhaps, but how else to set an example? He'd at least permitted her to live. Then she walked out on him. The desertion rankled. Disrespect on top of disloyalty.

On the other hand, he knew he'd wounded her terribly. Keeping her around didn't make any sense. Even an older animal can attack. If she wanted to go, he'd let her go. He didn't need her, not now with his businesses organized and under the watchful eye of an heir apparent.

~

It began as idle chat by a derrick man working up the coast of Wales for a small drilling company owned by Kemp. The pay was good, the accommodations decent for being at sea. A typical day involved intense physical labor alternating with stretches of tedium. The derrick man entertained his fellow roughnecks with an account of his sleepy town on the Pembrokeshire coast. Nothing much happened until the arrival of an enigmatic woman. Supposedly she dwelt at the edge of a cliff with two men and an old crone. Rumors flew amongst the residents. Some thought she might be a witch. Others thought a family of spies lived outside their village.

The first Arkady Dyukov heard about the story was from a cousin he'd recommended to Kemp for a shipboard position. The grateful relative invited Dyukov to dinner in London at a hangout favored by working-class Eastern Europeans. Over copious amounts of vodka, the tale of the mysterious group emerged.

"I bet she's in hiding," his cousin guessed.

Something about the anecdote made Dyukov take notice. He knew all about the ex-employee, about her special talent and the cruel plan his employer designed when she dared to fall in love. He was surprised it had taken her so long to leave. On the other hand, her timing made sense. At that point, she was fifty years old. An old woman. How could Kemp object? He noticed his boss didn't take her exit lightly. At least his son Paul found a way to move him past it. The old man's fixation wasn't good for business.

Now Dyukov felt compelled to look into this absurd story, if for no other reason than to put it to bed.

He confirmed the presence of the woman and two others outside a small town near the Bristol Channel. A younger man sometimes joined them, probably a son, or so the informants speculated. The husband, who went by the name Brian Davies, seemed to be the only one who ventured into town. He appeared an affable sort, comfortable talking about sea-related topics, although not about his family. The man spoke fluent Welsh. He politely declined all invitations to dinner or church, alluding to his mother's illness and his wife's preference for staying at the cottage.

Dyukov needed pictures. He went to Swansea and from there up the coast where he hired a local fisherman to take him out on the water. On the third day, his patience was rewarded. A woman came out from a stone cottage to sit at a bench that offered what must have been a breathtaking view of the Bristol Channel. He took photos with a digital long lens. They came out grainy, but Dyukov had little doubt about the subject. Somehow the woman Kemp sought to punish had ended up on the coast of Wales with her family alive and intact.

He had a bad feeling about all of it. He also knew he had to tell his employer.

From the day Victor Kemp learned his former assassin had outmaneuvered him, he found it difficult to eat, sleep, or concentrate on work. The happily reunited family living peacefully near the small fishing village represented an insult to his authority. He had let the woman go in the belief she would live out her days in misery. Once again, she'd gotten the upper hand. She had to pay for that. He would take care of it personally. He would end them all.

"Boss, if she's there, it's because she got help. For all we know, someone may still be protecting them. Is it really worth the risk?" Dyukov might as well have been talking to the wall. Kemp had made up his mind.

Paul was aware of Kemp's peculiar relationship with the corporate security manager. The woman had been with the organization a long time. Polite, efficient, attractive in a nondescript way, and very knowledgeable, she counseled prudently and expertly on security issues. Gossip had it she possessed a set of exceptional and unconventional skills that Kemp found valuable. No one knew what those were. She stayed aloof from coworkers and gave away nothing.

Once, though, Paul had seen her observing his father during a meeting. In her veiled blue gaze, the son caught a glimpse of contempt or something worse: hatred. Had he imagined it? Did his father know how she felt? Kemp fumed when she resigned. Paul calmed him. Now, five years later, something agitated the older man. Paul believed it was related to the woman. He couldn't say how he knew; he just did.

He confronted his father over lunch.

"What is she to you, this woman who used to work here? She's been gone five years, yet she still bothers you.

"Paulo, please."

"I remember how you were when she left, Papà. Angry, but not for long. You calmed down, focused on the work. Now you're upset again. Worse than before, I think. The company is doing well. Our profitability is assured. It's her. What did she do? Steal information? Go to work for a competitor?" He regarded his father steadily. "Don't lie, not to me. I will know."

Kemp looked into his son's blue eyes and knew the truth of those words. "She cheated me, Paulo. She robbed me."

"Of what?"

"Of revenge." He waited for his son to press for details.

Paulo spoke at last. "You said you trusted me."

"I do."

"Then we must recover what you're owed. Okay?"

"Okay."

With that one word, Kemp set in motion the events that would end with the death of the only person he had ever truly loved.

Chapter Eleven

Spies of a certain age have limited choices. They might retire to the country. They might go into politics. They might serve as analysts away from the field, contributing their expertise to threat assessment or profiling. Or they might teach, either inside or outside the intelligence community. Having lived a sort of forced semi-retirement for several decades, Brian had no intention of puttering about. He briefly considered a late-life career as a full professor, but he didn't want to submit to ivory tower politics. Fortunately for my husband and any future students, MI6 called in the person of the chief himself.

Grayson Tenant is a career SIS officer. The Foreign Secretary appointed him to the chief's position just after 9/11. C, as he's known ("It all sounds so James Bond," I once told Brian), is the only member of the Service known to the public. Information about his private life is released sparingly. His wife Jane is a solicitor. He has two daughters, Adele and Elsie. They're still in their teens, which must present its own kind of headache for a man in the spy business. Brian assures me their Facebook profiles are a study in atypical adolescent discretion.

Grayson was typically direct during the call.

"I wouldn't blame you if you chose retirement, Foster. Years in hiding and apart from your wife; raising a son while helping to bring down an international criminal. Hell, you've earned a break. I don't see you exclusively as the pipe-smoking cardigan-wearing type. We can make better use of your talents. The position I have in mind keeps you largely in London. Very little globetrotting. You can still teach part-time. I understand University College has a fine linguistics department."

The upshot of that conversation and a follow-up meeting has resulted in Brian's dream job, or so he claims. He remains a senior intelligence officer. He deals exclusively with maritime crime, a perfect fit. He works as a first-tier analyst, interpreting information collected by field officers and making recommendations. He also serves as SIS liaison to the Shipping Defence Advisory Committee, which is a joint effort of the Chamber of Shipping and the Ministry of Defence. He may receive occasional field assignments, he tells me, an announcement I meet with suspicion.

"Nothing dodgy, Suzie; I promise. I'll mostly advise. I report straight up the chain, all the way to the Home Secretary. The work's important."

I agree. Curbing maritime crime is vital to British security. This is an island nation dependent on seaborne trade. Nearly all UK goods are moved over the water. The country's seaport industry is the largest in Europe. The sheer volume of legitimate traffic in and out allows contraband to be smuggled more easily. Illegal transport is an economic drain. Piracy disrupts the flow of goods. Trafficking brings international criminals to British shores. Organized gangs run interference at the docks in return for a share of the profits. The higher the stakes, the greater the danger.

Brian's cup of tea, you might say, especially as he gets to teach without putting up with the backbiting common to every tenured faculty member in every university everywhere.

His new job interests me for other reasons. The unlawful cargo Brian and his group seek to stop includes people. Human trafficking is big business. The World Health

Organization has labeled it an epidemic. The number of persons being moved into and throughout the UK alone is rising dramatically. Desperation and depravity feed the operation on both the supply and demand sides. Much time and money are going into efforts to stem the tide. Unfortunately, short-term prospects for eliminating the scourge are bleak.

During my long and difficult career, I was trapped in a destructive professional relationship with an unforgiving man. I don't deny the pathology of that association or the physical and psychological consequences to me. I'm trying to understand what kind of person I became, what kind of person I might still be. My long-dormant rage remains unresolved. I'm unsure which issues I've buried and which have simply morphed or dissolved with time.

One thing is true: I was never physically battered, starved, or imprisoned. I was in fear for my life, but I lived well. I had the love of a good man. Although I was apart from him and from my son a long time, I knew they waited for me. I can't presume to understand the suffering or anguish of someone who has been kidnapped or forced to live as a sex slave.

I feel an affinity for victims of this sort of abuse. I want to help them. I want to root out the causes, ferret out the perpetrators, fight the good fight. Channeling my anger, I suppose. Despite my aversion to overt involvement, I've found myself drawn in.

There are dozens of UK organizations dedicated to eliminating human trafficking. As helpful as these organizations are, there is some overlap among them. I've chosen to support Freedom to Hope because of its on-the-ground efforts in Cambodia and the Ukraine. Changing a culture that devalues and victimizes its most vulnerable citizens is unimaginably difficult. I can only hope the next generation is a more compassionate one. Meanwhile, money draws both men and women in as predators, not just product. Cutting into demand—making it less profitable—falls in part to Brian and his crew. This particular nonprofit focuses primarily on the victims.

I've offered to help on an ad hoc basis. Since I'm not a staff member or a counselor, my value to the organization is as a contributor. I don't know how to be a fundraiser; I simply don't know the right people. Instead, I donate as generously as possible and find myself on a committee planning the ubiquitous gala. As I stuff envelopes and chat up the other members, I marvel at where I am at this point in my life: in the company of London society ladies instead of at the mercy of a pitiless criminal. How odd.

Dr. Ankit and Mrs. Riya Chadha, the organization's major patrons, have offered to host the affair at their Kensington home. He's a world-renowned heart surgeon. She chairs the Freedom to Hope board and sits on several others. Their house in the city is rumored to be worth more than twelve million pounds and has been featured in *Home and Design*. In their late forties, they're drop-dead gorgeous, like movie stars. Betsy Harrigan, who is co-chairing the event, tells me they have three unusually gifted children. The eldest is earning top grades at Oxford, the middle child is a topnotch equestrian, and the youngest is a musical prodigy of some sort. A superstar family.

I tell my husband I'm not one for hobnobbing. He reminds me it's for a good cause. He's right.

The night of the gala, I opt for a simple amber sheath made by an up-and-coming designer I like. It works with the simple gold jewelry I've chosen. Brian looks his usual smart self in a business suit. I've managed to sell tickets to Tommy and Maggie, who in turn have purchased two more for friends. I'm not sure if this represents the best way to ingratiate myself into the good graces of our future in-laws.

The evening is an unqualified success. There are the usual speeches, including a moving presentation by a human trafficking victim. Afterward, we organizers circulate. I've been asked to serve as an "awareness leader," which I take to mean someone who makes sure the guests understand how desperately we need money. I've armed myself with facts and figures and acquit myself rather well, I think. At any rate, I get several gentlemen and at least two women to go for their checkbooks on the spot.

"You are absolutely terrific at this." Betsy is enthused over my performance. She's a good-natured woman, perhaps forty-five, with soft blonde hair and pale skin that flushes easily. The epitome of English wholesomeness. Husband Jack runs an enormously successful retail operation. Money wouldn't necessarily earn them a place in high society; however, Betsy's people apparently go all the way back to before the Magna Carta. Their one child isn't unusually gifted, but they've put him through all the best schools. Now he manages one of his father's stores.

She looks lovely this evening. Her black Marc Jacobs dress flatters her figure. Her jewelry is a clever combination of heirloom and new pieces. Her carefully pinned hair is just beginning to come undone. She's also perspiring, which I put down to excitement and not discomfort.

"We need to make better use of you, Suzanne. Starting now." My friend is both earnest and insistent. Before I know it, she has me by the elbow and is steering me toward a couple standing quietly to one side. I estimate him to be in his early fifties. She appears to be about ten years younger.

"Suzanne Foster, I would like you to meet Lord and Lady Westcott."

"Good to meet you." The lord is whip thin but fit, with lots of tousled brown hair. His tone is sincere, his handshake firm, his smallish hazel eyes warm. A consummate politician. "Call me Mark. And this is—"

His wife cuts in, her manner both gracious and reserved. "Annabel. Or Annie, which I much prefer. Pleased to meet you."

She extends her hand. It's mannish yet soft, the wide palm and blunt fingers at odds with the salon polish. Her plain features are softened by expertly applied makeup, a few pieces of high-end jewelry, and a well-cut dress in the most beautiful shade of ruby red. She's a bit shorter than I am and nicely proportioned. Her dark shoulder-length hair frames a broad flat face. Pale eyes, upturned at the ends, assess me from under heavy eyebrows. Her smile reveals a prominent set of incisors.

"I overheard you speaking to another group about the plague that is human trafficking." The woman speaks in an upper-class dialect. "I must tell you, your approach is brilliant: calm, informed, but with an underlying urgency that compels your audience to listen."

Betsy beams to my left.

I ought to be thrilled. Instead, a great weight settles on my chest, as if I'm being crushed. What is going on? My natural wariness sets in. Have I been poisoned? I look at my untouched wine glass. Unlikely. Heart attack? No, the sensation is more generalized. Panic attack? Possibly. But why?

I force myself to respond. "That's very kind of you to say so."

Annie is regarding me quizzically. Her head is cocked slightly to one side, her mouth turned down. A slight crease appears in the middle of those thick brows.

"You're American. Have we met before? I feel as if we have. Perhaps a long time ago?" She lifts her voice slightly at the end, appropriate for a question. Yet there is an insistent quality behind the words, as if she will not be contradicted.

I know that tone, the voice in my head warns. The pressure increases. Definitely a panic attack. I remind myself to breathe. "I don't recall."

She regards me with crystalline eyes. "You might have known me by my maiden name—Annabel Kemp."

I've never fainted; I won't start now. I don't want to lose consciousness. I want to turn back time or teleport myself across the room or out of the building entirely. Anything is preferable to standing here, unable to move.

"Mind if I drop in? I'm Suzanne's husband, Brian. Brian Foster." He's approached quietly to slip his left arm under my right, all the while chatting up my new acquaintances. I don't bother to wonder how he knows I'm distressed. I simply lean gratefully.

"Hullo, Betsy," Brian continues. "Great turnout tonight. What a lovely dress. Lord Westcott, your most excellent reputation precedes you. Lady Westcott, I presume. How delightful to meet you."

The small group preens under his lavish attention. "Please, call me Mark," insists Lord Westcott once again. Betsy fluffs her hair while Annie favors my husband with her distinctive smile.

"I must borrow my spouse for a minute, if you don't mind. My lord, my lady." Brian dips his head and, almost as an afterthought, lifts Annie's hand and kisses it in a manner at once respectful and amused, as if he knows they're engaged in an outmoded ritual. She blushes, which perhaps keeps her from noticing how carefully Brian studies her. Then he whisks me away.

We stay another half an hour. The time crawls by. I exchange the requisite pleasantries. I drink a glass of wine, only one. I even make small talk, although words are sticking in my throat. My husband makes some excuse, and we head for our coats. Betsy waylays us to declare the evening an absolute triumph. She seems thrilled with my modest efforts to pull cash out of reluctant donors. I might be pleased if not for the pervasive sense of dread.

As soon as we're in the cab, I turn to Brian. "Is there any doubt?"

"None at all. I spent a fraction of the time with him that you did. Trust me, though, I remember his face. She looks just like her father, more's the pity."

I've slowed my heart rate some. The roaring in my ears has receded. My mind tries to process this turn of events. I always knew Kemp had a family in London. His daughter married while I still worked for him. The wedding made the British society pages. I may have overheard him boasting to a colleague about how well she'd done for herself and how much he looked forward to being a grandfather. He said none of that directly to me, of course. I would have killed him on the spot.

The daughter clearly didn't make the connection. She didn't remember we met once when she visited her father's office. I might have looked different. I used another name. No doubt she'll dismiss the thought from her mind, put it down to misplaced curiosity or an imperfect recollection, and move on to other matters.

If only I could.

Chapter Twelve

Daniel Guzman preferred London to Rio. Cleaner, for one thing. More cosmopolitan, for another. And without question, safer. His mother's relatively high profile back home had always made him and his older brother Paulo potential targets for kidnappers and terrorists. In London, he was simply another wealthy playboy. True, the city suffered from a dearth of nearby beaches, and the weather was often atrocious. He could always fly to the Mediterranean.

He hadn't expected to end up in the UK. During college, Daniel spent every weekend partying and surfing in the Hamptons. In the winter, he headed to Miami or Cuba on his Brazilian passport. After graduation, he moved to Manhattan. He naturally attracted people of means who assumed he was one of them. He had some capital but not nearly enough to support his desired lifestyle. Luisa kept him on a relatively tight leash where finances were concerned. He hated that, hated not being able to spend what he wanted when he wanted. He liked money, not only for the things it could purchase but also because it facilitated access and influence. Like his father, Daniel had a taste for power. Unlike Kemp, he lacked discipline.

He hoped to accrue wealth without laboring too hard. Residential real estate promised quick returns. He worked for his mother, then his friend, showing modestly priced apartments and earning an even more modest commission. Daniel had a talent for client relations. The friend urged him to obtain a broker's license. This he did, to the delight of his parents. Now he would rule the market. With apartments and town homes selling for as much as forty million dollars, he expected to make enough to support his lifestyle.

Regrettably, the supply of high-end residences was in inverse proportion to the number of predatory agents. Daniel found himself up against aggressive men and women who knew everything about stepping on or over rivals in pursuit of the Big Commission. His three languages, his natural magnetism, even his mother's connections weren't enough to ensure his success. He moved from agency to agency, hoping to get the one big sale that would create a nest egg he could invest. His goal was to flip properties for profit. Yet the opportunities never materialized or were snatched away as soon as they appeared.

His thirtieth birthday came and went. He worried his allowance might be curtailed. His mother indicated she planned to slow down, perhaps even retire. She remained a stunning woman in late middle age and a force in her profession. She'd succeeded in building a business while raising two sons. She was independently wealthy. Now she wanted to go off and paint somewhere. Worse, she had no intention of turning over the reins of her company to him.

"You are charming, *meu amorzinho*, and the clients love you. But you have no head for business. Besides, why would you return to Rio when you're having so much fun in New York?"

Kemp was likewise disinclined to dole out money to his youngest, although he offered him a job. "You can prove yourself as your brother Paulo has done."

Paulo, always Paulo. The golden boy, the apple of his parents' eye, the success story. Where did that leave him? Daniel loved his brother, but he hated him as well for setting an impossibly high bar. Paul was everything the younger man was not: smart, responsible, hardworking. A bit dull, as far as

Daniel was concerned. The elder brother had even forgiven Kemp his absences as the boys were growing up. Family, however imperfect, meant a great deal to Paulo. Saint Paul, Daniel nicknamed his brother, who lacked only a halo.

Daniel viewed his life through a filter of disappointment. He resented growing up without a father. He hated that no one came to his soccer games except Paulo, when he wasn't parrying and thrusting or whatever he did with those swords of his. On occasion, the younger son even begrudged his hardworking mother. His father's controlled largesse toward his illegitimate sons didn't impress him, and it didn't keep him from suffering the covert looks and overt insults that came his way. Paulo didn't seem to notice or care that kids at school whispered about them.

Daniel, on the other hand, got into more than one fight over being called a *desgraçado*, a bastard. He once received a suspension that caused his mother to interrupt a meeting so she could pick him up at school. He refused to tell her why he'd fought. She yelled at him, reminding him what a disappointment he'd proven to be.

He was a bastard; that fact could not be denied. At least he admitted it. He decided to become a very wealthy bastard. True, he had limited access to his parents' money, but he wanted his own. No one teases a rich man. He already had a reputation as a clever and attractive boy. He could use that. He would use that. If his approach disappointed Kemp or Luisa, he would turn his back on them as they did on him.

Then his father and brother died in a mysterious explosion. Or so his preternaturally calm mother called to report.

Luisa flew to London immediately following the accident. There was no one to bury, yet she insisted on attending the memorial service. It must have been hard, although she never let on. Daniel offered to fly over, but she ordered him to wait in New York. He fretted about being kept away, but what could he do? He did as he was told.

Finally, she summoned him. He arrived to find her distracted and preoccupied. He assumed it was grief or shock, along with the need to oversee a slew of decisions both personal and professional. He knew little about his father's business dealings but guessed provisions had been put in place in the event of the old man's death. Perhaps the company would be sold, which meant a payout could be forthcoming. Daniel expected to receive a portion of any profits. That would go a long way to mitigating the pain of losing his brother.

The trip to London produced one big surprise. His father survived, severely injured but likely to recover. That fact could never be made public, because the "accident" had been an act of sabotage. Luisa alluded to a former employee, a woman, who wanted his father dead. She wouldn't elaborate further.

What she did share with Daniel was pertinent information about Kemp's activities over the years. He'd been far more than a prosperous entrepreneur. He'd been a master criminal, one involved in certain operations that made him enemies. This necessitated that they maintain the fiction of his death. Luisa assured her son that most people respected his father. Daniel got the impression most people also feared him.

The younger son went through the motions of helping his mother sort out the arrangements. Most of the time, he served as little more than a shoulder for her to lean on. Even after pulling back the curtain on Kemp's activities, she kept certain details to herself. She spent much of her time with

Arkady Dyukov, going over what Daniel felt certain were plans for the future.

Daniel understood that his parents trusted Dyukov. He didn't like the man; he considered his father's lieutenant ill-bred. Moreover, if anyone should be making decisions during Victor's convalescence, Daniel felt it should be him. After all, he was the heir.

He decided not to voice his objections. Neither his mother nor his father realized that he already knew quite a bit about Kemp's operation and had for years. Paulo had confided in his little brother.

He visited his father as much as he could stand. The sight of the man's face made him physically ill, as did the maimed right hand. It was like something out of a horror movie. It wouldn't do to be weak, however. As the days passed, he began to appreciate the depth of his father's resolve. Kemp had lost some business advantage. Yet he seemed willing to work clandestinely, if that's what it took for him to regain a level of influence. Although Daniel wasn't yet privy to his father's new plans, he guessed Victor Kemp wanted to regain a degree of leverage, if not power.

As he became familiar with London, Daniel decided he was in the right place at the right time. Here, as elsewhere, money bought anything and overcame nearly everything, including barely suppressed xenophobia and racism. Unlike Rio, London's poverty was tucked out of sight. Crime against the wealthy wasn't an issue. Foreign investors with full wallets were welcome in every quarter. Cranes clotted the streets. Luxury apartments sprouted like weeds along commercial streets or loomed at the edges of venerated historic districts. Most of the new dwellings served as investments for those wealthy enough to make London their part-time playground.

Daniel aimed to ingratiate himself into this set. The influx of cash meant new restaurants, new clubs, and more social events than he could cram into his calendar. He relied on old friends, new acquaintances, and intuition to get him where he needed to be. He preferred "by invitation only" gatherings. Private parties made for excellent hunting. Daniel fancied himself something of a hunter. His quarry usually involved underage girls.

While Kemp recuperated and Luisa attended him, Daniel watched them both. His mother carried on, but she remained visibly shaken by Paulo's death. As for his father, he would not discuss the incident. He stowed his grief away along with his anger. Daniel understood; he had a lifetime of practice at cataloguing but also covering over the offenses against him.

He couldn't understand why the old man didn't retire. He asked his mother.

"Why does he stay here? Why does he want to keep working? He could go anywhere in the world to heal. South Africa, New Zealand, even Brazil. Why not buy a small island in the Caribbean? He has enough money, doesn't he?" Daniel reminded himself not to sound too anxious.

"It's not about the money, Daniel. Your father has unfinished business. Besides, he likes to work. You could learn something from him."

Daniel nodded and smiled. Her attitude infuriated him. He didn't appreciate being shut out of the family business. Nor did he feel he deserved a lecture on the virtues of industriousness. He felt himself to be resourceful enough.

Unbeknownst to Daniel, Luisa had spoken to Kemp about putting their son to work. "Something aboveboard," she implored Kemp. "I'm worried enough about what Daniel does with his time, the people with whom he associates."

Kemp agreed. "He can work as a docker. Physical labor will toughen him. He'll stay in London; I can keep an eye on him. We'll get him a visa and a temporary union card. Arkady can make that happen. If he proves himself, I'll consider bringing him into the business."

"Manual labor." Luisa feigned mock horror. "He will find it unlike anything he's ever done." She managed a tentative smile. Kemp felt his own pain recede.

"Mi querida." He reached with his good hand to lightly touch her face.

~

Daniel expected London winters to be dreary, enlivened only by the holiday social season. He anticipated heading somewhere warmer after the first of the year, perhaps back to Brazil to chase the waves and work on his tan.

Instead, he found himself moving a portion of the forty-three million tons of cargo that came through the Port of London annually, most of it via the Port of Tilbury in Essex. He rose at 5:00 every morning in order to make the one-hour-and-twenty-minute ride away from the city. Oftentimes, he didn't even bother going to bed.

The job managed to be simultaneously backbreaking and boring. Daniel worked alongside a multitude of foreign nationals and hardened locals. Sweating from exertion, shivering as the north wind cut through their clothing, they loaded and unloaded what seemed to be an endless number of crates and containers. Most of the men probably welcomed the steady paycheck. Good for them. Daniel hated almost everything about the experience.

Arkady Dyukov stopped by every so often, no doubt to report back to his boss. Daniel initially thought he might be asked to do something on behalf of his father, perhaps a job related to criminal activity. He looked forward to proving himself.

Kemp's lieutenant quickly disabused him of that notion. On the first day, he insisted to Daniel that his father ran a completely legitimate transport business. Yes, Kemp used a new identity, but that was to protect himself from people who wanted him dead. Otherwise, Dyukov never spoke directly to Daniel, only to the foreman, a rough-looking Croatian named Sergei.

After a few weeks, Daniel realized he'd been put at the docks not to help but to be taught a lesson.

He kept his counsel; he also kept up appearances. He accepted every after-dark invitation extended to him. Young newcomers, some of them still in their teens, appeared regularly at pop-up clubs in some of the shady neighborhoods. They were thrill-seekers with time on their hands and money to burn. Daniel knew how to show them a good time. Sometimes he met and made himself available to their mothers. He'd always been able to do without more than a few hours' sleep or none at all, if it came to that. He had access to whichever pharmaceuticals he required to get him through a hard day and an even harder night.

Daniel spent six months listening and learning at work and at play. Some of his new nighttime friends had interests that dovetailed with his own. Their parents occasionally had dealings that would have drawn scrutiny had they not been so powerful. One was a dictator, another a banker, another a solicitor in service to a Chinese tycoon. An older woman Daniel sometimes entertained ran an international high-end online escort service that prided itself on discretion. She explained her profession warranted caution.

"If my client list ever becomes public, I will be dead. So, it isn't, and I'm not."

The information he picked up during his day job proved equally compelling. British law enforcement actively patrolled the docks and the waterways—the Port of London had no fewer than five separate entities sharing these duties—yet the smuggling trade flourished. Gangs infiltrated the unions and organized their own bypass systems. Despite the volume of trade at the port, Daniel tried to look out for the cargo vessels painted with a bird of prey and owned by "Francesco Guzman." The father he never had, he thought sardonically. He had little doubt Kemp's vessels would at some point carry contraband. He wondered what kind.

Chapter Thirteen

In the days following the charity event, I find it impossible to go anywhere. I choose instead to keep to our cozy flat. Since I don't want Brian to worry, I pretend to have a head cold. He plays along, bringing home spicy Thai food and laying in a supply of excellent tea.

London in early December is a study in contradictions. The weather is miserable, monochromatic, and chronically damp. Night seems to appear in the middle of the afternoon. On the other hand, the streets are festooned with holiday decorations. Houses, shops, streetlamps, and park benches glitter. Pop-up markets line the Thames and crowd the parks. They sell nearly everything, from wool jumpers to hot grog. You've never seen a more determined group than the shoppers and revelers who populate the stores and pubs. Be gone, dark, they seem to be saying. We will overwhelm you with our gaiety and our money. I find it exhausting.

Betsy Harrigan calls to ask me out for tea. I put her off as kindly as I can. To my great surprise, not to mention distress, I receive a handwritten invitation in the post from Annabel Westcott, inviting me to lunch.

"Go, Suzanne. Meet her for lunch. Otherwise, you'll drive yourself crazy."

Brian and I are preparing for bed. I'm ready to hop between the sheets, having been in my flannel nightgown all day.

"How am I supposed to sit across the table from the daughter of the man who stole my life and tried to end my family?" I demand.

"Nothing connects Annabel Kemp to anything her father did. She's the wife of a politically savvy noble and by all

102

accounts a generous contributor to several charities. She probably adores her children and owns a rescue mutt."

I laugh in spite of myself. Brian has again worked his magic on me.

Four days later, I'm sitting opposite a younger, softer version of the man I dreamed of killing until the day he died.

We've scheduled lunch at Balthazar, a tony replica of New York's fabled hot spot. We settle into a dining nook and peruse the menu. I doubt I'll be able to eat.

Annie appears exactly on time. Her outfit reflects the craze for all things Kate Middleton. No surprise. Prince William's new bride influences the wardrobes of nearly every British woman between the ages of fifteen and fifty-five.

My lunch companion wears a short taupe-colored trench coat over a simple shirtwaist dress with an asymmetric neckline and elbow-length sleeves. Very smart. The color is eye-catching, a blue that reminds me of twilight. It works well with her dark hair and eyes. Though not conventionally beautiful, Annie projects a sort of confident, effortless sophistication. Her jewelry is understated: small gemstone studs, a simple necklace with a charm and a bangle. I'm in a gray cashmere/wool jacket and black wool slacks. Good quality but deliberately subdued. An outfit unlikely to catch the eye.

We lay the starched white napkins on our laps and begin a conversation about the charity. There's enough to talk about. The waiter hands us menus; we both choose curried chicken salad and iced tea. Annie seems delighted.

"Look at that. Great minds think alike."

My chuckle sounds more like a gurgle.

"I hope you'll consider a seat on the board. I know—" She puts up a hand in case I object. I fight the urge to run from the room. She is her father's daughter, right down to the gestures. "You're new, Suzanne, and you don't know anyone. Besides, you don't want anyone to pry into your husband's business, not that anyone would."

I must look surprised.

"Come, now. Mark sits in the House of Lords. Unlike a great many of his colleagues, he makes a point of being active. He strongly supports the work of the Ministry of Defence. Did you know he once served as an officer in the Royal Navy? Brian is very well respected in SIS. I doubt they'll ever allow him to retire."

If I were writing a movie script, I couldn't have come up with a more ominous line. I remind myself that Annie isn't channeling her father. I doubt she knows anything about my past. Or does she? Time to find out. I take a huge sip of water and nearly gag on an ice cube.

"Do you mind if I think about it a bit? I do want to contribute." I hesitate before continuing. I hope I can sound more off-handed than I feel about my next question. "Say, did you ever figure out how we know each other?"

She frowns, unsure whether I'm teasing or not. "I didn't. Did you?"

"I may have met you once at your father's New York office. I worked for him for a number of years."

Her reaction causes me to reconsider everything I'd guessed about Annabel Kemp Westcott. She registers alarm, along with distaste. I'm not sure what to say. I decide I must at least proceed with caution.

"I worked for years as a corporate security manager."

"Corporate security manager. It almost sounds glamorous."

"I hope so. My title never changed, I'm afraid."

Annabel raises a formidable eyebrow. "That sounds like my father."

"At least my salary increased."

"It must have been interesting work."

That's one way of putting it, I think. "I'd been studying to be an engineer. But after I joined your father's company, my career took a different path."

To say the least, my insistent little voice remarks. I want to scream at it to shut the bloody hell up.

"You worked for him a long time."

"Decades," I reply. The silence stretches between us. The waiter brings the breadbasket, which gives me a moment to collect my wits. I decide to go with a tiny bit of honesty. "The experience had its moments of stress, to say the least," I offer.

Her laughter cascades across the table. It breaks the tension. "Aren't you the master of understatement?"

"Don't misunderstand me. The pay was very good, as I said, and the job made use of my talents." I grab again for my glass. Good thing it's not wine; I'd be thoroughly plastered by now. "In those days, women had fewer options. I wouldn't have found a remotely comparable position elsewhere."

"Yet he didn't promote you. And I have no doubt he was an exacting employer."

"He could be." I clear my throat. "Did you see a lot of him growing up?" I don't want to talk about any of this. I have to.

"Not much. His business had him in New York quite a bit. Also, Brazil. Rio mostly. Sometimes he traveled to Eastern Europe. He was a bit of a cipher, at least to me. I suppose women found him appealing. At any rate, he appealed to my mother. I know why she attracted him. She was well-placed and good-looking. She was also manipulative and quite adaptable as long as certain of her needs were met. I am none of those things," she adds.

"You're quite attractive." I say what needs to be said.

She waves her hand. "Not important. I grew up wanting for nothing. Mummy wasn't an attentive sort, but she made sure I went to the right schools and showed up at the proper events. I saw Father a few days every month. Believe it or not, many of my friends had fathers who traveled for work. Or they pretended to. Really, they all had mistresses stashed in flats around the city. Some of them even had second families. At least my father kept his in Brazil."

"Really?" I couldn't hide my shock.

Her laugh is light and easy. "Oh, I figured it out early on. It really wasn't all that difficult. I found two boxes my father had hidden in his closet, and I unwrapped them. Baseball mitts, accompanied by a short note. I decided it was Spanish or Portuguese. I also found mailing labels for Rio de Janeiro. You may have gathered I was a bit of a snoop as a young girl. It seemed a useful skill to cultivate."

A neglected only child. How familiar that sounds. I'm suddenly in mind of the Emily Dickenson poem about the nobody who recognizes a kindred spirit. In spite of myself, I sympathize with this poor little rich girl.

"Two sons, I assumed," Annie says. "That would have delighted Victor Kemp. He brought one into the business, as I recall. You must have met him during your time there."

"How on earth did you know?"

"A few years after I married—I was pregnant with Aidan, my eldest—Mark came home with a tidbit about Kemp's company he'd seen in the business section of the *New York Times*. 'I know you don't care about him, Annie,' he says to me. 'I just thought you'd find it interesting that the company has appointed a young Brazilian lad as CEO. Ink barely dry on his MBA, from what I can gather.' I'd already told Mark I suspected my father had two illegitimate sons. I'm unusually close to my husband, you see. We don't keep things from each other. But he was right about one thing: I didn't care. I processed the news, but I had no desire to follow up.'

"Did you know—?"

"Did I know the memorial service I attended was likely for my half-brother as well as my father? I did. The irony was not lost on me. I admit I looked around a bit, curious to see if I could spot the mistress or the other son. Not that I'd know what they looked like."

She leaned in. "You must understand, Suzanne; I hardly knew my father, and I never loved him. I was happiest when Victor Kemp wasn't about. Not that he was cruel to me, not in the least. In fact, he behaved as a doting uncle might. He took me shopping and to dinner. He inquired after my activities and seemed to take great pride in my accomplishments, such as they were. He even gave me away at my wedding.

"But he—what is it my children say? He creeped me out. There was an animal quality to him beneath an oh-so-thin veneer of civilized behavior. I fear I'm sounding typically English and wholly prejudiced. I promise you it wasn't that he was middle European. I'm half of whatever he was, as is plain to see. No, he seemed devious and dangerous. Children can sense these things, you know."

She shrugs. "I just didn't like him. I certainly didn't like being around him, not at all."

I'm impressed with her prescience.

"Yet you came to see him in New York."

Annie looks almost mischievous. "Yes, it must have been sixteen years ago. Curiosity compelled me. I went over to see friends and thought I'd pop in. Victor—I found it hard to think of him as Father at that point—invited me to dinner, but I insisted on lunch and a visit to the office. He seemed a bit taken aback, I must say. I gather he was used to controlling absolutely everything and everyone. I'm not sure what I hoped to accomplish. A meet-up with the half-brother, perhaps? Wouldn't that have been something? Did we resemble each other, do you recall?"

"Not at all." What I recall is that sixteen years ago, Paul Guzman was the financial officer at his father's company. Meanwhile, I was pretending my family was dead by the hand of the man for whom I continued to work.

"I didn't run into him, as it happened. Perhaps I was kept away whenever he was there. I ran into you, though. I'm sorry I don't recollect. Nor do I remember anything odd about the workplace."

"There wasn't anything to see."

She throws me a sharp look. "Of course, if my father were involved in something he didn't want visible, he would have established a legitimate business as a front, wouldn't he?"

I say nothing.

"Security consultant. What an interesting job. You'd have been on the lookout for corporate espionage, that sort of thing. Perhaps there was more you did. With my father, I imagine there was always more."

Stop now, I think. Somehow, the message is telegraphed across the table. Annie reaches for my hand.

"I have no business pushing you, Suzanne. Your history with Victor Kemp seems to be a sore subject. The fact is, he wasn't easy to be around. We both know it. Truthfully, his death didn't distress me at all."

I don't dare respond.

"Do you know what? I'm a great believer in letting the past stay in the past. Especially when the present is so much more beguiling. Besides, I've been simply dreadful about monopolizing the conversation thus far." Annie claps her hands, as if to banish bad thoughts from the table. "Let's talk about your son's engagement to the delightful Kate Edgerton. Tommy and Maggie have asked us to the party they're throwing." She stops suddenly. "That's not a problem, is it? Not awkward or anything? Because I can certainly bow out."

Against any and all odds the universe might have presented, I genuinely like this woman. "Absolutely not a problem. We'd be delighted to have you there."

"Splendid!" Her smile, infectious instead of chilling, is nothing like her father's. "Kate is really a marvelous young woman. We sit on at least one charity board together. She has a wicked sense of humor, as you must know. Terribly smart as well. I've seen photos of Michael. Gorgeous. I can't wait to meet him. What a couple they make. I mean, in addition to being impossibly good-looking, they have complementary professional aspirations. How did they meet? Has a wedding date been set?"

Her soothing prattle washes over me, carrying away all traces of anxiety. Annie Westcott is a nice person, observant and shrewd, yet with an empathy utterly lacking in her father. Her provenance hasn't dictated who she has become. Neither has mine. I'm the daughter of a deluded drug addict and a conniving narcissist. She is the daughter of my worst enemy. But he is dead and gone, and here we sit, talking about the future.

"I would love to fill you in," I say as our waiter approaches with our salads. "Should we splurge on some wine?"

I am suddenly famished. We settle in for a leisurely meal, two ladies who lunch.

Chapter Fourteen

Victor Kemp carefully chose the contraband he carried. Once he'd established his business, he began to add goods of questionable legality or items that were banned outright. Clients who needed to ship things covertly paid more, starting with a sixty-five percent down payment. He had no moral qualms about what he transported. He didn't care whether his vessels contained cocaine or purloined medical supplies. He had no interest in whether the consignment went to a brutal tyrant or a bloodthirsty rebel group. He employed a team of lawyers to structure airtight contracts and used another team of enforcers to make certain his terms were met. He expected his clients to be equally exacting should cargo be lost or damaged en route.

Kemp never intended to transport human cargo. In his previous dealings, he had refused to deal with sexual slavers or traffickers. He didn't trust them. Too many variables came into play. Too many things might go wrong. Further, those on the purchasing end of the business catered to a specific type of individual he loathed: wealthy sexual predators.

Victor Kemp didn't hold human life in particularly high regard. He had killed or had underlings kill scores of people over the course of his professional life. He never allowed obstacles of any kind to interfere with his plans. He simply believed enslaving people to do one's bidding represented an exercise in vanity, if not sadism. Housemaids, gardeners, nannies, cooks, and caretakers kept by force would never provide the highest level of service. Fear was a tool or a weapon, not a form of payment.

As for sex slaves, Kemp reckoned that men (or women) who had to buy children to satisfy their needs suffered from some deficiency. He understood solitary addictions like gambling or drugs. Addictions that involved domination he rejected as a failure of will.

So, no human cargo. That should have been the end of it. Except he was being pushed to reconsider by Daniel.

His second son surprised him. He lasted six months in the job at the docks. Kemp wouldn't have guessed Daniel had the fortitude, especially given his nocturnal activities. Society columns mentioned the dashing bachelor rumored to be the son of a Portuguese shipping magnate. Victor admired his son's bravado and at the same time disliked his indiscretion. He winced when he read (on a social media site Arkady pointed him to) that his son was keeping company with some very young women. This was not the sort of reputation anyone associated with Kemp/Guzman ought to cultivate. Furthermore, consorting with children was illegal.

When Daniel extended an invitation to lunch, his father nevertheless accepted with pleasure. He welcomed the chance to get out. Too often, he felt like a prisoner in his own home. Besides, he looked forward to sitting down with his son. He knew Daniel did not come to him merely for social reasons. Something was on the younger man's mind.

Daniel had arranged for them to dine in a private room in the back of a trendy eatery. They entered via a well-hidden and thoroughly enclosed garden. The son had dressed in a smart jacket and slacks. He exuded confidence and vitality. His face had lost all traces of softness; his body appeared hard and lean. Despite differences in color and build, Victor recognized a replica of his younger self.

More noticeable, Daniel showed no indications he led the late-night lifestyle described in the media. Perhaps the reporters exaggerated. Such things were common, especially when it came to the British press.

The restaurant opened out onto the Thames. A light wind ruffled the water. Flower boxes dotted the patio railing. London embraced spring, especially those rare days of blue skies and gentle breezes. Kemp wore a wide-brimmed fedora pulled down on the right side. He turned his head to catch the sunshine. He was in mind of a beautiful spring day, not quite a year earlier, when a fishing boat entered the calm waters of a channel off the Irish Sea.

Daniel ordered for them both. Ceviche appetizers, salad, steak, and a fine bottle of red from Portugal's Douro Valley. Kemp approved. He'd noticed restaurant fare in London had improved greatly over the forty years he'd lived there.

They conversed in Portuguese during the first course. Kemp enjoyed practicing the language. He also recognized how hungry he was for small talk. Arkady didn't have any interest in banter. Daniel excelled at it. This didn't surprise his father. The son's patience did, though. He'd always been a bit demanding, his sense of entitlement compelling him to insist on immediate gratification. Spoiled, Kemp assumed, as younger sons often are. Now Daniel waited, looking for the appropriate moment during the conversation to introduce a new topic.

As the waiter set down the filet mignon, he began.

"I've brought you a proposal, Papà." Daniel switched to English. The global language of business. "I've put a lot of consideration into this, so I trust you'll give it the hearing it deserves."

Kemp nodded without speaking. He noticed Daniel's expression tighten before he continued.

"I've found a way to improve your profit margin," the young man began.

"I'm listening."

"It's time you brought me into the business. I don't need to keep working on the docks."

"I agree. I have another position in mind for you."

"Actually, I have something to suggest to you." Daniel smiled, emboldened. He took a sip of wine, then continued. "I've met many people in my short time in London, notwithstanding my work schedule. In fact, I have come into contact with potential clients who would benefit from your services, clients with unlimited resources."

No one has unlimited resources, Victor thought. "What sorts of clients?"

"These are people who need to get goods from one place to another, goods that might not meet certain legal requirements."

"What makes you think I'm any longer involved with such things?"

"I know you and I know what you're up to. I also know you like the money, the power, and especially the thrill that comes with outsmarting others. Your move into shipping was brilliant, and so was giving yourself enough time to establish a perfectly aboveboard trade. I'm sure you've been in touch with former competitors to offer them your services. I'm simply proposing you add new clients."

"You're presuming quite a bit, Daniel. Perhaps you've misunderstood something you overheard. Or some confidence your mother shared with you."

"Neither one, Papà. I pay attention. I understand prudence better than you might think. No one knows about Victor Kemp's survival, let alone what became of his second son. Or even that he had one."

Kemp ignored the note of bitterness. He put down his fork and regarded his son. "Let's get back to the business at hand. You suggest an expansion. I'm curious as to the specifics of your proposal. For instance, what would be your role in all this?"

"I can be the broker. Some of the clients I bring in will have specialized cargo."

"Specialized illegal cargo."

Daniel pretended he hadn't heard.

"I've already suggested to them we can facilitate any transport. I'm related to the owner of a shipping company, one that has built a sterling reputation in far less than a year. Top-quality vessels, no problems with piracy, no issues with mutiny, clean, safe transport. That sort of thing. I hope you don't mind if I play off our connection. We do share a last name, after all."

Victor's eyes narrowed. "Are you trying to push me into a corner, Daniel?"

"No, not at all. If I were doing that, I wouldn't have remained for nearly six months in that crappy hellhole you chose for me, working my ass off side by side with the scum of the earth."

Daniel stopped, drew a breath, and continued. "I'm offering my services. I've been on the outside long enough. It's time for me to be let inside. Paulo is gone. I'm here. You need me. And I can help you."

Kemp said nothing.

"I know your ships carry contraband. There's no need to pretend otherwise. That being the case, we can do even more. I'm not talking about transporting drugs or stolen artifacts. Those are low-level items. No doubt nuclear or bioweapons fetch a higher price, although such cargo can be dangerous. But what about people?"

Victor heard the note of eagerness in his son's voice.

115

"The best commodity to carry is the one that is hardest to send and most in-demand. Weapons can be transported in the lining of a coat. For God's sake, there are now experiments underway that will let people print guns! Illegal substances can be replicated in a lab, of course. Moving bodies is harder, yes. But the demand is skyrocketing. It's a multibillion-dollar business with no signs of slacking off. Governments are divided in their policies for dealing with the export and import of humans. Response is weak. Many countries don't consider missing people to be nearly as critical as, say, missing antiques." He paused to catch his breath.

"People are a liability, Daniel. They take up space. They eat, they drink, they shit, they get sick, and they die. They make the worst cargo and the worst investment possible."

"They are by far the easiest consignment to offload."

The two men could have been talking about livestock or handbags.

"Victor, look." Daniel leaned forward, intent on making his point. "This is the wave of the future, at least the immediate future. Free labor keeps costs down. Whole families are used. Men, women, even children." His eyes flashed.

Kemp caught the change in his son as the discussion proceeded. The thought of human trafficking excited Daniel. This wasn't simply about commerce. Some unmet need drew the younger man to the venture. The father wondered, not for the first time, what motivated his son. Was he trying to impress Kemp? Did he hope to stand up to the memory of his dead brother? Or was there something darker at work? Did he have a predilection for young girls or small children? Kemp didn't care to speculate. Whatever it was, it rendered his son fallible.

He sat back in his chair and spoke carefully. "I am in the shipping business. I don't buy anything except vehicles and employees. And access. I don't sell anything except the services of my fleet for purposes of transport. Is that absolutely clear?"

"Of course, Papà."

"The new clients must be thoroughly vetted. Contracts will need to be drawn up. My lawyers can take care of that. We require a new payment structure. We must charge more, as we will be taking on far more risk."

"Naturally."

"We must allow a few months in order to set certain procedures in place and to determine what we can reasonably manage. We will not use one of my current ships but rather one we procure by other means."

Victor paused. "Finally, I am not in the business of serving the personal penchants of my employees. No one touches anything I transport. Is that understood?"

Father and son exchanged a look. Beneath Daniel's studied nonchalance, Kemp sensed both calculation and hunger. Below that, he picked up an undercurrent of resentment. Daniel was an immature child in a man's body. That didn't make him less treacherous. The older man might have said no. He suspected Daniel would have found another way to entangle himself with the trafficking business. His son might be a fool or a great businessman— or both. Kemp couldn't yet know. He would have to keep a sharp eye on this undertaking.

He knew what his son saw. An old man coming to terms with a new reality. The prodigal son returned, empowered. A tougher version of his old self. Someone who'd spent time with hardened men, many with nothing to lose.

As for Kemp, he saw a no longer young man who'd been stockpiling disappointments and harboring grudges for years. An opportunist who knew what he wanted, or rather, what he believed he deserved. Someone who didn't know enough to fear Victor Kemp, aka Francesco Guzman.

Someone who should have.

Chapter Fifteen

Ubatuba, Brazil, is a small city located east of São Paulo and down the coast from Rio de Janeiro. Its reputation for excellent surfing is rivaled by its standing as one of Brazil's rainiest locations. Dedicated board riders who know to avoid high season and most weekends can count on having pristine beaches and perfect waves to themselves.

Unless a body shows up.

The corpse that two surfers found in the early hours of a bright December morning initially became the business of São Paulo's Civil Police. The department sent its lead investigator to the morgue, an experienced detective who'd seen this sort of thing before. Murder was not unusual in and around Brazil's larger cities. Neither were washed-up bodies.

The state coroner determined the corpse had been in the water perhaps eighteen hours. Unusually cold ocean temperatures had kept it in relatively decent shape forensically, although a saltwater predator had chewed off part of the right leg. Female and young, likely between twelve and fourteen, of Asian descent. Water in the lungs occurred postmortem. The girl had broken her neck, possibly prior to going into the water or as she fell. The coroner found opiates present in the system and faint markings on the remaining ankle. Perhaps a tattoo or an inventory marker.

"She was a virgin. I have enough to tell that. Yes, we can tell such things. You never know when it might be relevant."

A small, efficient-looking woman with long graying hair pulled back into a bun, the coroner amused herself by watching reruns of "CSI: Miami" and American college football. Now she picked up the dead girl's hands.

119

"Something else. I've found traces of steel shavings underneath her fingernails. Her hands are bruised along the outside."

"From fighting off an assailant?"

"More like she pounded them against metal."

"A steel-reinforced wall."

"Against which she clawed, scratched, and beat her hands. Maybe trying to escape."

The detective looked down at the child who'd been treated so cruelly. His own daughter was eleven.

"I hate this job," he said.

He left to call his chief, who concluded the girl on the beach represented something too large for his department to handle. He in turn called in Brazil's Federal Police. An agent arrived in Ubatuba from Rio. It took him less than an hour to recommend contacting Interpol. Law enforcement tended to ignore issues of sovereignty when it came to cases like this.

~

"More beer, Suzanne?" Charlie Campbell gestures at my nearly full glass.

"I'm fine, thanks."

Charlie refills his mug and Brian's and takes a long draught.

"Much better. All right, where was I? Oh yes, my best friend has the nerve to ask me if and when I plan to retire. I suppose he thinks I'm past ripe, having given thirty-five years of my life to Her Majesty's Secret Service. No doubt some of the younger lads are thinking the same."

"Charlie, I was joking," Brian protests. "You'll outlast us all, mainly because you're damn near irreplaceable. Who else has a dozen accents at his disposal? Don't forget; I've seen you pretend to be a Texas oil baron." Brian turns to me. "His fussy French bureaucrat is better than the real thing."

It's true; the wily Scotsman has perfected the art of playing many parts while remaining inconspicuous. Though Charlie is cagey about his birth year, I imagine he's somewhere in his fifties. You couldn't describe him as tall or short, fat or thin. His hair is brown going to gray. I swear his eyes change color every time I see him. His voice is pitched in the middle of the normal masculine range, although he can make it higher, lower, lighter, or heavier as required. His features are unremarkable. They're also symmetrical, which is unusual. I'm told he's a wizard with makeup and wigs and so forth. He rarely seems to need props of any kind. He's escaped from some sticky situations, Brian tells me, because witnesses have trouble describing him.

One other thing: Charlie is strong. Not just physically, although he's demonstrated impressive skills. What distinguishes Charlie is his strength of character. He is quite simply a man of sound principles: self-aware, self-confident, loyal, and passionate about his work, his family, and his friends. There is no one on earth Brian trusts more. I feel the same.

We're having dinner together, as we often do when Charlie gets down to London. He lives in a small town outside Glasgow with an old collie and a patient wife. He has a son about Michael's age, I believe. About every four weeks, he comes here for business, or so he says. Since MI6 retains offices in Glasgow and Charlie is on the road much of the time, the so-called business seems to be about having a sit-down with people he likes. We're delighted, whatever the reason.

We're meeting in one of London's countless pubs, a place my husband insists is underrated and thus overlooked by the tourists. It's noisy and cheerful in the main room, the perfect antidote to a bleak December evening. Brian and Charlie go back to speaking in the shorthand of longtime friends. I'm enjoying the sound of two men reveling in each other's company without paying attention to what they're saying. Then my ear catches the words "human trafficking" and I tune in.

"Charlie, even if the girl that washed up on a beach in Brazil turns out to be a victim of human trafficking, how does MI6 get pulled in?"

Charlie takes a mouthful of meat pie and washes it down with a swig of beer.

"You know C is pushing for greater international agency cooperation, right? Especially since we're under fire for overreach in the last few years."

"Every spy group in the world is under suspicion these days. Frankly, the politics shouldn't be the concern of either the analysts or the operatives."

"They aren't, laddie. I still do my job, and you do yours. But it's all to the good that some of our intel makes its way to multinational organizations like Interpol and OSCE."

The Organization for Security and Cooperation in Europe deals with a broad array of "security issues," like the spread of arms, protection of national minorities, preservation of the environment, terrorism, and human rights violations. It's an ambitious agenda. Input from law enforcement and intelligence agencies is generally welcome. Interpol, for instance, has an ongoing partnership with OSCE.

"Brian, you know everything's global," Charlie continued. "Money laundering, nuclear proliferation, slavery, and every kind of terrorism you can think of. As of right now, OSCE and Interpol have hooked up to fight human trafficking. Other agencies have been brought on board. There's a great deal of political and public interest in and support for efforts to stop it, wherever and however possible. At least there is today."

I can't fault Charlie for his cynicism.

"Suzanne has put some effort behind a group doing solid on-the-ground work in the area of trafficking." My husband speaks with a touch of pride I find charming. "She convinces the smart set to give their money to something other than the art and fashion industries."

Charlie looks at me. "Might that be Freedom to Hope?"

"How on earth did you know?"

"I dinna ken; I guessed. Jenny donates a small amount every year. She tells me the group does good work. She's all for savin' bairns."

Jenny is Charlie's wife. I remember they lost a daughter to crib death.

"Let's recap." Brian has pushed back his uneaten sandwich. "This dead girl has been traced back to a sizeable network operating out of Cambodia. The biggest trafficker by far in that region is a Chinese national named Bai Jie Heng. The man is wanted by at least forty governments. He's only gotten stronger. In the last few years, he's grabbed control of smaller operations. He supplies from half-a-dozen origin countries and traffics to at least that many destinations, though he favors the Americas. He might have some competition, but he's got more local officials in his pocket than any ten newcomers. You know this, Charlie."

"I do. His specialty is young girls, both Asian and Caucasian. Plenty of those in the 'stans these days."

Uzbekistan, Turkmenistan, Tajikistan, Kyrgyzstan, and Kazakhstan have fallen on hard times. Grinding poverty and indifferent or corrupt officials conspire to push desperate families into selling their children. Young women hoping for a better life sign up with questionable "agencies" to pursue work abroad. These countries have added greatly to the supply of sex slaves in the last decade. All this I've learned from my involvement with Freedom to Hope.

Brian is unimpressed. "Charlie, I'm your biggest fan and perhaps your greatest friend next to your wife. I'm no mind reader, though. You said this case came to your attention and you thought it should come to mine. Why? Yes, human trafficking is horrible. Yes, the ringleader in this instance is a bad guy. We've been after him for years. The children he sells are by way of the most devastated regions in the world, some of them having been dumped by Mother Russia. No surprise. Old story, old chap."

Charlie carefully folds his napkin. "Old story, yes. New route."

Brian and I both sit up at that. Charlie has our full attention.

"Assuming the seller, the product, and the destination are unchanged, ask yourself what's different? What would bring this to our notice? What's changed is the route: east to west, far south of the tip of Africa, using a well-equipped vessel that doesn't seem to require refueling and always manages to avoid both the pirates and those pitifully few areas where maritime law is in effect. It's likely stolen; the number of phantom ships traveling the globe is in the tens of thousands."

"Stolen and re-outfitted. Tell me, Charlie, who uses that particular route?"

"I thought you might ask, my friend. It's followed almost exclusively by completely legitimate vessels, at least as far as we know, owned by a Portuguese businessman we've only just learned about. Name's Guzman. Francesco Guzman. Although that may not be his real name."

Someone enters the pub just then, accompanied by a bitter winter gust that temporarily displaces the warm, close air. That's not why I suddenly feel cold.

Chapter Sixteen

Arkady Dyukov watched his boss pace back and forth. The open office space seemed too small to contain the man's fury. Yet when he spoke, Victor Kemp used the measured tones of someone conducting a business meeting. Dyukov wasn't fooled for a minute.

"The body was traced back to one of our ships. I don't need to know how that happened. A branded body washed up on shore, someone suspected human trafficking, and suddenly every law enforcement agency is on it, along with a hundred watchdog groups. Which is why I never wanted any of this." He stopped himself and expelled a lungful of air before resuming. "What I must know is how this child ended up off the ship and into the water. What have you learned?"

Dyukov gave a quick recap. The ship docked at Rio at midnight four days earlier, where the middleman scheduled to take delivery of his human cargo found the body count down by one. Kemp's associates moved quickly to minimize the damage. They quarantined the crew at an abandoned police station inside one of the city's worst favelas. Since the group had nothing to useful to say, they'd been eliminated. The captain remained in isolation at a separate location until he could be interrogated. The ship meanwhile had been pulled into a private dock and taken offline immediately.

The loss of a vessel represented a serious decline in income. Of greater concern was any injury to Kemp/Guzman's reputation. The company had never experienced a problem delivering cargo. As a precaution, it carried special insurance against loss. Within hours of hearing about the missing girl, Kemp arranged advanced payouts to the cargo's owners. The money mattered far less than appeasing the sellers. Victor Kemp had no illusions about the kind of people he was dealing with.

"I want to talk with the captain. Now."

The skipper, an experienced seaman from Cyprus, had a lot to say. The man must have been startled to find himself in front of a computer screen speaking with a heavily bandaged man who introduced himself as the ship's owner, Francesco Guzman. They spoke in English, their common language. The man told Kemp that twenty girls were loaded at Phnom Penh Port into a steel-encased room with a bucket that served as a commode at one end and overlapping mattresses at the other. They received three meals a day.

"We made sure they were reasonably comfortable, Senhor Guzman."

"I'm sure you did."

"The crew knew the girls were strictly off limits. The problem was the guest."

"What guest?" Off screen, Kemp clenched his left hand, but his voice revealed nothing.

"A Chinese man got on with the cargo. He claimed to be a nephew of the cargo's owner. I was told never to allow passengers under any circumstances, Senhor Guzman. This man insisted. He even gave me your son's telephone number to call. I did so and confirmed that Daniel Guzman extended permission for this man to board. He said he'd promised the man's uncle. I assumed you knew. What was I to do?"

The captain now rushed through the rest of the story, eager to unburden himself and appear cooperative. The nephew, who he described as a weasel-faced little man with an appetite for young girls, decided to sample the wares. He let himself into the enclosure in the middle of the night. One crewmember reported he hurt the girls. The captain stayed out of it, unsure how to proceed. One night, though, the Chinese man forgot to close the door. One of the younger girls slipped out.

"They weren't chained up, sir," the captain told Kemp. "I'd never do that. They were compliant, but the man, he treated them badly. This one girl scrambled up and over the gunwale like a little monkey and jumped right off the side of the boat. A crew member reported hearing a splash. It was all hands on deck, believe me. We could see coast lights at that point, but we were still miles from the shore. The poor girl didn't stand a chance. Broke her neck as soon as she hit the water; I'm sure of it. We briefly spotted the body and tried to pull her out, but it was dark and we could not manage."

"What happened to the Chinese man?"

"We locked him in his room and called ahead to report the problem to your representatives. Your man in Rio has made arrangements to return the nephew to the uncle's agent."

Kemp nodded. His people acted correctly. Kemp/Guzman was responsible for the delivery failure. The client would deal separately with his imprudent relative and with the fallout from the sibling or in-law whose son he had caused to disappear.

The captain stared at the screen, his expression beseeching. "I hope I handled everything according to your satisfaction, Senhor."

"You did what you had to do, as we all must." Francesco Guzman waved his hand. It was the last thing the captain saw before the guard standing behind him shot him.

Kemp signed off and turned to Dyukov. "Find Daniel," he ordered. "Now."

~

Daniel Guzman had been looking forward to a well-deserved afternoon off in the company of two stunning young ladies. Exactly how young, he couldn't say. He'd been careful not to ask. If he had to hazard a guess, he'd say fourteen. Not as young as he liked but young enough.

The text annoyed him. A summons from his father, yet not from his father. Victor Kemp didn't text. No, Arkady Dyukov had issued the terse command for a meeting to take place within the next two hours. Not dinner. Not even cocktail hour, which meant this was not to be a social occasion.

Daniel didn't appreciate being ordered about, especially by Dyukov. He put it down to language barriers and cultural differences. The Russians and other Eastern Europeans could be brusque to the point of rudeness, he found. Luckily, he'd inherited not only his mother's good looks but also her Latin sensibilities.

The text came in at 1:30 p.m. and Daniel showed up at the office at 3:29, just under the implied deadline. He intended to make a point. He might need to remind his father that their new venture had increased profits. Eight months after he came to Kemp with his proposal, five months after they'd outfitted a single ship to accommodate human cargo, business was booming. Daniel thought it was time to add another vessel or two. Perhaps his father concurred. Possibly he planned a midafternoon celebration. Daniel had no problem drinking champagne any time of day or night.

"So," he said, his smile wide, his air jovial. "What urgent business requires my attention?"

"Sit down, Daniel." Kemp directed his son to an uncomfortable-looking chair.

Daniel unwrapped his scarf slowly. He took his time unbuttoning his coat. He wanted to get the lay of the land. Kemp didn't sound happy; as far as his son could read his face, his father didn't look pleased, either. Daniel couldn't say what had caused the downbeat mood.

He looked around with distaste. The surroundings wouldn't help anyone's disposition. Too antiseptic, too barren. The place cried out for a decorator's touch, not to mention decent furniture. He ought to have a desk for himself and one for the secretary he intended to hire. And partitions, as the current arrangement did not permit adequate privacy.

He sauntered over and sat down opposite his father, crossing his long legs and adjusting the crease of his perfectly tailored pants. Arkady Dyukov stood to one side of his boss like a sentry. Dyukov: ever-present, ever loyal and, to Daniel's way of thinking, ever annoying. That might also need to change. He considered speaking in Portuguese to keep Dyukov in the dark. He chose English. Might as well keep things polite. Besides, he had nothing to hide.

"How may I help you, Father?"

"We've had some disturbing news about one of our shipments, specifically the cargo bound for Rio from Phnom Penh."

Human cargo, Daniel thought. Victor Kemp still refused to name it as such. Ah, well. Technically not Daniel's responsibility once he signed the client, but he guessed his father would try to pin any problems on him. He kept his expression agreeable.

"I'm sorry to hear that. We've had no difficulties with the four previous deliveries."

"How do you know Zhang Li Tao?"

The abrupt question caught Daniel off guard.

"Tao? He's, ah, the brother of an acquaintance of mine. I met him at a party here in London last year."

"Where the two of you no doubt indulged your taste for underage girls."

"I'm an adult. My personal life is no concern of yours."

"It is if it has clouded your judgment. What made you believe you had any right to invite him aboard one of our vessels?"

Daniel felt as if the ground had shifted. He half expected to look down and find himself dangling over a yawning abyss. Stay calm, he ordered himself.

"I didn't see a problem. Tao was doing some business in Phnom Penh for his uncle. We were shipping his cargo, you may remember. The uncle thought it might be valuable if his nephew were allowed to see another side of the business."

"That is a lie!" Kemp slammed his fingerless fist on the desk. "His uncle knew nothing of his nephew's unscheduled trip. He is, however, aware of Tao's predilection for very young girls, which is why he would never have sanctioned this arrangement. He is not a fool. Unlike his nephew and my son.

"Just a minute—"

"A young girl died on that ship, Daniel. Or rather, she escaped during one of your friend's visits to the room where the cargo was kept. She jumped overboard rather than suffer his indignities. Her body washed up along the coast of Brazil, not far from one of your former surfing spots. Her disappearance has caused our client great inconvenience and cost us dearly, as you can well imagine. I suspect it also cost your friend his life. His uncle is not a forgiving sort."

"What?" Daniel leapt out of his chair.

"Sit down and listen carefully. We have taken steps to clean up after your mess. It's bad enough that this incident has angered an important client. As you can imagine, or perhaps you cannot, the girl's death has attracted the interest of Interpol and others. They are asking questions, Daniel. Do you understand what I am saying? We are now vulnerable. Suspected. Exposed."

Daniel didn't speak. He couldn't; he could scarcely swallow.

Kemp walked around the desk and bent over his son. His face came so close to Daniel's it nearly touched. The younger man wasn't sure which disturbed him more, the puckered skin or the cold eyes. He stifled the urge to turn away.

"I am not inclined to let this go, Daniel. If you were anyone but my son, you would be dispatched by now. Be that as it may, I'm a civilized man, not an animal like some of the people you have mixed us up with. There's also your mother to think of. She's had enough grief to deal with. Therefore, you will survive. Know this, though; we will no longer transport human cargo."

"That makes sense." Daniel tried to speak in a normal tone, one that did not reveal his fear.

Kemp straightened and clamped his left hand down hard on his son's shoulder. His strength surprised Daniel. The younger man couldn't have moved if he'd wanted to.

"I'm not finished. From now on, you will have nothing to do with my business. Nothing. I can't make you change your name, but you will cease to identify yourself as my relative or as the relative of Francesco Guzman. As for how you earn a living going forward, I don't care. If you want to return to the docks, I might be able to arrange that. You might also consider marrying a wealthy woman. Perhaps someone older, someone who will turn a blind eye to your faults.

Kemp pushed even harder, his fingers digging into Daniel's shoulder. "You have one month to figure it out," he said. "One month, Daniel. And don't think of going to your mother. On this, she will not defy me." He removed his hand.

"You may go."

Daniel managed to propel himself into the winter dark. It was not yet four o'clock. It could have been midnight. A harsh wind blew off the Thames. He shook, not with cold but with fear. He had misjudged everything about the operation: the hazards, the complications, his friend's fecklessness, and the uncle's brutality.

Most of all he'd underestimated his father. Kemp had risked everything to come back from the dead. Daniel had approached his father's business as a lark. Now he'd jeopardized the entire undertaking. Worse, he'd earned the older man's enmity. He began to see how unsafe that might be for him.

He sank onto a bench and looked across the choppy waters. He must find a way to get back into his father's good graces. To do that, he needed to address the root cause of Victor Kemp's problems. Daniel wasn't at fault, not really. All of the troubles that led to this debacle could be traced back to what happened in Wales. Perhaps farther back than that. Everything Victor Kemp had experienced over the past year and a half, all the pain and loss, could be tied to that woman, the one Paulo called a thorn in their father's side. She had worked for him; according to Paulo, she had also murdered for him, which made her dangerous.

Now she was retired. A former assassin but still a threat. No matter. Daniel knew she lived in London. He even knew her name: Suzanne Foster. She was the problem. He had no doubt her removal would be the solution.

Chapter Seventeen

Today is the shortest day of the year. Dusk arrives at 3:00 p.m. I'm sitting in an overstuffed armchair, my legs folded up under me, an afghan across my lap, a cup of tea close at hand. Normally I don't mind these brief afternoons. The flat is well lit and inviting. A small gas fireplace offers at least the illusion of warmth. We've furnished the place comfortably. There's plenty of room by London standards, yet I feel as if the walls are closing in on me.

The rising star Victor Kemp brought into the company—Paul Guzman—was Kemp's son. Most everyone suspected as much. He looked a bit like his father around the eyes. I always assumed Guzman was the mother's name, a fact Brian confirmed. They'd had eyes on the mistress for years and on her two sons, at least until they left home.

As for Paul, the young man had turned out to be a valuable employee, streamlining practices and raising profits. I remember an earnest sort, a bit self-effacing, almost ethereal, with soft blond hair and wide upturned blue eyes hidden behind scholarly looking glasses. Not at all like his father in personality. Yet he must have entered into Kemp's underground world at some point. Then he died in the boat explosion. How hideous of Kemp to drag his son into his revenge fantasy.

Guzman. As Brian reminded me, the name is ordinary, the Portuguese equivalent of Smith or Jones. Nothing suggests the owner of a fleet of cargo ships is related to the mistress of my mortal enemy or his bastard children.

I continue to obsess, not a week after Charlie drops his bombshell. Brian has promised to check around and report back. He may be able to get information from his Interpol buddies. I promise not to worry. It's almost impossible not to.

I toss off the blanket, grab my cold tea, and head to the kitchen area to pop the cup in the microwave, still ruminating. Paul had a younger brother who never came to the office. I imagined him as an over-indulged second son. He didn't appear at the memorial service either, not that I paid a lot of attention. He'd be somewhere in his thirties by now, I realize. Old enough to run a shipping business, providing he had the talent and discipline. I'm not sure he had either of those, but what do I know?

The key in the door brings me back to earth. Brian is home early, marking the official start of the holidays. He's off next week. We plan to spend Christmas with the kids in the old stone farmhouse in Wales. Tommy and Maggie Edgerton will join us at some point. It promises to be jolly, providing I can get through tonight.

When Maggie suggested holding an engagement/ holiday party at their townhouse on the Friday before Christmas, I considered it a terrible idea. Most of the schools break a week or more before the holidays. Government offices close several days before Christmas, and only the most dedicated sort work after that. The vacation exodus is normally well underway by now, with Londoners getting out just as the tourists arrive. Who would stay around for a party?

There's also the guilt factor. The bride's parents traditionally absorb the cost of the wedding, which will likely be exorbitant. I know we're handling the rehearsal dinner. What's the protocol for an engagement party? Should we have chipped in? I have no idea. We've proposed dinner out, but Maggie won't hear of it.

"You're hosting six of us for a week in the country. And our house looks so lovely all dressed up for the holidays. We so want to show it off."

I don't say what I'm thinking; no one will show up to admire it.

I needn't have worried. Maggie and Tommy have clout. Additionally, the lure of an excellently catered party with free drinks is enticement enough. Only a few people have declined. Even our children's friends are willing to put off their destination vacations. Perhaps they're planning to work right up until Christmas Eve. Michael and Kate run with an industrious set.

Since the festivities are tonight, I need to pull myself together. First, though, I throw my arms around my handsome husband just as he walks in. I let him go so he can hang up his coat. He turns back to me, ready to address the questions he knows I've been compiling all day.

"Francesco Guzman is supposed to be a lifelong bachelor. No family. No link to anyone named Paulo or Paul. Nor does he seem to be connected to Luisa Guzman, Kemp's mistress and Paul's mother. In all the years we monitored Luisa, we never encountered anyone named Franco. You do know she had another son with Kemp named João."

"Yes, although I never met him. Victor never talked about him, except in passing. Paul mentioned a younger brother back in Rio who planned to move to New York. I think the two of them were close, although I can't be sure. The younger one would be in his thirties now. That's all I recall."

"We lost track of the second son some time ago, I'm afraid to say. I had our people run a search for a João Guzman in Rio and in New York. We turned up thousands of names, as you can imagine. When we filtered for someone the proper age, we were left with five men. Believe it or not, not one of them has relatives named Luisa or Francesco.

He stopped and searched my face.

"You know I'd do anything to ease your mind, Suzie. Let me ask you this: did Victor Kemp ever involve himself with any aspect of human trafficking? Think carefully."

"I don't need to think at all. He hated the idea. He said so on several occasions. It wasn't about the morality of it. He had an aversion to potentially unmanageable entanglements. Humans are messy and capricious, he told me. He meant they were difficult to control. Victor Kemp wouldn't have touched any part of that trade, and I don't see him involving his offspring."

"There you have it. Francesco Guzman is not Victor Kemp. Now if I'm not mistaken, we have a party to attend. I've picked up a bottle of Krug for Kate's parents, and no, I won't tell you how much it cost. Less than they're shelling out for this bash, I'll wager."

"We both know Tommy and Maggie are thrilled to be hosting. And it was very clever of you to pick up such a classy gift. I'm sure they'll appreciate it." I glance at the mantelpiece clock and gasp. "Oh dear, I really have to get moving if I want to be ready."

Brian pulls me to him once more. He smells clean and masculine and warmly familiar. I look up into the face I love and see the glint in his green eyes.

"Let's at least get you out of this robe. Although I can't be responsible for what happens after that. I imagine you can dress quickly enough, when all is said and done."

I don't argue.

~

Three hours later, we pull up to the elegant city dwelling of Lord and Lady Edgerton. They've got a country home as well, but Maggie loves to be in London. The townhouse is located in an upscale neighborhood adjacent to Green Park. Brian and I had planned to walk there by way of Hyde Park and its holiday markets. Our afternoon diversion has put us behind schedule, though it's improved my mood.

For all that, we've arrived pretty much on time, even a bit early. I'm wearing a high-neck, deep-green silk sheath by a designer named Niu Niu. Brian looks quite handsome in jacket and tie. We're more than presentable.

Potted pines festooned with tiny white lights frame the door, which is covered by an enormous wreath. We're ushered into the narrow foyer by a polite young person in white shirt and black slacks. A formal dining room to our right sits adjacent to an ascending staircase. The ornately carved banister is draped with fresh pine boughs. Flame-shaped bulbs flicker in the wall sconces that run along the hallway and up the stairs. The effect is as intended, as if the house were lit by candles. We've stepped into a Victorian Christmas.

To our left is a cozy library with a gas fireplace. Seasonal carved pieces sit on the mantle, among them a Father Christmas, a delicate looking reindeer, and a snowflake. A fat tree decorated with cut-glass ornaments squats next to a bookshelf of old books. First editions, no doubt. The room appeals to Brian, I can tell. I tug on his sleeve to keep him moving ahead.

The action is in the back of the house. Maggie has completely redone the rooms to suit the entertainment needs of a socially active couple. The space combines a family room with an enviable kitchen boasting a double oven, a six-burner Viking range, and a granite-topped center counter. One young woman oversees food preparation. Another puts the finishing touches on a table laden with delectables. Two fresh-faced waiters are circulating with trays. The bar looks predictably well stocked. Glass patio doors open onto a small deck and a pocket-sized back yard. Its gardens lie dormant, but the tiny lights strung around the fence and wound through the tree branches brighten the area.

Two men in suits stand on either side of the room, backs to the wall, hands folded left over right in front of them. Brian identifies them as security. Their presence comforts me.

I'm happy to have a chance to chat with our hosts. Tommy receives our gift with pleasure. He pounds Brian on the shoulder.

"Excellent choice, old man. We'll save this for New Year's in Wales."

Within an hour, the house is crowded with a mix of young and mature adults. Kate and Michael (I can't call him Mike, as his chums do) have arrived with a group of their friends in tow. The young women are dressed in black dresses and impossibly high heels. The men wear jackets without ties. The Edgertons have invited approximately sixty people. It looks like everyone has accepted and then some.

Annie and Mark show up with Betsy and Sam Harrigan. They greet us warmly. I'm stuck by the incongruity of my situation. How did it happen that a woman who spent so much time hiding, faking, hurting, and being hurt has ended up with real friends? Don't go there, I remind myself. Tonight is about celebrating.

Brian, ever attentive, nudges my arm. "Let's get drinks in everyone's hands. What do you say?"

"I say it's a marvelous idea. I just want to give our future daughter-in-law a hug first."

Kate Edgerton is a magnificent-looking woman in a green dress not dissimilar from my own. I smile at that. What distinguishes her physically isn't so much her athletic figure or even her warm hazel eyes, though both are appealing. It's her hair, a full mane of auburn curls that tumble past her shoulders. The image of redheaded grandchildren running around the stone farmhouse fills me with delight.

Standing to one side is Harry Goldston. Stout and red-faced, Harry is every inch the proverbial stalwart friend. He worked in Africa with Michael and Kate. Widgy is with them, looking for all the world like a version of Prince Harry.

The others I don't recall meeting, like the blowsy blonde woman in the too-tight, too-short dress who is hanging onto her escort for dear life. I've never seen him before, either. He's a bit older than the others, in his thirties, and handsome in a vaguely predatory sort of way. His dark hair curls at his collar; his dark-brown eyes turn up at the end. He looks familiar, probably because he's a type. Latin playboy, I decide. Someone as attractive as he is ought to be filled with preening self-confidence, yet he appears uneasy, even anxious.

The hairs on the back of my arm stand on end.

I'm a firm believer in intuition. So is Michael. He's had plenty of reasons to stay alert throughout his life. I've no doubt his senses are fine-tuned to pick up on various hazards. Yet, as I watch him tonight, he appears relaxed, focused on his friends and his future bride. He's not in the grip of any sort of premonition. I can't say the same for me. My spidey sense has kicked into high gear.

"Suzanne?" Annie comes up behind me and rests her hand on my arm. "Is anything wrong?"

She follows my gaze. The dark-haired man realizes he's being watched and looks back at us. Astonishment flits across his face, followed quickly by a look of anger so naked Annie and I pull back. Which of us is he glowering at and why? I'm staring at his face, then at the hand that's emerging from his pocket. Before I have time to yell, he's pointed a gun and fired in our direction.

I move to block Annie, unsure where the gunman is aiming and how good his aim might be. The bullet nicks her in the elbow; she cries out. I hear a second shot, but I don't know where it ends up.

I'm half-supporting my friend, who is holding her arm. Mark and Brian are instantly with us. Annie is remarkably self-possessed for a shooting victim. On the other hand, she is babbling, which might just be shock.

"Is Suzanne hurt? Is someone else? I heard another shot. Where is security? Did you catch the gunman?"

Mark gently tells her to shut up. She subsides, her face ashen.

The security men and several other capable looking-individuals have rushed Michael's group. I assume they've wrestled the man with the gun to the ground.

"We need a doctor!"

I hear my future daughter-in-law's voice and my head snaps up.

I push my way into the tangle where a moment ago a group of young people stood, most of them with nothing more than fun on their minds. Except one. I note the absence of the dark-haired, dark-eyed shooter and spot Brian running for the door. Then I see my son lying on the floor, and everything else fades away. Three sets of hands rest on his stomach: his, Kate's, and Harry's. Six hands covered in blood.

"Mrs. Foster, he threw himself in front of the gunman."

Harry is sweating heavily, pressing for all he's worth in order to keep God knows what from leaving my son's body.

"Christ, there's so much blood!" he exclaims. "Come on, man. Hang in there."

Kate is on Michael's other side. She's gone white, but she stays composed. She repeats her orders for water, for a doctor, for something to staunch the wound. The friends move off, all terribly efficient. The young woman from the kitchen rushes over.

"Let me help; I'm a nursing student," she says. She reaches over Harry's shoulder. Now there are four pairs of hands on my son.

Someone has brought over a pile of snowy linens from the dining room. Those will be expensive to clean, I find myself thinking.

"Harry, let her in." My not-quite-daughter-in-law catches the young man's eye and looks in my direction.

Brian appears suddenly, shaking his head. The gunman has gotten away. Clever bastard. No matter. I saw his face. I have an idea who he is. I might even know who sent him. I'll take care of them both in due time.

He lives, I think before I can stop myself. There's no time to process that revelation, so I file it for now.

I kneel by my only child, next to the kitchen helper/nursing student. She's used up nearly all the linens and is trying to decide where the helping hands can do the most good. I reach in to offer another set. Perhaps a mother's hands can do what no one else's can. The garnet blood soaks into my emerald silk dress. Red on green. A holiday party gone horribly wrong.

"Michael, I'm here," I whisper. I look down at my son. He's drained of color. His eyes stay closed. I take his icy red hand in my bloody warm one and squeeze. I imagine he squeezes back, but I can't be sure. In the distance, an ambulance sounds, its two-note refrain propelled by a single directive: hurry!

Chapter Eighteen

Daniel ran the entire length of Green Park, stopping once to reach under a park bench and retrieve a bag. Exiting at the northern corner, he entered a busy pub called Henry's Cafe Bar. He kept his head down, as if he were reading something on his phone, and pushed through the jovial holiday crowd to the men's room.

Removing his black cashmere jacket, he folded it and set it to one side. He pulled several items out of the bag he'd retrieved and put them on: blond wig, glasses, and a rain jacket. The mirror showed a scholarly-looking man with slightly disheveled hair. I look like my brother, he thought. Stuffing the jacket in the bag, he thrust it into the trash and headed back into the bar.

Daniel had dropped the gun in a park sewer after wiping it quickly on his coat. The swarms of Metro police and SIS combing the area would find it soon enough. The Serbian who'd sold it to him swore a semiautomatic would be perfect for his needs, even though Daniel hadn't told him how he intended to use it. Perhaps semiautomatic Glocks were the go-to weapon of choice for criminals. Daniel took the gun without mentioning he'd never used a firearm, never even seen one up close. It wouldn't do to look weak. He figured he paid ten times the value of the weapon. He hadn't been in a position to object. Weapons were scarce and Daniel's timeframe exceedingly compressed.

The night his father all but disowned him because of the incident with the pedophile, Daniel concentrated his anger on Suzanne Foster, aka Susan Smith, the former assassin. The woman had brought so much havoc into their lives. Kemp had tried and failed to kill her, but she had turned the tables. Paulo had died and his father had been critically injured. Daniel intended to finish the job once and for all. Then he would return, triumphant, to bask in his father's gratitude and respect. The only question was how.

The answer appeared serendipitously that very night. At an after-hours club party, Daniel overheard a platinum-haired woman complain about finding an escort for a posh little engagement party she wanted to attend. The girl was both too plain and too old for Daniel's taste. She looked to be a hard-living twenty-five. It was obvious she came from money, which she was willing to throw around.

The name Kate Edgerton meant little to him. Apparently, she was the privileged daughter of a British lord. Her fiancé, he noted, had an interesting résumé that included time spent abroad in Africa and Wales, of all places, before he came back to London and asked lucky Kate to marry her.

"What did you say his name was?" Daniel decided to chat up the girl, see what she knew. "I wonder if we might have run into each other once or twice."

"Michael Foster. I doubt you would have met. He's a good-looking sort, but serious. Not usually the kind to show up at a party, if you know what I mean."

Daniel did. After taking her home and causing her endless amounts of pleasure, aided by copious amounts of alcohol and Ecstasy, he proposed he serve as her escort. She eagerly accepted.

Getting hold of the gun meant he had to return to the docks with a wad of cash. That proved much easier than trying to figure out how to smuggle a gun into the home of a sitting member of Parliament. He considered bribing one of the catering crew and rejected the idea. They were more likely to be searched than the guests. Daniel couldn't imagine a pat-down, but visitors might be wanded or passed through a security system on their way in.

Once again, fortune smiled on him. Daniel had a piece of metal in his left knee, the result of an old soccer injury. He often carried a medical card to help him move more quickly through airport security. It didn't always work, but he guessed entry into a private party might be easier. He decided to strap the gun high up his inner thigh as he'd seen it done in movies and pray to a god he didn't believe in.

He scanned the house as they approached. Everyone entered through the front door and handed their coats to some obsequious fool. He saw no obvious security precautions, although he presumed a couple of hidden cameras must be trained on the property. He ducked his head, pretending to listen to his date's inane prattle. They slid into the Edgerton home along with half a dozen other young people he didn't know. He grabbed a glass of Chardonnay from a passing tray and favored the young server with a dazzling smile. She blushed. His date didn't notice. Daniel felt powerful and in control. Being good-looking made life so much easier.

Excusing himself, Daniel made his way to the powder room. He locked the door, unstrapped the gun from his leg, and transferred it to the pocket of his jacket. Then he leaned over the toilet and threw up.

He was about to kill someone in a crowd that no doubt included ex-military and security types. He'd never seen his target before, although he'd found a blurred photo online from a recent event. The picture accompanied an article about some charity that helped victims of human trafficking. Oh, the irony.

Daniel brushed at his jacket, adjusted his tie, and smoothed his hair. Nerves were to be expected. His plan was either bold or disastrous. He was either insane or incredibly brave. He took a moment to study his reflection in the mirror. Brave, he decided. He popped a breath mint, brushed at an imaginary bit of lint, and nodded at his reflection. What did his college roommate used to say?

"Let's get this show on the road."

~

It had not gone as intended. Daniel had no familiarity with a gun's recoil. He had no idea how difficult it was to shoot under pressure and in close quarters. The Serb said the Glock's accuracy made it impossible to miss the target. Then again, the man didn't realize Daniel would come face to face not only with his adversary but also with his father's daughter.

He knew it instantly: same lowered brow, frosty eyes, and full lips. The female version of Victor Kemp was much younger and well dressed, but the resemblance was obvious. Not a good look for a woman, Daniel decided. He imagined she had an impressive set of teeth, though she wasn't smiling. Rather, she appeared puzzled. Why was she standing with her hand on the arm of the woman she should have hated? How could those two know each other? Were they friends?

The possibility that Victor Kemp's beloved legitimate child was in league with the woman his father hated enraged Daniel. He pulled the gun, briefly lost control as he tried to move his arm into position, and fired. He could have sworn he aimed at Suzanne Foster, but the bullet hit his half-sister. He barely had time to register his mistake before some idiot next to him tried to disarm him. The gun went off a second time, directly into the man's gut.

The mayhem that followed helped. He dropped to the floor as if he'd taken the bullet himself and rolled outward, knocking a few people off their feet. Crawling through the tangle of arms and legs, he jumped up and got as far as the hallway before a security man appeared from outside.

"Help!" he cried. "In here! Someone's been shot!" He waved the man to the back of the house and tore out the front door.

Outside the bar in his disguise, Daniel took a moment to check the news on his phone. Reports of a shooting at the home of Lord and Lady Edgerton identified two victims. A guest, Lady Annabel Westcott had only been grazed, but the second victim, Michael Foster, was rushed to the hospital in grave condition.

Holy shit, he'd shot the son! He could still turn this to his advantage, couldn't he? Okay, the first bullet hit his father's daughter. That might anger the older man temporarily, but he would soon realize she hadn't been seriously hurt. Daniel would point out the obvious: she'd been associating with the enemy. If he'd mortally wounded Suzanne Foster's only son, his father would have to be pleased, wouldn't he?

He made his way to the building in Wapping, working out the story. It was just after 9:00 p.m. He suspected his father would still be downstairs working. Daniel pulled off his wig and glasses and leaned on the buzzer before easing off. It wouldn't do to seem frantic. He looked directly at the security camera and shivered with relief when he heard the door click. At least his father was willing to see him.

He heard the sound of animated chatter coming from the lower level. His father was watching the news. That wasn't good. Daniel wanted a chance to explain before Kemp jumped to conclusions based on sensationalized outside reporting. Although an enormous flat-screen television adorned the back wall, the old man sat in front of his laptop. Arkady Dyukov stood just behind him as usual, leaning over his shoulder. Sure enough, some reporter was going on about the shooting. She even played an interview with one of the guests. Everyone sounded terribly excited. Daniel wondered if the blonde he'd abandoned had taken her turn in front of the cameras.

"Papà."

"You have something to report." Kemp closed the computer.

"I do." Though not invited to sit, Daniel pulled out the chair opposite his father and plopped down. He could hear his teeth chatter in the sudden stillness

"Get the boy a whiskey."

Dyukov went to fetch a bottle. Kemp turned back to Daniel.

"Talk to me."

Encouraged by his father's interest and attention, Daniel succinctly recounted the evening's events, taking care not to embellish or exaggerate. He omitted only two points: he didn't reveal he recognized his half-sister, or that he actually intended to kill Suzanne Foster.

"I wanted to hurt that woman as she has hurt us. Surely you understand that. She stole my brother. She stole your son." He saw Kemp grimace. "She's the one who caused your suffering. I decided killing her son would be the best possible punishment." Daniel didn't actually know whether Michael had died, but saying it out loud added legitimacy to his presentation. He paused, waiting for the other man to speak.

"Go on."

"I'm sorry I didn't let you in on my plans. I believed this was the safer course of action. I hope you will forgive me. You must know how much the honor of our family means to me." He looked at his lap, feigning a modesty he didn't feel.

Dyukov came back with the whiskey. He set it down in front of the younger man and resumed his post. Daniel emptied the glass, squared his shoulders, and looked directly at his father, man to man. When Kemp spoke, his voice was low so that Daniel had to strain to hear him.

"Let me get this straight. You obtained an illegal handgun and somehow managed to smuggle it into a party at the home of a high-profile member of the House of Lords. The lord in question has a daughter who is engaged to the son of a man who used to spy on me and a woman who used to work for me. You planned to murder my former employee's son in as public a setting and in as noisy a manner as possible and then escape undetected.

"Instead, you wounded the young man—no, he's not dead, at least not yet—which will guarantee that his mother will now dedicate her life to finding the person who shot her son. The police will also search for the shooter, aided by the finest intelligence agency in the world and likely the royal family itself. The gunman's compulsion to brag will lead them to a Portuguese businessman named Francesco Guzman, if they can find him. Even if they can't, even if it ends there, the woman, one of the most cunning people I have ever known, will have made the connection to her sworn enemy. She will determine he is alive and behind the plot to kill her and wound the assassin's son."

"But you weren't the shooter."

"Shut up." Kemp's voice had gained strength and fury. He leaned across the desk as if to strike Daniel. Blood suffused his ghastly injury. "My God, how stupid can one man be? I cannot believe you share my DNA. Come to think of it, maybe you don't."

"Papà, how could you say such a thing?"

"You haven't just risked everything, Daniel; you've ruined it. You told people that we were connected. You hurt and perhaps killed her child, never mind he is engaged to the daughter of a prominent public figure. You did so in as public a manner as is possible. You left my enemy alive to hunt me. Most unforgiveable, YOU SHOT MY DAUGHTER!"

"I—that was my half-sister?" Daniel could barely get the words out.

"You knew that, you son of a bitch, just as I know you intended to kill the woman, not her son. You missed. You fucking missed."

Kemp stood. "You've pushed me to the breaking point, Daniel," he said. "I will not tolerate you anymore. Not personally and certainly not professionally. This will break your mother's heart, but it has to be done."

He drew a small pistol from his desk and trained it on his son.

"Please, no. You can't do this. You won't."

Kemp kept the gun pointed at Daniel for several seconds. With a sigh, he lowered his arm.

"You are right about one thing. I won't kill you. It would require me to lie to your mother, and I don't want to do that."

He turned to Dyukov, who had been standing quietly off to one side. Arkady Dyukov, the man he had trusted for years, the one man since Paulo's passing who had truly behaved like a loyal son.

"Take care of this, please."

He lay the weapon on the desk and walked away.

"Papà!" In that moment, Daniel sounded like a little boy pleading for his father's affection instead of his own life.

"With pleasure, boss." Dyukov gave a tight smile, picked up the pistol, and put a bullet between Daniel Guzman's eyes.

Chapter Nineteen

Nothing exists outside this room. Surely life goes about its noisy business. I simply don't care about any of it. My heart and soul live within these four walls, bathed by night in the ambient glow of a table lamp and by day in filtered sunlight through sheer curtains.

St. Mary's Hospital is a highly rated trauma center that has the advantage of being relatively close at hand. As we come tearing in, I have a passing thought about the other people who come here, other patients who are sick and injured, other panicked families consigned to wait. I dismiss them all from my mind. There is only my son.

I've been in the hospital twice before. Once, when I was nine, my parents dropped me off at a nearby clinic when I complained of a sore throat. They promptly forgot about me. Two days later, they returned only because the kindly doctor who treated me tracked them down at City Lights Bookstore. If I'd been feeling up to it, I might have begged him to let me stay.

Michael's birth occasioned my second visit, not quite twenty-eight years ago. How happy I was, notwithstanding my husband and I were terrified of being discovered. I sprawled in the bed, spent. Brian stood to one side, along with a grinning friend of ours. What was his name? I saw the smiling doctor and nurse through a happy haze of drugs and exhaustion. On my chest rested an impossibly tiny human. You are mine and I will never let you go, I remember thinking. My fierce possessiveness startled me.

Yet I did let him go, didn't I? He spent his childhood without a mother but with a target on his back. Others shielded him, to be sure. His innate common sense

154

protected him. I used to think my love did as well, but that's a foolish conceit. The present circumstances give lie to the notion.

This room, whose contours I perceive only vaguely, is larger than most hospital rooms, I suppose. It feels smaller, perhaps because I've scarcely left it the last thirty-six hours. There are so many people crowded in here, it seems. Friends have stopped by. I heard someone whisper something about "saying goodbye." I put it out of my mind.

Tommy and Maggie stand a respectful distance back from their daughter. Kate sits on the right side of Michael's bed, holding his hand. She is as immobile as a statue. I see tear tracks but no tears on her lovely face. The English and their reserve, I note. The thought is a loving one.

I'm half kneeling in front of the armchair I've pulled by my son's bed, across from the machine monitoring vital signs with implacable insistence. I am the only information you need, it declares. In that moment, it speaks the truth. Beneath the surface of my calm, I am a roiling cauldron of unquenchable fires and bestial urges. I need to scream, to tear, to rip open someone's throat or pierce his heart. I want to take a life, one life in particular.

Perhaps I am not yet a former assassin.

My husband stands behind me, his face etched in grief. If only I could ease his suffering, but I can't. I can't see anything but Michael's closed eyes. I can't hear anything but his labored breathing through that God-awful tube and the beep-beep-beep of the panel. I can't feel anything except tightness in my chest. Brian squeezes my shoulder. I look up. The numbers on the panel are dropping; the monitor's peaks have spread father apart, as if the landscape were flattening. Too low and too slow.

Michael draws a breath, as deep as any I've ever managed, and releases what seems like every last bit of air he's ever taken in. Then he stops. The peaks disappear and so do the beeps, replaced by a single drawn-out note. Kate's plaintive "no" adds a peculiar harmonic urgency. The outside comes crashing in, all screaming alarms, stamping feet, and shouted orders. We're out the door, displaced by entering medical personnel. I resist being pushed away; I reach back to touch my son's cold forehead. "Don't leave us, Michael," I plead. "Can you hear me?" The words linger for a moment before being carried away by a gust of frigid air. I call out again, "Don't go."

PART THREE

Chapter Twenty

Memory changes us. That is, our recollections figure in what we do, what we fear, and what attracts or repels us. Memory shapes our habits. It also shapes our future. I know how to clean, load, and fire a weapon because familiarity and repetition have imprinted these actions on my brain. I remember how to kill because I've done it before. I am likely to kill again despite promises made and best forgotten.

As my son lies suspended between life and death, I think of the people I love or respect, people who know what I've done. Brian and Michael. Grayson Tenant, who for two decades kept me sane by keeping me apprised of my family's whereabouts. Charlie and his friend Fred. Possibly even Kate. They assume I had no choice. They've never questioned further.

I do, though. I ask myself whether I am predisposed to kill. Am I an abomination or merely a product of my culture or environment? I'm an American, after all. D. H. Lawrence declared the essential American soul to be "hard, isolate, stoic, and a killer." Lawrence, a British novelist and essayist, found himself reviled later in his life as a pornographer. I suppose we could take his assessment with a grain of salt. At the same time, the description provides both explanation and cover.

Perhaps my run-in with Victor or someone like him was inevitable. I can't say. I had to learn the art of self-preservation early on. When your father is an unsuccessful poet dependent on heroin and cocaine for inspiration, you learn to disappear. When your mother, an opportunistic beauty with no time for a daughter, takes up with a variety of disreputable men, you stay hidden. Until one man comes along and tries to make you do something you don't want to do.

Not Victor. Stuart.

After my mother threw my father out, I lived under the slit-eyed scrutiny of strange men for three years. I tried to be careful around these interlopers. I kept my anger in check. I didn't want confrontation. I just wanted to be left alone.

I was not yet fifteen when Stuart made his move. A plain and slender girl, I dressed in androgynous, oversized clothes from Goodwill. Nothing about me should have tempted him, except if he found my very unavailability perversely suggestive.

One January afternoon, I sat at our rickety kitchen table trying to study. Lisette was at work. Stuart was napping, I thought. Then I felt his heavy hand on my shoulder. He leaned in and whispered in my ear, "You smell good."

"I've got schoolwork," I said and shrugged to dislodge him. No good. He pushed down hard, aiming to keep me in place. Time to move. I rose with effort, planning to retreat to my loft upstairs. He blocked my way.

"Come on, sweetie," he cajoled. "You're old enough. Hell, I'm as close to your age as to your mom's. I'll make it good for you." He pressed against me, reeking of sweat and rosé.

I put a hand on his chest and said, "No." He ignored me, caught up in his determination or desire.

I killed him.

I should say, I meant to kill him. Being young and inexperienced, my timing was off. I missed the carotid artery, but I hurt him.

Lisette came home to find her lover on the floor clutching his pulsing throat while her daughter scrubbed blood off the cheap parquet. She didn't panic, my mother. She called our local police precinct to frantically report the near-rape of her daughter by a man she had trusted.

"Put away the cleaning materials," she commanded after she hung up. I did as I was told. Then I watched with fascination as she cut her hand. "I need credibility," she told me. "Now sit down on the couch and don't say a word until I tell you to."

When the two policemen arrived, she explained she came to her daughter's defense with a broken glass. In the struggle, her hand and the assailant's throat were cut. One of the men, a handsome guy whose long hair suggested he spent his off-hours surfing, commended her on her bravery.

"Self-defense," Surfer Dude announced. "No doubt about it." He took her hand tenderly. "Do you need that cut looked at?" he asked, his soft brown eyes gazing into her blue ones. I thought he was going to offer to stay the night.

The policemen remained until the ambulance came to peel Stuart off the floor and take him to the hospital. Lisette promised to come to the station once she'd made sure I was okay. They were all breaking some sort of protocol, but no one seemed to care. A couple of neighbors appeared, drawn into the hall by the excitement. Now Lisette had a wider audience to entertain. She played her part to the hilt. I stayed on the couch. My mother explained to her sympathetic listeners that I'd been thrown into a temporary and mildly catatonic state.

When everyone had cleared out, Lisette came back inside the apartment, closed the door, and turned on me.

"I thought I was going to pass out in front of the police. You cut a man's throat! With a piece of glass! Jesus Christ, you almost killed him! What kind of person does that? Are you insane, Suzanne? Have I raised a crazy person? Oh God, what if he dies? What were you thinking? Never mind. I don't want to hear it. Do you even understand what you've done? Do you realize who you made me lie to? To the police. To our neighbors. Are you happy now? Is this what you wanted? God Almighty!"

"Stop, Mom. Just listen. The guy came at me. He threatened me. He was going to rape me! I had to defend myself."

Lisette was having none of it. "You didn't have to do that! There are so many other ways—God, I don't even know who you are anymore. I can't look at you. You need to get out of here. Do you understand me? You have to leave."

"Mom—"

"I mean it, Suzanne. Get your things and go."

"But where?"

"I don't care. Just go. Now!"

It hit me then; my mother wasn't afraid for me. She was afraid of me.

I left, found shelter elsewhere, and didn't speak to her for six years. She knew where I was, but she never asked me to return home. Even after our tentative reconciliation, I still asked myself why she treated me like a monster instead of a frightened girl. She was wrong, wasn't she? Or did she see something I didn't, know something I couldn't?

I will myself back to the present.

Michael lies in a bed. I've panned back and forth between him and the machines that monitor his vital signs countless times. He looks weak. The numbers remain unchanged. Which image do I trust? Neither offers the slightest hint of what is to come.

I look around. Pale-yellow walls are hung with what appears to be original artwork. Sheer curtains flutter over Venetian blinds. A couple of floor lamps provide soft ambient lighting, except when someone on the staff enters and throws on those hideous overhead lights. Overall, the room combines the features of an upscale corporate hotel with a guest bedroom.

I have two vantage points. I either wait in the armchair or decamp to the hallway. Handsome wall fixtures mitigate the harshness of standard issue fluorescent illumination. Wall-mounted television monitors on either end are set to a low volume. One shows sports, I think, the other a BBC channel. A central nurses' station, very high-tech, completes the picture. Chairs and at least one seating area provide options for visitors.

I never sit in the hallway. I pace. I keep my head down, unwilling to risk eye contact. I memorize the path beneath my feet: well-traveled, low-pile textured carpeting the color of chestnuts. A red fleur-de-lis appears every couple of meters or so to break up the monotony.

From time to time, as I sit with my son, the door opens. I frown at whichever nurse enters to read a screen or change a drip. I've apparently terrified most of them. They can sense the murderous rage that burns just beneath my flat affect. I heard an orderly warn another to "mind the tigress."

They have no idea, no idea at all.

Then there is Nancy Okorie. A tall, slender, black-skinned woman, she manages to be efficient, patient, kind, and quite strict when necessary. Brian tells me she is from Sudan. She's just a few years older than my son. I imagine she's dealt with plenty in her lifetime, including murderous mothers. I don't scare her. I respect that. As a result, I'm inclined to heed her bidding. I also trust my son's care to her completely.

I am fixated on the flowers that fill the room, massive quantities of them. Many people have sent fruit baskets, as incongruous as that might seem. No teddy bears, thank God, but a huge wreath from someone. Of course: it's nearly Christmas. Friends of Michael and Kate have pooled their resources to buy a garland of brightly colored out-of-season flowers that must have cost them a fortune. Discrete arrangements arrive from Tommy and Maggie's many friends. Some of them likely attended the holiday party where the shooting occurred. I don't expect anyone included a card that said, "Merry Christmas and thanks for a lovely evening."

We've made our own friends in our short time back in London. Brian, in his dual roles as professor and SIS analyst, hears from colleagues. A beautiful bouquet from C is among the gifts. My fellow volunteers with Freedom to Hope deliver confections. Even the shooting club to which we belong sends a small offering. How odd that seems in the present context.

Michael has miraculously escaped injury to the solid organs. He's in a private room, attended by a well-regarded military surgeon Tommy Edgerton has brought in. Most doctors in the UK lack experience with gunshot victims. This surgeon is able to remove the bullet. The doctor is initially guarded but optimistic. With any luck, my son will make a recovery.

Except that as luck would have it, Michael has not one but two critical episodes in the first seventy-two hours. The second crisis, an infection that causes a dangerous spike in his temperature, requires we remove all plant life from the room. Just as well, since the space resembles an unkempt English garden or a flower shop on delivery day. None of us wants to take anything home, not that we leave, except to change and snatch a bit of sleep.

Kate takes over the job of relocating all of it with Widgy's help. The poor boy is beside himself. Michael is the older brother he never had. Unable to stay in the room for more than a minute, he takes over delivering flowers to other floors. Kate provides direction and sometimes accompanies him. They present the floral gifts to each of the nurse's stations, placing the plants and flowers next to plug-in desktop Christmas trees and wilting poinsettias.

My future daughter-in-law also keeps a list of gifts so that we can issue thanks at a later time. The task keeps the two of them marginally occupied. It's good for Widgy and for Kate, who otherwise wouldn't leave the room. She's as immoveable and as stubborn as I am, or so Brian notes with a touch of admiration. I love her, both for her steadfast nature and her love for my son.

Lord and Lady Westcott have opted to make a generous donation to the hospital. Annie Westcott, her arm in a sling, has stopped by twice. If I have any sympathy to spare, it's for my new friend. She's been dragged into Victor Kemp's ongoing narrative through no fault of her own. I don't yet have proof, but I am certain her half-brother fired the shot that wounded her and so grievously injured my son. So is she.

During the first days, I sense the reassuring presence of my husband. From the beginning, Brian takes charge, as I am unable to do so. He's once again the patient teacher with whom I fell in love nearly thirty years ago. He gently instructs the nurses to work around me, keeps well-wishers at bay, and keeps his concerns about my well-being to himself. He simply urges me to eat, to walk around, even to nod off in the chair. Since I won't leave the hospital, he brings a change of clothes.

I don't deserve him. He doesn't deserve this. But most of all, the man who shot my son doesn't deserve to be walking around while Michael fights for his life. I push that thought down where it lurks, a predator just beneath the surface.

Chapter Twenty-One

By the end of the third day, my perspective has widened. It's as if I've lifted my head. I take note of how Michael's precarious position has impacted others: Kate, Tommy, Maggie, and most of all, Brian. He was the present parent. He raised our son into manhood. It could be argued that he's closer to Michael than I am, although I don't know how one measures such things. I spent years imagining that any nurturing instincts left after my loveless childhood had been obliterated over decades in service to a monster. Five years with my family, even in hiding, has given me reason to hope.

I will not lose that hope now. Nor will I let it be drained from my husband.

I emerge from my black hole to catch Brian just as his resolve begins to crumble. He loves Michael fiercely and hasn't allowed himself to imagine a world without him. I hold my beloved close, whisper reassurances I may not fully believe, and give him permission to weep silently against my shoulder. At some point, dear Kate comes upon us. I open my arms to include her in our group.

To all outward appearances, I've regained my strength. Most importantly, I no longer terrorize or concern those around me. I appear both steady and reliable, able to weather the storm and help others do the same.

Appearances, though, can be deceiving.

At some point, I remember to call Lisette. Michael is her grandson, I reason. She needs to know what has happened to him. Maybe I simply need to tell her.

We first reconnected six months into my university life, well before I met Victor Kemp. I discovered she'd remarried and then shed her Santa Barbara husband and several years of couples' swaps for the tamer environs of Boca Raton. She'd decided to become a writer; she wanted to focus on her career. Her first book had attracted both an agent and a publisher. It had the makings of a serial.

"Why not move to Key West?" I asked her. "Isn't that artistically more fitting?"

"Oh, please, I'm no Hemingway," she replied with surprising candor. "Boca's close enough to Miami; I can still have some fun. I'm divorced, not dead."

That earned her a laugh from her peripatetic daughter.

Lisette managed to stop talking about herself long enough to compliment me on how well I turned out. Though she didn't take any credit (I would have laughed her off the phone), neither did she apologize for her shortcomings as a parent. I realize I didn't need her to.

"You've really turned your life around, Suzanne," she said.

"So have you, Mom," I told her.

Now I hesitate before calling. I've deliberately kept her at arms' length. She didn't even know I had a husband or a son until a year and a half ago. She hurt me by sending me away so long ago. I would say I've repaid her tenfold with my lies of omission, notwithstanding I was trying to protect her.

To my surprise, she insists on flying into London from Florida. "I can catch a flight—I can charter a plane, for God's sake—and be there tomorrow," she says.

It's been years since I've spent any significant time with Lisette, but I doubt she's changed all that much. I can't imagine bringing her out-sized personality into the mix. I'm not sure any of us could handle her mix of virtuousness and attention-seeking. Which is to say, the last thing any of us here needs is more drama.

With the skill born of decades of practice in both active and passive resistance, I gently turn her down. She handles the refusal with equanimity. We talk a bit more. The conversation comforts me.

When she says, "I love you, flower," I remember strolling down a city street long ago with my beautiful mother. She picked a daisy, affixed it to my barrette, and pronounced me a "little flower." She either didn't notice or didn't care that she'd leaned into someone's private garden to help herself. So like my mother.

I smile at the cell phone and sign off with, "I love you, too, Mom."

Michael's infection shifts him in and out of a semiconscious state. He mumbles or falls silent. His heart rate races and slows; his temperature rises, backs down slightly, and climbs again. People come and go: vague shadows, familiar faces. We've sent poor Harry Goldston home twice now, once to change out of his bloodstained clothes, another time because he nearly fell over from exhaustion.

While I pretend to be taking it all in stride, I feel panic hovering close by. Shouldn't Michael's problems be resolved? Shouldn't he be on the mend? There's no sense in demanding information from the surgeon; he's in a wait and see state of mind.

Juliette calls from Brussels. Now director of a respected lycée, she has coped in recent years with her own health scare and the death of her husband, Guy. Brian discourages her from hopping a high-speed train to London, promising instead to provide updates.

Michael's cousins also check in. Jules agrees to stay put. It's nearly Christmas, and he's got a large family and a job with a bank that does not grant him banker's hours. Younger brother Simon won't be dissuaded. We expect he'll show up any day now, assuming he acquires permission from whatever agency he now serves. Most people believe he's attached to a do-good nonprofit organization. Brian and I know the truth, or a portion of it. Like uncle like nephew, it seems.

He arrives on Christmas Day. Simon is a good-looking man, mid-thirties, of medium height, with a strong chin covered by one day's stubble. It lends him a raffish air. A piece of his chestnut-colored hair flops over the lightly tinted square tortoiseshell glasses that partially obscure his indigo eyes. He's dressed in jeans, work boots, subdued flannel shirt, and drab-olive jacket. The outfit looks utilitarian and probably cost a fortune. Simon gives off the air of a hip scholar or the founder of a state-of-the-art tech company. He is neither.

"How's my cousin?" His tone is light. He squeezes Michael's unresponsive hand before turning to us. "What can I do?" he asks.

My answer surprises me. "Pray."

I'm not a religious person, not in the least. I enjoy certain holiday rituals, especially those that revolve around family, friends, and food. I'm still learning to relax in the company of others after so many years on my own. I will no doubt come to see the value of relationships in all their forms. The number of people who have supported us in the last few days alone testifies to the enduring power of love and friendship.

These are human connections, though. I have no evidence that anything else is watching out for us. My version of hope, insofar as I have any, exists without either expectation or faith. That makes it open-ended and unpredictable. My hope insists on action, because what else is one to do? We're on our own. Brian has decided I'm an existentialist. He's not wrong.

The problem is, there's nothing to be done.

Perhaps Simon takes my advice and calls on a Higher Power. I don't. I involve myself in a one-sided discussion with . . . something. Fates, furies, that part of myself I can't forgive. Late into Christmas night, I argue, cajole, plead, threaten, and bargain while the others stand sentry over Michael. Around the world, people are celebrating the birth of the Redeemer. I'm negotiating in order to spare my only child, one of two people who have served as my personal saviors.

~

"Mamà?"

Cracked, weak, but unmistakable, my son's voice lands on the last syllable of the word before skittering up. Michael spoke French the first several years of his life. He didn't have much occasion to call for his mother then, but he does now. I jump from the settee, move over to the bed, and take his hand in mine.

"Ici, chère."

Brian jumps out of the chair where he's been dozing. He comes over, his face filled with wonder.

"Dad?" My son shifts back to English, which sounds just as beautiful to my ears.

"Welcome back, son. I'll be right back." He kisses Michael on the cheek and sprints out the door.

"Where is Kate?"

"Just down the hall, dear heart. I imagine your father's gone to get her."

Nancy, now my favorite nurse, charges in. She is either prescient or in possession of impeccable timing. She glances at the monitor and puts a hand to my son's forehead. Then she nods briskly, causing her colorfully beaded braids to sway.

"I would say his fever's broken," she says. A wide smile splits her dark face.

Simon strolls into the room with a "hey, kid, welcome back." Not a moment later, Kate bursts through the door with Brian just behind her. Artfully avoiding Nancy's outstretched arm, she crouches next to the bed and rests her head gently on Michael's chest. He lifts a hand to stroke her hair.

Brian reaches around Nancy's right side and lays his hand on Michael's forehead.

"Son." He speaks so quietly I may be the only one who hears him.

"Out, now, the lot of you," Nancy commands us. "I need to check some vitals and get this boy changed out of his gown. He's soaked through." She herds us to the door.

We tumble out of Michael's room, all talking at once. It's 9:00 a.m. on December 26. Five days have passed or perhaps an eternity, depending on one's perspective. I consider that Michael's recovery on Boxing Day has spared us from clichés delivered by well-meaning friends about Christmas miracles. I'm being churlish, which I put down to relief on top of stress and sleeplessness. If I've learned anything this week, it's that many people truly care about our family. Whatever is out there or up there clearly has a sense of life's absurdity.

Katie has moved to the waiting area and is talking excitedly on her cellphone, likely with her parents. Widgy, who has been sleeping in a chair in the hallway, is doing an odd little jig. Simon is grinning at everyone. Brian announces he's famished. Everyone laughs. As we wait for the doctor, I expect to feel a spiritual wash of gratitude overtake me. Instead, dread pushes past my relief. Yes, my son lives. As does the man who has put him here. For now.

Chapter Twenty-Two

Even by Victor Kemp's reduced standards, this was the most miserable holiday season imaginable. Over the past month, he and his associates had invested—no, wasted—time and effort cutting their ties with human traffickers. That meant canceling lucrative shipping contracts with very dangerous customers during a busy time of year. He brought his personal lawyer in to handle the tricky negotiations with clients and offer bribes or concessions where necessary. Kemp had little doubt other methods might also be needed.

He blamed Daniel for pushing him into transporting human cargo. He might have blamed himself for agreeing to such a scheme. He might have faulted himself for allowing his eldest son Paul to accompany him on his personal vendetta eighteen months earlier. He might have, except Victor Kemp wasn't given to self-recrimination. Each of his sons made his choice.

The only rebuke he deserved was in not dealing more harshly with Daniel after the incident with the dead girl. Bad enough he had to deal with an infuriated gangster whose cargo had been lost. Worse, the debacle brought the company to the attention of several international agencies. He couldn't be sure, but he couldn't take chances. Everything Kemp had rebuilt as Francesco Guzman had been imperiled by Daniel's carelessness.

What had Kemp done about it? A slap on the wrist in deference to the boy's mother. Then Daniel had caused irreparable harm with his foolish plan to shoot the former assassin. At a party hosted by a member of Parliament and swarming with security! On the heels of the disaster at sea! How could any son of his be so stupid?

Now Daniel's latest rash act promised potentially greater scrutiny. It put Suzanne Foster on notice. The law enforcement and intelligence agencies might not connect a headstrong, party-loving Brazilian to an Eastern European criminal entrepreneur presumed dead. Eventually, though, she would.

Victor Kemp knew when to cut his losses. Daniel had to go.

Dyukov called in a team of specialists who could quickly establish a series of false leads. They left evidence at Daniel's flat of a hasty departure. They wiped his phone records and added charges to credit cards. Someone matching Daniel's general description traveled to Dubai. Another lookalike boarded a plane for Auckland. A third left for Moscow under the name Daniel Grubman.

The efforts paid off. The hunt slowed while the hunters spun off in different directions.

Kemp wished he could find a way to get rid of Daniel's date, the woman the young man escorted to the party. The trashy-looking girl from the posh family was all over the news, going on about her close relationship with the would-be killer. Dyukov advised against it. As he predicted, the media realized she knew almost nothing, not even that her escort had been carrying a gun. They moved on; her brief fling with fame evaporated.

Unfortunately, she'd put the name Guzman out to the public. Authorities were quoted as making headway in tracking down the gunman's father.

That could never happen.

In the midst of a frenetic forty-eight hours, Kemp heard from Luisa. He'd been dreading her call, but there was no avoiding it. In Rio for last-minute business, she had made arrangements to spend the holidays with her lover and her son. As if they were a normal family. He thought it nonsense. Yet he couldn't help but be touched by her desire to behave as other people did.

Though they often video-conferenced, she called this time from a prepaid cell phone. Her sultry voice was pinched with worry. They spoke in Portuguese.

"It's all over the news, Victor. Is it true? Did Daniel shoot those people at the party?"

"It seems he did."

"Why would he do such a thing?"

"If I had to guess, I'd say he believed he was doing me a favor, trying to kill the woman he holds responsible for both my injuries and his brother's death. He obviously didn't think it through. He missed and shot the woman's son." Kemp didn't mention that Daniel had also shot his daughter, although the news wire had reported on the minor injury sustained by Lady Annabel Westcott. He hoped Luisa wouldn't bring it up.

"He was trying to kill the woman you chased up to Wales? The former assassin, Susan Smith?"

"I think so."

"How does he know about her?"

"Perhaps his brother told him."

"And how did he get a gun?"

"Not from me. He undoubtedly made contacts from his time working on the docks."

"That's insane."

"It was. It is. Trust me, Luisa, I would never in a thousand years condone, let alone recommend such an act."

He could hear her breathing into the phone.

"I know that. But where is he now? Has he contacted you?"

How he hated to hold back from her. Luisa had been his mistress for nearly forty years. She bore him two sons, dealt with his long absences, and even, on occasion, used her considerable professional clout on his behalf. She put her career on hold and came to stay with him while he lay in agony recovering from the mishap that killed their oldest son. She found a reliable surrogate to cover Kemp's interests on the board. All this she did without complaint.

Kemp supposed Luisa understood her remaining son's foibles, perhaps better than Daniel himself. If anything, she was inclined to forgive, an inclination the father didn't share. She understood that as well. At some point, she would draw her own conclusions about the fate of her youngest. Nothing would be gained by telling her everything in that moment.

"He's probably in hiding."

She didn't respond.

"Luisa, I realize you planned to return to London. In light of these events, I think it's better for you not to come here. There's nothing you can do. I'm not even certain you ought to remain in Rio, although I leave that up to you. I doubt the authorities will connect you with Daniel Guzman. Your children are—were—named Paulo and João." He silently berated himself for that slip.

A few seconds went by. Then Luisa spoke, her tone restrained.

"I will take care of things from my end."

"I can help—"

"I don't want your help."

Once upon a time, he wouldn't have permitted anyone to talk to him like that. No one refused Victor Kemp. He alone decided when someone said yes or no to him, with one exception. He had allowed the former assassin to leave, only to discover the magnitude of her deceit. Never again, he vowed.

Except this was Luisa. He had repaid her loyalty by causing her further distress. A smart woman, she must have sensed he was withholding information. A proud woman, she would take matters into her own hands. She was through with him. He knew it.

Yet he continued. "I will be moving out of this building and probably out of London altogether," he told her. "I will task a realtor with the sale of the property. Not you; you don't need the attention. Naturally, you'll receive a portion of the commission. I'll also be consolidating my business ventures. I may even sell a portion of them. Whatever interests you have will be honored."

"Fine." She sounded utterly neutral. They may as well have been concluding a business agreement.

He felt an unfamiliar pang. If she left, the humanizing qualities she brought to his life would disappear. Against his better judgment, he asked the question he had no right to ask. "Do you know where you will go?"

Silence.

He cleared his throat. "I trust you will contact me when you've settled. I'll do the same."

"Goodbye, Victor," she said and disconnected the call.

~

Arkady Dyukov was not given to sentimentality. True, he practiced an old-world version of fidelity, but its roots were pragmatic rather than emotional. He couldn't imagine betraying his boss. Nor did he ever question Kemp's advancement of first one and then the other of his sons. They were polished, educated, and connected in ways a

Russian roughneck, even one good at math, would never be. They were also blood, and that counted for much.

Paul had been an intelligent young man, dedicated and knowledgeable. He treated his employees with respect and his father with appropriate deference. Dyukov appreciated that. His loss had been a blow to Kemp and to the company.

Daniel turned out to be something else. Vain, spoiled, and shallow, he learned nothing from his six months working on London's docks. Six months against a lifetime of privilege hadn't been enough to toughen the boy up, let alone develop a sense of responsibility. Dyukov had tried to warn his boss. But Kemp had a soft spot for his wayward son. Even after Daniel endangered his father's entire business, Kemp let him off with a demotion. Dyukov would have removed at least a finger or two or perhaps something lower down.

The shooting proved to be the last straw. Dyukov never doubted his boss would take the necessary steps. The trusted enforcer would have killed the son even without permission from the father.

As for getting rid of the corpse, Dyukov treated it as a pesky garbage disposal. He spoke with a few professionals he knew who were experts in such things. He persuaded mostly with American dollars, sometimes mixed in with a few threats and made arrangements through a sister shipping company. Lye worked as well as anything to dissolve tissue. A body in a Teflon-lined barrel could quickly be reduced to nothing more than a few bones. The container could be dumped in the middle of the ocean. Illegal but necessary, as were so many things Dyukov did for his employer.

He couldn't say how he felt about the mistress's apparent departure. Dyukov used women exclusively for sex. He never treated them roughly; he always paid them fairly. He had no need to do otherwise. He'd never been in any kind of relationship. He preferred to avoid emotional entanglements. His enjoyments ran to vodka, pirozhki, and the occasional wager on a race or sports event.

All in all, he was a simple man, familiar with the rules governing both fealty and authority. His only concern related to how Luisa's exit might affect his boss.

Victor Kemp had married into London society. Dyukov saw that as a strategic move. Luisa Guzman exerted a different sort of pull. Perhaps she fed into Kemp's vision of himself as a successful and wealthy businessman who could have whatever he wanted: fine clothes, fine homes, a beautiful mistress, and a socially prominent family. At some point, Kemp grew genuinely fond of the Latin woman. The arrival of two possible male heirs appealed to his ego in ways his massive empire could not. Or so Arkady Dyukov surmised.

Now that portion of Kemp's life was gone. Dyukov could only hope the fallout wouldn't affect business.

Even before Daniel's latest and most disastrous blunder, Kemp ordered key alterations to the way he did business. He could not and would not touch human cargo ever again. Nonetheless, he chose to stay in shipping. He didn't wish to waste the time and money he'd invested. Francesco Guzman had to retire, though. A thoroughly original identity had to then be established.

A new entity incorporated in Madagascar and headquartered in Melbourne purchased the four shipping companies previously owned by Senhor Guzman, along with their vessels, clients, and routes. The legal documents listed a South African named Johan Krüger as the owner. Krüger was known to be interested in resurrecting struggling maritime companies. The ships now flew new flags, carried new registrations, and used alternate shipping routes.

Kemp/Krüger named his newest company Monachus, the biological category belonging to the Mediterranean monk seal. An ancient and critically endangered species, the mammal survived hidden in caves underwater or tucked into rocky cliff sides. Kemp found the symbolism appropriate. He ordered his ships adorned with a silhouette of the rare animal.

Frederick Weber, Kemp's personal attorney, led the legal team that handled the paperwork for the new company. Over the last decade, Weber had acted as Kemp's personal consigliere. He'd been with the firm much longer. The German-born lawyer didn't hesitate in reaching out when news of the shooting first made the news. He even volunteered to fly to London.

Dyukov didn't care for the man. He resented Weber's education, his opportunities and advantages, and especially his friendship with Kemp's son, Paul. He found the man slippery, his easy grace masking a sense of entitlement. Though Arkady Dyukov wouldn't admit it, he also viewed Kemp's reliance on the lawyer as an impediment. Dyukov had come to believe that with Daniel's demise and Luisa's departure, he would hold the coveted position of favored son, blood or no. He intended to make that happen. No fancy German-born solicitor from New York would get in his way.

Dyukov had once caught Weber gazing at Paul Guzman with something akin to desire. The enforcer had no interest in whether the lawyer was gay. Unlike his boss, he cared nothing about anyone's private life unless it interfered with work. This was something different because it involved Kemp's beloved son.

He didn't know how far it went or whether the apparent attraction had been mutual. With Paul dead, would it even matter? It most definitely would to Kemp. While Dyukov had no concrete evidence, he didn't imagine he'd need much to provoke a reaction in his employer. He kept his impressions to himself. He might decide to act on them one day, but not yet.

Weber ended up remaining in New York. He and Kemp spoke twice a day by secure video feed or telephone line. Dyukov was included in these conversations, which reassured him as to his position within the hierarchy. Together, he and Weber promised Kemp's most important clients the same level of service from the new company. Dyukov demonstrated his worth in other ways. Kemp's new operations needed an intricate underground network of criminals, bribable officials, and dupes. Dyukov made sure the infrastructure continued to function effectively.

His sources let him know the Foster boy had survived. He reported to Kemp.

"And my daughter?"

"Superficial wound, exactly as reported. The bullet hit her elbow. She'll be fine."

"You took care of the other matter? I don't need details."

"Everything is taken care of."

"Good."

Relocation now became a priority. Kemp had already moved into a discreet boutique hotel across the Thames, preferring to be away from the East London building. Papers were burned, information downloaded to flash drives, laptops trashed, security systems disabled, and any recordings destroyed. Now the older man discussed more permanent solutions with both Dyukov and his lawyer.

The enforcer contained his irritation at Weber's continued involvement. He couldn't begrudge the other his dedication or his accomplishments. Through back channels, the attorney found a buyer for the Wapping building. He flew to London to conclude the transaction and remained a few days longer. The three men weighed various relocation considerations, including access to excellent medical help. Then Weber went back to New York.

Dyukov listened, observed, and weighed in from time to time. He appreciated that Kemp valued his opinion. The man's recent losses—his son dead, his mistress gone—appeared to have stripped him clean, purged him of any concerns save building his empire. Kemp would never again entertain notions of legacy or family. His life now revolved strictly around his work. Dyukov presumed revenge would figure into future plans, but he couldn't be sure. Kemp had fared worse than Suzanne Foster. Perhaps the obsession with the former assassin had played itself out. The man was first and foremost a businessman. Sometimes one had to cut one's losses, regardless of the pain, and move on.

One thing he understood: wherever Victor Kemp went, Arkady Dyukov would also go. He'd always been Kemp's most reliable man. Now he was more, raised up by virtue of circumstance, combined with his own patience and unswerving fidelity. Notwithstanding Weber's talent as an attorney, he would never earn the degree of trust enjoyed by the ambitious Dyukov. The lieutenant intended to show Kemp how invaluable he could be. The thought pleased him.

Chapter Twenty-Three

The digital clock read 6:45 a.m. on the last day of the old year. Ambient light from streetlamps crept around the curtains. London stirred in the dark, dawn's first appearance at least an hour away.

Brian Foster propped himself up on an elbow and watched his wife breathe in and out. Suzanne lay on her left side with her back to him. One arm was extended under the covers, the other wrapped protectively around herself. She looked to be deeply asleep. Brian hoped she was, although he doubted it. The position was one she adopted in Wales. She'd kept a pistol under her pillow.

He wanted to stroke her face, but he didn't want to risk disturbing her. Even in the shadows, he could see that she'd hollowed out in the last week. He'd feared for his son's life so much at times that his chest hurt. He still feared for his wife. Beneath the reserve and years of enforced self-discipline lay a darkness unresolved even by the leveling influence of her family.

Brian knew something about human psychology. Genetics and environment both played a role in shaping the psyche. He'd grown up in a loving home with two parents devoted to their family. Brian and his sister had never lacked for attention or inspiration. Friends and cousins provided an endless supply of playmates. The siblings had access to the best of French and British traditions from which to draw.

Yes, Peter Foster's accidental death had been a tragedy, but it had been within the realm of the ordinary. Adult children lost parents and survived. Brian had certainly done so, though his family had faced some financial challenges for a time.

Suzanne's early life lacked stability, to say the least. True, she'd remained physically in place within a single neighborhood in San Francisco. On the other hand, she'd been essentially rootless, a child whose parents' gross neglect constituted abuse. She'd chosen her own guardians, beginning with the people who took her in when her mother threw her out. Then she met an older couple who looked after her when she briefly ended up homeless in Seattle. She'd even found herself a mentor in the Army. Suzanne knew what she needed: structure and a sense of belonging, a way to feel connected. Family.

She didn't choose Victor Kemp, though. He chose her. She found herself in his sights because she killed the men she thought hurt her roommate. Why on earth did she get involved? She hadn't been in any imminent danger. Killing those people didn't necessarily guarantee her safety, although she might have believed it would. Why did she act on behalf of a woman she didn't really know? Was she motivated by youthful hubris? Blood lust?

Brian didn't believe his wife to be a psychopath. He wasn't naive or blinded by love. He relied on analysis. The killing in Nashville spoke to Suzanne's sense of justice, her instincts for dealing with a perceived threat, and perhaps a degree of misplaced confidence. He supposed most men who found themselves in the same position wouldn't think to question their motives, let alone their actions. Suzanne did, as much as she protested otherwise.

Brian likened her years with Kemp to being a captured soldier forced to work for the enemy. She'd been, if not brainwashed, then thoroughly intimidated. She undoubtedly felt herself to be in jeopardy.

He understood that feeling. Even his line of work, which relied mostly on information gathering and assessment, became dangerous from time to time. He'd twice taken a life and caused the deaths of several others over the course of his career. Leaving aside the body count, how different were her actions from his?

If Suzanne didn't try to explain away her past (and neither he nor Michael ever expected her to), she clearly worried about what that past had made her and what it had done to her family. Pragmatic and initially taciturn, she developed the habit of apologizing for putting them all in harm's way. Michael finally asked her to stop.

"If anyone's to blame, it's the maniac who's pursuing us. Okay? Let's focus on bringing him down, and we'll all sleep better."

After they succeeded in doing just that (or so they believed), they returned to London. Freed from the strain of hiding and fearing, Suzanne nonetheless remained guarded, on the lookout for threats from without and within. Only recently had she agreed to see a therapist in order to sort through her experiences and, as she put it, "come to terms with what I am."

"What you are is a brave, resourceful woman," he assured her.

"But do you think I'm also a natural born killer?"

Suzanne had posed the question just six weeks earlier as they lay together under their goose feather comforter. Brian considered before he answered.

"We all are, aren't we? I mean, we're all geared to survive."

She raised her head, her blue eyes fixed on him. "That's what my friend Skeeter used to say."

"Your Army instructor."

Suzanne had trained under Jon "Skeeter" Hutchinson, a marksman with the infamous 9th Infantry Division. The division became a model for the Army's first sniper school and set some sort of kill record during the Vietnam War. It's no surprise they formed a connection, especially after she learned he was a closeted gay man. Two outsiders bonding over a rifle.

"He was in a position to speak to the issue, don't you think? And you said he'd made peace with it." This is what passes for intimate pillow talk between people like us, Brian remembered thinking, people who not only see but also fully immerse themselves in the muddy underbelly of the world.

He looked her full in the face, his green eyes intense. "If what you're asking me, Suzanne, is whether I see you as someone who kills without compunction, the answer is no."

"I have, though, haven't I? Killed without compunction. So how can you say that with any assurance?"

"Because you ask the question. Because my answer matters to you. Because you care how your past actions and even your present impulses affect those closest to you. Because your question indicates the presence of compassion. And because I love you."

He worried the last bit was too cavalier. He did love her, mightily. But love was a complicated tangle of generous and narcissistic impulses. Attraction played a role, as did affection. Most of all, love acted as a mirror of one's own sense of worth. Suzanne made him feel strong, intuitive, even privileged to have access to the real woman hidden from the rest of the world.

She reached a hand to his face in the dark, her touch soft against his cheek.

"I love you, too." Then she fell asleep.

That night, after she dozed off, something else occurred to him. Long-distance killers, whether behind a scope or in the cockpit of a bomber, have the luxury of being removed.

The reality of modern warfare was that the warrior didn't have to look into the eyes of the target. It didn't change the soldier's duty, but it might change how that soldier felt about killing. Brian's two experiences had involved close encounters. Suzanne had a few of those, but she never stayed around, never looked down at the lifeless bodies of her victims. For all her experience with death, she had little blood on her hands.

That wouldn't stop her from exacting revenge on Victor Kemp, if he lived. If he lived. She remained convinced he did. No body had been found, no evidence of life. Kemp had been seventy when he went into the water. Even a young man would have been unlikely to survive the sea, let alone the blast. That Kemp may have seemed impossible. Stranger things had happened, though.

One thing Brian knew: the woman who appeared so fragile and drained as she slept would strangle the man with her bare hands if she had a chance.

He slipped out of bed and padded into the kitchen, only a bit surprised to find his nephew dressed and with his laptop open on the tiny kitchen table.

"Good morning. I didn't want to risk waking you by making coffee. Or are you a tea drinker?"

"Coffee in the morning, tea in the afternoon. I'll get a pot going. I don't know if we've got much to eat, though. We were expecting to be in Wales."

"I picked up some milk and some pastries last night. Figured those would do."

Simon set out two plates and a box.

"Here you go. Belgian patisserie. I actually located an open shop. Oh, and Mamà sent along some cheese and dried fruit, which I put in the fridge."

"It's good to have you here."

It was an understatement. Next to his son, Brian loved Simon most of all. How he would have liked to keep Michael in a relatively stable situation with his Belgian relatives instead of leaving and returning, only to run again. All to prevent Victor Kemp from discovering he hadn't succeeded in murdering the Foster family. The very thought of Kemp produced in Brian an all-consuming hatred hotter than any flame. Suzanne wasn't the only one to feel the full effects of a deep rage.

"Are you all right?" Concerned, Simon pulled out the chair. "Sit down, okay?"

"I'm fine. Tired." Tired and old, Brian thought. His sixty-third birthday had come and gone with a minimum of fuss, just a quiet dinner out with Suzanne. His doctor assured him everything was in working order and then some. Sixty-three was the new something or other. But Brian understood that a life of subterfuge had worn on him. He would be eternally grateful to SIS for insisting he keep on working, albeit discreetly and in disguise, during his twenty years on the run. It took a secretly sanctioned operation to wipe out the scourge that had ruined their lives.

Now he questioned whether they had truly succeeded.

"Uncle Brian, I have something to discuss with you relative to Victor Kemp. I think you'll find this very interesting."

"Do tell."

The two men turned to see Suzanne standing at the entrance to the kitchen, wrapped in a lavender fleece robe, her tousled dark-blonde hair spilling over the collar. She looked rested, although dark smudges remained under her eyes. Husband and nephew popped up at the same time, nearly bumping heads. She laughed, the sound magical to

189

Brian's ears. He hadn't heard her laugh in some time, hadn't known if he ever would again.

"Don't worry, you didn't wake me. It was the smell of coffee. Honestly, I can't think of a more luxurious way to get up in the morning. Well, unless . . ." Suzanne caught Brian's eye and they both blushed.

"All right, you two, not in front of the young person. Auntie, may I get you a cup?"

She inhaled, took a sip, and sighed with contentment.

"Perfect. And stop calling me Auntie, Simon. Unless you want me to feel old."

"Phtt, you are ageless."

"Thank you. That's just what a woman wants to hear early in the morning. Wait, are those mattentaarts? I love them! Where on earth did you find an open bakery? Simon, your resourcefulness astounds me."

She bit into a cheese-filled pastry and groaned with delight. Her sugarcoated grin lifted Brian's heart.

His energy had surged with the appearance of his wife. Her skin was pale, almost translucent. She looked beautiful. Her appetite had clearly returned. He noted with amusement that she reached for a second pastry before she finished the first. All of this suggested that at least superficially, Michael's terrible ordeal hadn't done his mother any permanent damage. What it had done to her emotionally—what it had done to them both—was something they would discover in time. Right now, they needed to deal with a host of unanswered questions.

As if she'd read his mind, Suzanne put down her pastry. "What is this interesting news you have, Simon?" she asked.

Uncle and nephew exchanged a glance. No sense in keeping anything from her.

"I've been checking regularly with my contacts. I know you've got plenty of resources at your disposal, Uncle. And you've got Charlie to help and your other colleagues. Given how preoccupied you've been . . ."

"Call me Brian, Simon. And don't worry about hurting my feelings. You're as equipped as I am to gather intelligence. Perhaps more so."

The Metropolitan Police Force, also known as New Scotland Yard, led the investigation into Daniel Guzman's motives. Because the incident occurred at the house of a member of Parliament, a special operations group within the force known as CTC, or the Counter Terrorism Command, had been activated. CTC worked closely with the domestic and international counterintelligence divisions, MI5 and MI6, as well as with other intelligence partners. Brian had no concerns about slipping out of the loop. That didn't make him any less grateful for Simon's engagement.

Most people who knew (or thought they knew) Simon Vauclain believed he was employed by Friends of Europe, or Les Amis de l'Europe. The ostensibly nonpartisan think tank had been around for more than forty years. Its staying power owed to its efforts to remain relevant and widen its appeal. Though it began in Brussels, it developed over the decades a decidedly pan-European approach and a focus on citizen involvement. As far as anyone knew, Simon worked as director of social media.

In reality, he was employed by a non-aligned, nongovernmental organization so clandestine most agencies around the world didn't know it existed. Like his uncle, Simon spoke several languages. Like Charlie Campbell, whom he greatly admired, he excelled at morphing into whoever he needed to be. His job also involved activities that required mental and physical prowess, or so Brian once confided to Suzanne.

"Super-spy stuff. Think James Bond, then double it."

"He must report to someone, Brian. Who is it? Who signs his paycheck?"

"I don't know, and I don't know who does know. I assume his bosses are the good guys, all things being relative."

Now Suzanne wrapped both hands around her mug and gave Simon her full attention.

"Please go on."

"There's a coordinated effort to locate Daniel Guzman, as you can well imagine. I don't need to tell you, Brian, heads are going to roll over the security at Lord Edgerton's party. Basically, it failed. It's not like Guzman snuck in a plastic pistol he made from a 3-D printer. He had a Glock, for God's sake!" Suzanne flinched, but Simon didn't seem to notice. "Initially, intel had him hopping a flight to Dubai or maybe Christchurch. Still other leads pointed to an escape to Moscow or Chicago. Each of these leads turned out to be not just false but deliberately constructed to throw us off the scent."

"In other words, he could be anywhere." Suzanne's voice was flat, but Brian picked up on the underlying tension.

Simon shook his head. "He could be, assuming he had all sorts of sophisticated help. Which he clearly had. His phone records have been wiped; his computer is missing. The Met's only clue as to where he's been the past two years comes from an assortment of people he partied with. They're being questioned, at least those who aren't off on some sort of holiday. I doubt anyone will give up anything useful. For one thing, it's not at all clear that anything Daniel told them is true."

"What about the father? I mean, Francesco Guzman?"

"Ah, now there's an interesting story, Uncle, er, Brian. The senior Guzman sold his company just two weeks ago."

"That's remarkable timing, wouldn't you say, gentlemen?" Suzanne seemed curious but not fearful.

"Absolutely," Simon agreed.

"I'll follow up from my office. Simon, do your sources know where he might have gone?"

"He's reported to have retired, although the location is unknown. One woman at his headquarters"—Simon drew air quotes around the word— "claims he decided on Costa Rica. Only he's not there. Or if he is, he's living under an assumed name. We've checked. Another thing: none of the staff remembers Francesco Guzman mentioning a son. Not that they actually met the man. The conversations were all by telephone."

Suzanne took a sip of coffee. "I understand the elder Guzman never married."

"Correct, at least according to what we've been able to find out. So, what is his relationship to Daniel Guzman? Illegitimate or adopted son? Grandson? Nephew? Interpol has no DNA for either of the Guzmans."

"And both of them have disappeared."

"Yes."

"What do either of you know about Daniel Guzman's mother?"

"According to the few people we've contacted, Daniel never talked about a mother or any siblings, only about how rich his old man was and how he was in the shipping business."

"You do know Victor Kemp's mistress is—was named Luisa Guzman."

"We know. It's a common name."

Brian looked down at his mug. The thick coffee obscured the bottom of the cup. "There's still a lot left to uncover."

"If it's any consolation, there are any number of agencies still looking, including my group. If there are layers, we'll pull them back."

"There are always layers." Suzanne set down her cup and left the room.

Chapter Twenty-Four

When I was a child, I met an author at City Lights Bookstore who'd written a young adult novel I loved. I can't even remember the title, but I recall a quote from the book: "Belief creates its own reality." The heroine's father says it to explain what he calls his daughter's overactive imagination. As it turns out, she's not making anything up. She simply sees more than most people do. She's able to get at the truth beneath the truth.

To peel back the layers.

The media spins the holiday shooter, as they call him, as a disturbed young man seeking attention. The explanation is simplistic. I doubt anyone in any agency now hunting him believes it. While some members of the press may be trying out that story on a gullible public, a handful of reporters will dig deeper. What will they find? What false evidentiary trail has been built in advance of the digging?

I have no proof Daniel Guzman is Victor Kemp's son. I'd never seen the man with the gun before; at least I don't think so. He did look familiar, but my memory might be playing tricks on me.

Even if he were Kemp's son, who's to say he had it in his head to kill me? Perhaps he really was aiming at Annie. He may have learned she was his half-sister and resented her legitimacy. Not unheard of. Even if I were the one he wanted dead, why wait until now? What motivated him? Misplaced sense of duty? Delayed revenge? It seems a stretch.

Most notably, Guzman's actions were so reckless as to be the work of an amateur. No one connected to Victor Kemp, including the man himself, would have sanctioned, let alone ordered, such a crazy stunt. Yet Daniel Guzman's disappearance has been nothing short of masterful. He's vanished without a trace. That suggests he had expert help. Which then begs the question: was the shooting a diversion? If so, what is the main event? Nothing else has happened, although the principals are being watched by a protective detail for the time being.

My efforts to sort through and arrange the puzzle pieces have given me a headache. I hoist myself up from the breakfast table where I've been worrying a piece of toast as thoroughly as I've worried my mind. I need to stay sharp. Michael is being released from the hospital this morning. He requires daily interaction with a nurse for another week or two as well as six weeks of physical therapy.

Initially, the doctors suggested a care facility, but I couldn't bear the thought. At the same time, we knew we couldn't properly accommodate his needs in our small flat. Tommy and Maggie generously proposed their townhouse. We demurred. Neither Brian nor I believed taking Michael back to the scene of the crime makes sense.

Enter Brian's place of employment. Not the university but rather Her Majesty's Secret Intelligence, which has come through in fine fashion. Apparently, SIS maintains a high-end safe house for valued assets inside a well-maintained and well-guarded luxury highrise. While it might not suit the requirements of a Russian oligarch or a Saudi prince, it's surprisingly spacious and perfect for our needs.

Our temporary home has two bedroom suites, one at each end of the flat. The den doubles as a guest room. There's a library, a small front sitting room, an alcove with a table that seats six or eight, and an open kitchen outfitted to impress a professional cook. The windows are double-glazed and likely impenetrable. You can't exactly air out this place. Nor is there a balcony. We do have a private lift and access to a lovely walled garden at ground level. The building even boasts a fitness room and small pool.

We've managed to snag Nancy Okorie for a week of private duty nursing. Without a doubt, the pay is part of the appeal. I like to think she also enjoys working with a young patient with Michael's determination. Kate is staying in the den for a while. She'll eventually join Michael in the master suite, but who knows when that will be? In the meantime, she's arranged to work remotely for a week or two so she can help Nancy oversee her fiancé's recovery.

Brian thinks it's a splendid idea. "Between those two women, he'll not be able to slack off," he chuckles. "They'll have him running laps if he's not careful."

He won't be in danger, I think, noting the watchful eyes of the men and women placed unobtrusively around lobby. What happens when we leave, though? I keep those observations to myself.

We hoped to get Michael checked out before his birthday, but what with the holidays and all we had to settle for a celebration in the hospital. I wouldn't have predicted we'd be there rather than in Wales. Then again, I didn't know if my son would even see his twenty-eighth birthday.

Today I've hired a van with a driver who can double as a bodyguard. Michael, Kate, and Nancy are waiting at the entrance as we pull up. Kate and Michael have already taken care of the paperwork. He's even managed to sign himself out. He looks so weak sitting in the wheelchair, wrapped in scarves and a blanket. At the same time, he desperately needs a shave.

Your son is a man, I remind myself.

He stands on wobbly legs with Kate's help and favors me with a grin that melts my heart.

Twenty minutes later, we drive up to our temporary home. Michael lets out a whistle.

"Pretty swanky."

"Your father has pull."

We get him upstairs. He insists on looking around.

"Enough excitement, young man. To bed." Nancy points to his room, and her patient complies.

Between the nurse and the fiancée, the care duties are well covered. I'll have to balance my need to interfere against their impressive competence. Brian says as much as he kisses the top of my head and prepares to head out. I pull on his sleeve.

"I want to know everything you know."

"I promise."

~

During my working years, I was ostensibly employed to assess weaknesses and make recommendations. My title was corporate security manager, although I had no one to manage. Because I was young and female, I typed up my own reports as well as the notes at most meetings I attended.

Kemp's company stayed ahead of the curve in hiring and appearing to promote women in the workplace. In reality, the place was as sexist as any other company at the time, never mind my presumed value to my employer. It took me a dozen years to get a part-time assistant and a private office. Paul Guzman had all of those and more the day he joined the company. Then again, he was the boss's son.

The advantage of my experience is that I learned the value of personal follow-up. I remember names, faces, birthdays, anniversaries, number of children, kinds of pets, and any significant others who may be important to the people I work or socialize with. I never fail to acknowledge a kindness. If I come off as reserved, I'm nevertheless regarded as well mannered. In this day and age, my approach may seem old-fashioned. I don't think of it that way. It's a habit that pays off.

I suppose I have Victor Kemp to thank.

I'm willing and able to spend the day writing to all the people whose outpouring of support has meant so much to Brian and me. It doesn't feel like a burden or busywork or even penance, as it must to so many people. I'm grateful for the chance to acknowledge the human connection.

What the busywork doesn't do is address either my anxiety or my simmering fury.

Brian comes home at six, his arms filled with goodies from Harrods Food Hall. It's just the four of us. Nancy has gone back to her flat, presumably to pull together an overnight bag. She insists on staying with us for tonight, after which she'll turn over the graveyard shift to Kate. Michael's fiancée appears more than prepared to take her caretaking role seriously. She approves a small glass of craft brew for Michael.

I pretend to eat while watching them all. Michael looks stronger, especially with the indomitable Kate by his side. Brian appears more tired than usual, or maybe he's preoccupied. I suspect the latter when he looks at me across the table and uses sign language to indicate we need to talk.

After dinner, we send the Kate and Michael to the library, a clubby little room with a huge TV screen tucked behind some shelves. Nancy has returned and is unpacking in the guest bedroom. Both women have agreed on an 8:00 p.m. bedtime for Michael. The poor boy really doesn't stand a chance.

Brian and I are in our suite at the far end of the flat. We bring our chairs close together. He can't stay seated. Characteristically and almost comically, he bounces up and begins talking and pacing in front of me.

"There's no trace of Daniel Guzman. No hints or whispers, nothing except deliberately false leads that have taken investigators nowhere for nearly two weeks. Nothing."

"Which means?"

He stops and looks me full in the face. "Some of us think maybe Daniel Guzman didn't disappear on his own."

"He had help."

"Not exactly. It's more like he was made to disappear."

"Killed, in other words." I don't sound at all surprised, which appears to surprise Brian.

"Yes."

"Because he failed to complete his assignment?"

"Doubtful."

"Because he attempted an unsanctioned assignment that failed."

"Yes. And in doing so, he inadvertently brought attention to someone else who didn't appreciate it. Possibly his father."

I make to rise out of my chair.

"Hold on, Suzie. I'm talking about Francesco Guzman."

I sit back down. "Who has also apparently disappeared. And who may not ever have existed."

My husband kneels in front of me, an oddly romantic gesture. He takes both my hands.

"I know what you're thinking, Suzanne. Leaving aside the unlikelihood that a man half Kemp's age could have survived the explosion, there's simply no evidence . . ." His voice trails off.

THE FORMER ASSASSIN

No evidence that Victor Kemp is alive and responsible for the disappearance of his own son, the man who shot my son. Nothing to go on, except for the churning in my gut and the buzzing in my brain. Spidey sense.

Chapter Twenty-Five

Lisette Brooks loved southern Florida in late January, with its longer days and reliably warm temperatures. The dreaded tourist season didn't kick off until next month, allowing the locals to enjoy the area's natural bounty in relative peace and quiet. Snowbirds irritated her. They brought with them packed streets and crowded restaurants. Thirty years in Boca Raton allowed her to call herself a native.

She hadn't yet decided where to take her winter holiday. Like many of her acquaintances, she normally decamped in February. She spoke a bit of Spanish and often ended up visiting friends in Chile or Argentina, where she could be assured of a decent social life. Sometimes a man might factor into her decision about where she vacationed. Nevertheless, it always remained her decision. Lisette had sworn she would never again let any male interfere with her life's plan. She didn't need to. Money bought many advantages, chief among them the freedom to make arrangements at the last minute.

She didn't have any idea writing would make her wealthy. She became a novelist because she wanted to, and because she was prepared to work at her craft. As it turned out, she had a talent for telling suspenseful stories in which a strong heroine always overcame the problem or maneuvered around the obstacles that stood in her way. Love played a role at times, but the protagonist never reinvented herself for any man. The female leads skewed young but not too young, beautiful but not impossibly so, and educated but not unapproachable. Trained in a variety of martial arts and weapons use, they nonetheless relied first and foremost on their mental acumen. Her girls were clever, resourceful, and above all, independent.

Though she hadn't continued her formal education beyond high school, Lisette always read avidly. She wrote whenever possible, mostly journal entries about the life she wanted, and essays about the life she observed. She studied authors and their styles during her time at City Lights Bookstore. She also made mental notes about the customers, particularly those who gravitated to fiction. A good book, she knew, provided entertainment. A great book, she believed, celebrated its readers and treated them as members of an exclusive club. Lisette already excelled in the art of making people feel special. She used that talent as an author.

As a result, she became not simply a novelist but a hugely popular one. Her books regularly entered the bestseller lists and stayed there for weeks at a time. Critics called her "the thinking woman's Jackie Collins."

She created two series. For the second one, she used the pen name J. J. Boyle after her mother Janice. Her books were available in print and ebook format. Most of them had been recorded. One had already been made into a television serial starring a mid-list actress who found fame with the part. J. J. Boyle's debut novel had just been optioned for a film. Lisette arranged to consult on the project. She wanted to insure her loyal readers got the script they deserved. She also thought she'd enjoy flying to Hollywood and being treated like royalty.

Her global fanbase wrote letters and emails. They established clubs and social media pages and engaged in endless discussions centered on plot points and character development. Mostly female, they remained steadfast in their admiration. Lisette had never had much use for women in her younger years. Now she acknowledged their considerable consumer power. She liked having fans.

Meanwhile, she made money hand-over-fist, money she could never hope to spend. She didn't do book tours anymore. She occasionally consented to a reading, although she no longer trusted her voice to sound as youthful as she wanted. Her team—accountant, agent, assistant, attorney, and publicist—handled it all. All she had to do was write books.

Not bad for a woman at a certain point in her life.

Lisette moved languidly around the lounge chairs and toward her favorite semi-private enclosure where she could relax without being bothered. She looked forward to seeing her favorite cabana boy. It was a near daily ritual, this flirtation with the handsome young man who served her margaritas while she lolled on the chaise. Lisette never came down before four, in part because she wrote until then, in part because she preferred that time of day. The sun hung lower in the sky. She'd put in a day's work. Time for fun.

She wore the requisite oversized sunglasses and big hat. Her sheer cover-ups blocked the late-day sun while offering the outline of a still-shapely body. Even with all the time and money she'd invested, it was best at her age to present a peek of this, a hint of that, the mere suggestion of sensuality. Smoke and mirrors.

Lisette understood how the game was played. Wealth could slow the aging process. It couldn't stop it. She detested the idea of growing old. Who didn't? She'd been blessedly free of any health issues. Her joints, all of them original, functioned well. Her organs were apparently in mint condition. She lived relatively pain-free, an anomaly she appreciated. Skilled cosmetic surgeons had done whatever she decided her appearance required in as subtle a fashion as possible. Not for her the packed in, pulled back, sewn together look of so many of her contemporaries.

For years, she skirted the age issue. It made sense to maintain a certain air of mystery. The Internet and the increase in the number of nosy entertainment reporters made that increasingly difficult. She had a daughter in her fifties and a grandson who just turned twenty-eight. Once those facts were made public, anyone could do the math.

Women were judged by their age as well as their appearance, whether they were housewives, television stars, or best-selling authors. At the same time, everyone was becoming more candid these days. At least fame allowed for some narrative control. She could reveal details about her past life when she was ready. She'd once or twice indicated she had a family from whom she'd long been estranged. When pressed, she'd allow that it was all too difficult to discuss. The young reporters pushed, but Lisette Brooks was more than capable of holding her own.

After Michael's recent near-death experience, her outlook underwent a seismic shift. She'd always accepted her on-again off-again connection with her daughter. She realized she might have been a more active parent, might have paid more attention to Suzanne. But what could she have done? She had to deal with her lunatic husband. Once she got rid of him, she had to provide for the two of them. Her early choices hadn't always been wise, she conceded. At the outset, she'd been convinced her sullen and sensitive daughter was to blame for whatever she claimed had happened to her. These days, she wasn't so sure.

Though Lisette visited New York several times during the nineties to meet with her publisher, she connected with Suzanne just twice. Her daughter had grown into a most attractive woman. She'd clearly achieved some measure of success, though Lisette was in the dark as to what the younger woman did for a living. Suzanne refused to discuss work in any detail, though she shared amusing details about corporate meetings. An executive of some kind, Lisette surmised.

They dined both times at an out of the way bistro instead of the trendy place Lisette thought might be fun. Conversation touched on cultural and social events. Suzanne appeared to be adept in the art of polite conversation. She'd even read a few of her mother's books, which pleased Lisette more than the older woman let on.

At the end of one meal Suzanne insisted was her treat, the waiter returned with a credit card. He handed it back with a small nod and said, "Thank you, Miss Smith."

Lisette cocked an eyebrow.

"Nom de plume, mother. Like your J.J. Boyle. Although in my case, you might say nom de guerre."

Well, that's cryptic, Lisette thought. What was her daughter fighting? "Should I be calling you Miss Smith?" she asked.

"Why not?"

Suzanne clearly had secrets to keep. Perhaps she left a failing marriage or fled an abusive relationship. She might even be involved in some sort of covert operations. She'd once mentioned that military service had brought out her natural talent as a markswoman. Just like her grandfather, she noted. Lisette found the idea of an undercover daughter intriguing. It had the makings of a dramatic story.

Lisette didn't probe. She had no idea what might be considered appropriate inquiry between a mother and her daughter. She scarcely knew this expensively dressed woman who sat across from her. None of her business, she decided, though she experienced an unfamiliar tug of concern.

They stayed in touch by phone. More precisely, Suzanne called twice a year. Lisette didn't have contact information or any idea where her daughter lived. In 2006, Suzanne telephoned her to say she'd taken early retirement and would be traveling and out of touch for some time. Lisette didn't hear from her daughter for five years.

When they at last spoke, Lisette discovered more than she could have imagined. Suzanne and her family—her daughter had both a husband and an adult son, which was shocking enough—had been in hiding all that time. Her daughter couldn't talk about it except to say they were all safe. She allowed as she'd married a man who taught and did "government consulting." Lisette determined he worked as some sort of intelligence officer. Perhaps they worked together. His and her spies, which sounded dangerous but also oddly reassuring.

Suzanne was much more forthcoming about her son. She shared with her mother details about his plans to be an engineer and his engagement to a budding architect, the daughter of a member of the House of Lords. Michael was marrying into a noble family! The idea of a royal wedding thrilled Lisette.

Then the awful (and still unsolved) incident occurred. Lisette wanted nothing more than to fly to London and stand vigil for her only grandson alongside her only child. Family mattered, she realized. Even this late in life, perhaps especially this late in life. That she suppressed her selfish inclinations and remained in Florida as Suzanne requested surprised her. Maybe she wasn't too far along to change after all.

Besides, she'd been thinking about what a brilliant coda to her autobiography the reunion would make. Married to an addicted Beat poet, our heroine lived among pre-revolutionary types during the height of the hippie movement, then enjoyed a swinging couples-swapping life in 1970's California. Inspired by the feminist revolution, the budding writer determined to chart her own course. She found her destiny, became a renowned author, and reunited with her daughter. Her grandson married the daughter of an English nobleman.

It promised to be a bestseller. Lisette could almost see her agent salivating.

As she glided toward her regular spot, Lisette was surprised to see not blond and buff Rory but an older man. Lisette had a keen eye when it came to judging age. This man was perhaps in his fifties and quite well preserved. No, better than that: he was, if she had to be honest, absolutely gorgeous. A few strands of silver at the temples in a full head of otherwise ebony hair. Wide shoulders, broad chest, and slim hips owed more to nature than any gym routine.

A man, Lisette decided, not a boy with aspirations.

He'd been setting towels inside the small tent. Now he straightened, turned, and favored her with a gleaming white smile.

"Good afternoon, Ms. Brooks. I have everything set up for you. My name is Gabriel, by the way. Like the archangel." His English was impeccable, just the faintest trace of an accent.

"What happened to Rory?"

"Rory went back to school, I believe. The young are always bent on self-improvement, which is most admirable. I hope my presence does not disappoint. Let me amend that." He broadened his smile. "I will make certain my presence does not disappoint."

Good-looking and bold, Lisette thought approvingly. None of the obsequiousness that those serving the wealthy often exhibit. This man knew his place; he also knew his power. She arched an eyebrow and curved her lips ever so slightly.

"I have no doubt you will succeed."

~

Gabriel issues his report a week later.

"She's smart and careful. Not one to share. This one, she listens as much as she talks. Very unusual, especially for a woman. It appears she has accepted that I am an unemployed teacher hoping for better luck in the United States."

"Don't get too inventive. You are not the storyteller; she is."

The comment stung. Gabriel felt he deserved far better from his employer. He resisted an easy retort.

"I am aware of that. You might be interested to know I am using her predilections to great advantage."

"Of course you are. Please continue."

That's better, Gabriel thought. All he asked for was a modicum of respect.

"The woman has never been open about having a daughter. Now she intends to disclose all in advance of the union between her grandson and the child of some nobleman. She's quite taken with the whole notion. Naturally, any announcement will be tied to some sort of book promotion. She remains quite ambitious. The wedding date isn't set, owing to what she refers to as 'a tragic incident.' I made sympathetic noises and suggested she must have planned to fly over in her family's time of need. She told me she was asked to remain stateside. And here's where we run into a problem."

"What kind of problem?"

"She doesn't know where they're currently living."

Chapter Twenty-Six

Frederick Weber was just beginning to relax. Over the past year, he'd done everything possible to prove his worth to Victor Kemp. Following the problem with the girl whose body had washed up on shore, Kemp decided it prudent to make substantial changes. Weber applauded his employer's decision. Although he might have recommended leaving the shipping business altogether, he made every effort to expedite paperwork and renegotiate contracts. They retained some of their most valued clients. Not the human traffickers, thank God. Weber preferred sitting across the table from the attorneys for the world's most ruthless arms peddlers to dealing with sexual slavers and their minions.

His latest coup involved selling the building in Wapping for an impressive profit. The warehouse had been smartly upgraded. The property still had to move quickly. Daniel's name was all over the news. He'd disappeared. Weber suspected the absence would be permanent.

That Kemp asked Weber instead of Luisa to arrange the sale surprised the attorney. Perhaps Kemp's long-time mistress also found it wise to remove herself from the picture. He didn't know whether authorities might connect her to Daniel. He assumed she was taking precautions. He wondered if she planned to stay away. If so, he would miss her.

While Kemp could be challenging to work for, Weber prided himself on doing right by the man. He rarely allowed himself to think what might happen if he couldn't perform satisfactorily. At least he could look back and be quite pleased with his career trajectory.

Some twenty-five years earlier, Weber had just finished a discouraging year at a middle-sized real estate concern specializing in commercial properties. With a Harvard law degree in his pocket, he received a number of offers from established Boston and New York law firms. Three years at the prestigious school had soured him on the prospect of a large law firm with its legions of smart associates and cutthroat politics. The real estate job promised less pressure. It also turned out to be deadly dull and insufficiently challenging.

Then he met Luisa Guzman. She changed his life.

Luisa generally worked in high-end residential real estate. She had a property she wanted to help her client convert from apartments to mixed use. Frederick found a way to work around a restrictive zoning law. Luisa made her client happy and in turn suggested Weber might be happier with a firm at the cutting edge of the energy business.

Weber went to work at the age of twenty-six as one of five legal counsels for Kemp's global enterprise. Everyone who worked for Kemp's legitimate organization came with a recommendation, regardless of whether the job was in the mailroom or the marketing department. Luisa's endorsement carried special weight, Weber noted. He felt as if he'd struck pay dirt. The work was interesting. Better still, his generous base salary rendered concerns about bonuses moot.

Frederick Weber knew he presented well. He possessed both focus and flexibility when it came to interpreting the letter of the law. Socially nimble, he stopped just short of being facile. He spoke six languages flawlessly, including Mandarin. He dressed with understated elegance and played jazz piano well enough to impress listeners.

Women loved him. He pretended to love them back. The corporate world in 1987 wasn't the best place to be out of the closet. AIDS still posed a threat. While he wouldn't have dreamed of going to a gay bar, he joined a private club whose members were carefully screened. There he could relax and enjoy himself. Mostly he worked hard.

He remembered the employee who would later cause Kemp so much heartache. She went by the intriguing name Susan J. Smith, which sounded so phony as to be laughable. She spoke in a modulated tone that hid her origins. She kept her face a mask and rarely showed emotion. Somewhere in her thirties, she possessed an ambiguous beauty, with pale skin, blue eyes, and blonde-brown hair. Even her job title projected mystery: corporate security manager. She traveled half the time, to conferences or meetings, Weber assumed.

Susan Smith was good at her job. She designed solutions that addressed security weaknesses. She came up with suggestions for protecting against predatory competitors looking to steal information. All in all, she was a diligent worker.

Occasionally, she might approach Weber's group with questions about the legal implications of a safeguard she'd conceived. As technology began to play an important part of corporate life, she challenged the lawyers to think beyond contracts and mergers. Under her gentle prodding, they stayed abreast of developments in cyber-law. He liked the way her mind worked, always two steps ahead. He admired her self-possession, although he picked up on the sadness that colored their brief exchanges.

Weber kept his head down and his ambitions up. Within a decade, he'd risen to the position of chief corporate counsel. He was just thirty-six. When Kemp brought Paul Guzman into the fold, the younger man gravitated to the urbane attorney, referring to him as "my comrade-in-arms." They even resembled one another with their pastel blue eyes and fair hair. The unmarried Weber took the new hire under his wing socially, a move thoroughly endorsed by Kemp. The lawyer suspected a blood connection between Guzman and Kemp and considered how it might present him with an opportunity.

Unfortunately, something else threatened to interfere. From the moment he laid eyes on the young man with the good future, Weber experienced an attraction so strong it pierced his heart, scrambled his mind, and stirred passions he didn't know he could feel.

By that time, being gay carried less social stigma than it had when Weber began working. Being in love with the son of his employer, a hyper-masculine man with ambitions for his heir, was a riskier proposition. Weber was no fool, and he was not without discipline. Since he couldn't presume his feelings for Paul were mutual, he knew to keep his desires thoroughly suppressed.

He lived in a state of exquisite anxiety. Each day became about the anticipation of seeing the young man. Paul's office was down the corridor from Weber's, and he developed the habit of popping his head in to greet the attorney with a "Hello, Frederick, how are we today?" The plural never failed to send a shiver through Weber.

The men attended events together in the company of women. Weber relied on his long-time friend Clara, a beautiful and remarkably accommodating woman. Paul dated a series of young and, to Weber's mind, inferior females. Sometimes the two men went out for drinks with coworkers. Susan Smith never joined them.

Once, when the two of them found themselves at the bar ordering drinks for their table, Weber nearly let down his guard. They'd consumed plenty of top-shelf liquor at that point and were sloppily finishing each other's sentences. Weber leaned in and fingered the collar of Guzman's jacket. He allowed his hand to linger at the back of the other man's neck.

Paul jerked away as if he'd been bitten. He stared unsteadily at the other man.

"What are you doing, Frederick?"

Weber played it cool. He narrowed his eyes as if he were studying the inside of the man's shirt. He shook his head, sat back, and wiped his hand on a cocktail napkin.

"You've got something on your collar. I thought it was blood; thank God it's shrimp sauce. What the hell, Paul? Have you been napping in the hors d'oeuvres again?"

Paul roared with laughter and clapped Weber on the shoulder.

"If you only knew where this shirt has been, my friend."

The lawyer put his companion in a cab and walked seventeen blocks to his apartment, cursing his carelessness and praying the incident would be forgotten. It was. When he went into work the next day, everything appeared as it always did. Paul even stopped by to complain of a headache.

"I suggest you drink lots of water." Weber didn't look up when he spoke.

Only when Paul left did the older man let the air out of his lungs. He swore he'd be more cautious going forward, no matter the personal cost.

Not long after Paul's promotion to CEO, he proposed Weber become Kemp's personal attorney. His father's long-time advisor was retiring for health reasons, the son explained. Weber couldn't imagine declining. The salary matched something he might pull in as a member of a prestigious law firm, except he didn't have to share or pay back into the company. The favored son and new chief executive officer had recommended him. He'd now be read in on sensitive information. He might even have more interaction with Paul. Was there any downside?

Working closely with Victor Kemp might be one. If everyone carried secrets, Kemp probably had an armoire full of them. Beneath the bespoke suits and handmade ties, the man was a thug, or maybe worse. Weber had guessed as much the day he joined Kemp's firm.

He'd long suspected Kemp operated at two levels, one completely aboveboard, the other far beneath the surface of propriety or legality. The public corporation did well. Even during economic downturns, the enterprise as a whole prospered. Kemp grew his business carefully. He retained a fleet of smart financial advisors. He built a board of shrewd investors. Still, a cash-heavy company, even a cautious one, suggested something less than aboveboard.

Working in the shade could prove hazardous, even for an attorney with flexible ethics. Refusing the promotion that introduced him to Kemp's dark world would be more so.

~

Weber wasn't apprised of the specifics of Kemp's trip to Wales, only that it wasn't to be a fishing vacation as announced but a potentially dangerous undertaking. The lawyer thought to question Arkady Dyukov, the taciturn Russian who worked as a sort of overseer. He doubted the man would be forthcoming. The two had taken an instant dislike to one another. At least they generally operated within separate spheres.

Weber only knew the plans called for Dyukov to accompany Kemp, Paul, and three others for a portion of the journey and then wait in Bristol for further instructions. Weber couldn't understand why Paul had to make the trip—peace-loving, numbers-oriented Paul. The idea filled him with dread.

Three days after the explosion, Luisa Guzman sent Weber a ticket to London, along with a set of instructions. Weber hastily packed and grabbed a commercial flight out, his heart in his throat.

Once across the pond, Luisa apprised him of the entire horrific story. Weber didn't understand what Susan Smith had done to incur Kemp's wrath; she'd been gone five years at that point. He only knew Kemp's determination to exact punishment had led to the deaths of five people, including the man's own son.

Luisa assumed Weber would react chiefly out of self-interest. To that end, she assured him his services would be needed whether her paramour lived or died. Weber drew no comfort from her promise. Alone in his posh hotel room, he wept. Paul's death devastated him. Yet he refused to wallow in regret. He worked for a criminal, which made him indirectly culpable. You lie down with dogs; you wake up with fleas. So he showered, shaved, rested for a few hours, and went back to sit vigil in the apartment where Victor Kemp hovered between life and death.

As soon as Kemp's survival became assured, the lawyer commuted back and forth between London and New York in order to secure the business, ensure the lines of succession, and safeguard finances. He took a seat on the board and, together with Luisa's proxy, voted for actions that assured money would flow to one of his employer's secret accounts. He admired the mistress both for her loyalty and her acumen. She seemed in turn to value both his abilities and his willingness to handle all manner of arrangements. It made sense. Though remarkably resilient, not to mention resourceful, the woman was mourning her son.

As Kemp recovered, he relied on his lawyer to work out the details of his new shipping enterprise. Weber liked the focus. By serving those criminals with whom Kemp had formerly competed, they might remove potential threats. Starting over obviously appealed to Kemp's entrepreneurial side. Overseeing a single business afforded him the opportunity for more top-down management. Luisa considered it good therapy. The attorney drew up papers and negotiated contracts with his usual savvy and finesse.

Then Daniel arrived.

Weber didn't know the second son very well. He didn't like what he saw. On the subject of Daniel Guzman, he agreed with Dyukov. The young man had nothing in common with his older brother or either of his parents, for that matter. He was lazy, disrespectful, spoiled, and possessed of an outsized view of his value. Luisa proved to be predictably forgiving. Victor's indulgence of his second son's indiscretions surprised Weber. An only child, Weber maintained a polite relationship with his parents. Placing family above all else had always seemed unwise, even fraught. Daniel's series of blunders proved the point.

Weber sighed and returned to the present, which found him packing in his London hotel room. He looked forward to heading home. He welcomed a respite from the envy that radiated off Arkady Dyukov. The man had a pitiful need for his employer's approval; that much was clear.

The lawyer was comfortable in his skin at last. He'd resigned himself to a life absent intimacy but filled with other fine things money could buy. He didn't care what

Kemp thought of him personally. He only wanted to remain invaluable to the man until such time as Weber could negotiate his retirement or his employer died—whichever came first.

His phone pinged. A text. Weber hated the intrusion but appreciated the convenience of instant communication. He was still an officer of Kemp's legitimate empire, even though he was at the same time handling the legal affairs for the new shipping concern owned by Kemp's doppelgänger, Johan Krüger. In both capacities, he needed to make himself available. Speed-dial worked well enough, text even better. Weber sighed and picked up his phone.

It read: "do u still carry a torch 4 him?"

Weber frowned. He looked at the number. Blocked. He typed back.

"Who is this?"

"u must miss him even now"

Two emoticons followed, one kissing and one looking sad.

The lawyer's stomach tightened. He tried to think how to respond. Another text appeared.

"at least u have memories"

The note was followed by a blurred image. Weber sank to the bed, his heart pounding. The photo must have been a decade old, probably taken with one of those instant cameras. It showed Frederick Weber and Paul Guzman at a bar, their heads almost touching. Weber's hand was at the back of the younger man's neck as if about to embrace him. He knew exactly when this had been taken: the night the attorney came so close to exposing his true feelings.

Who had taken the picture? It must have been one of his coworkers. Who'd been at the bar with them? He couldn't possibly remember after all this time.

The cursed text pinged again.
"cute couple. did VK know about u2?"
Weber commanded his fingers to obey.
"what do u want?"
He stared at the screen, willing it to respond.
A response appeared:
"u will know soon."

Chapter Twenty-Seven

As Michael recovers, I fret and stew. It's not a comfortable experience. The fretting is bad enough; the stewing is intolerable. It's a matter of control, I suppose. Sitting around makes me feel powerless.

When we first came out of hiding, Brian questioned whether I'd be able to live a life of genteel inaction. "What are you going to do with yourself?" he asked. "I don't see you spending your time decorating the flat."

"What am I going to do? You mean, now that I don't have anyone to kill? Oh, I'm sure I can find something." I'd been joking (sort of), but his question hit a nerve. Brian's grimace told me I'd ventured over the line. Guilt washed over me like a wave. I reached for him.

"Honey, I'm sorry. Put it down to stress or shock or both. Trust me. I'm going to be occupied for at least a little while. I have to learn how to live without looking over my shoulder. That's going to take practice, you know."

He took me in his arms. "I understand, Suzie. You've been isolated longer than any of us. Your adjustment will be greater. But I know you. At some point in the not too distant future, you'll be bored silly. And then ..." He looked away, embarrassed.

"And then we'll find me something useful and thoroughly legitimate to do. I promise."

I meant what I said at the time. When we first came to London, all I wanted to do was walk down the street and smile at people, go out at night, perhaps make a friend or two. I wanted to live as Suzanne Foster, as a wife, a mother, and a human being. My involvement at Freedom to Hope has been both social and purposeful.

Yet I'd begun to feel restless even before Michael's attack. I don't need to work, but I want something to do.

On its face, looking for my son's shooter doesn't seem like a worthwhile project to take on. It's not as if the various law enforcement agencies hunting down Daniel Guzman have asked for my help. Nor do I begin to have their resources.

On the other hand, I'm not hampered by bureaucracy. I've no doubt Brian, Charlie, and Simon are following up on the possibility that Daniel Guzman is the son of my nemesis, if for no other reason than to establish motive. I can go further. I can find people who know if Victor Kemp is alive.

I'm sitting at the kitchen island on a wan morning in early February. The island is a marvel of design, with its cleverly concealed stovetop burners, small sink, and ample storage space. Even in a modern apartment like this one, I find it homey. This dwelling affords a number of places I can work or read. I happen to like to perch on the tall chairs and set my laptop and mug on the smooth granite surface. I also like having access to the refrigerator. I'm not a big eater, but I develop unusual cravings when I'm stressed. Today, I'm in hunger mode.

Michael walks into the kitchen wearing sweat pants, a hoodie over a T-shirt, and trainers. Nancy Okorie follows close behind in a green zip-up jacket over a crisp white shirt. Her dark slacks are pressed. They've just come from the small area on the second floor that serves as a gym. Nancy has been working with Michael. When we first learned she was credentialed as both a nurse and a therapist, we moved quickly to secure her services. She welcomed the extra work.

"I'll come every other day for two weeks, then three times a week for another month. After that, we'll see what he needs. If he agrees to keep to his exercise routine without overdoing it, he won't need me. He's young, strong, and motivated. He'll be fine."

Her confidence in her patient pleased me enormously.

In the five weeks he's been home, Michael has made remarkable progress. His color has returned, as has some of his weight. He can't go out, of course. At first, he was too weak. Now he simply accepts the gravity of his—of our—situation. He doesn't protest, although I'm sure he's feeling cooped up. Harry's the only friend who's been cleared to visit. He comes as often as he can. Kate practically lives here.

Nancy is another reason his mood is mostly upbeat, I think. She's strict with him but not impossible. They seem to get along very well. They're near each other in age and share a deep understanding of trauma.

Brian has gone to great lengths to explain to our son that healing will occur in intervals of six. The patient needs six days out of the hospital to get on a regular sleeping and eating schedule, six weeks of physical therapy, and six months before health is fully restored.

He's absolutely right, although Michael doesn't respond well to the idea he might need to wait half a year for anything. He's feeling a bit twitchy, as am I. In his case, it's a good sign, as long as he doesn't overdo his exercise routine.

My son opens the refrigerator and pulls out sliced beef, lettuce, tomato, mayonnaise, beet salad, and a couple of pieces of whole grain bread he pops in the toaster. Nancy shakes her head.

"Hungry as a horse. Hope you're well-stocked."

Michael puts a hand to his heart. "I'm recovering from a near-death experience, woman."

My heart pinches. Then Nancy gives him a light shove. I can't help but smile. It's like having two youngsters home from college. Or so I imagine; I missed that part of my son's life entirely.

"I need to get to work at the hospital. Michael, I'll see you in three days. Don't slack off. You'll be on your own after next week, you know." Nancy goes to the closet and pulls out her coat.

"Don't remind me. I don't know how I'll manage without you."

"You'll manage."

What a kind and understanding healer Nurse Nancy has been. I've gotten used to her calm presence, her efficient manner, even her low, lilting voice. It occurs to me I know almost nothing about her. I ventured an inquiry once and learned only that she is unmarried with a brother and mother who remain in her native country. When I asked if they might someday be joining her, she replied simply, "I hope so."

"I'm glad you two get along so well," I tell Michael as he wolfs down his sandwich.

"I like her, Mum. Her family's still back there, you know. The brother and the mother. The country has endured years of civil war. Their president is a brutal dictator, not that there's any other kind. The government killed her father. I'm not sure why. The brother is in prison. No reason given, no access to any legal representation. Even her mother, who isn't well, is under house arrest or something. Nancy hasn't seen them in years. She only got out because family members bribed all sorts of people so she'd have a better life. I want to figure out what we can do to help. She could use a hand, even though she's awfully resilient."

So are you, I want to tell him. But it's not the same thing and I know it. He has his family close by.

I marvel at how much Nancy has shared with Michael and how genuinely taken he is with her plight. The world is a terrible place, filled with cruelty and violence, some of which my son has known firsthand. Notwithstanding his experiences, he has retained a positive, even hopeful outlook.

"Your heart's in the right place, Michael. We can talk with your dad about all this when he gets home."

"Okay. What are you working on?" Michael changes the subject as quickly as does his father. I'm always startled by how easily they pivot away from one task or conversation or mood and embrace another.

I turn the laptop so he can see my work. "I'm making a list of people who were part of Victor Kemp's inner circle, at least as far as I can remember," I tell him.

Michael leans in to look at the screen, unconsciously crunching a bit too closely to my ear. I cover my smile.

"You weren't really part of that circle, were you, Mum? I mean, I guess you were one of his people in that you provided, ah, specialized services. But I always got the impression he kept you somewhat isolated and out of the loop."

"I think I can guess which few people he relied on. Kemp contracted out a lot, at least when it came to his illegal business. I imagine trust had something to do with his decision. He had one man beginning in the early nineties who seemed to pop up everywhere. A tough-looking sort. He didn't come into the office much, but I dealt with him at most of—" I falter briefly— "most of my assignments. I don't know that he's still with the organization."

I remember Arkady Dyukov. The man could have been Kemp's son; they were that easy with each other. They didn't really look alike. Dyukov also lacked his boss's urbane veneer. I imagine he felt far more comfortable on the docks or in rough bars than he did in a corporate setting. But Kemp and his henchman shared a similar savagery, albeit thinly disguised. I don't know if Dyukov liked to hurt people, but I guessed he was quite good at it.

Michael's voice brings me out of my reverie.

"Were any of Kemp's illicit types working in the legitimate company when you were there? I mean, they couldn't all have been lowlifes, right?"

I took a moment to consider. In addition to Dyukov and occasional contractors, Kemp had someone else in his employ who performed services similar to those I provided. I know this because my employer saw fit to tell me so without identifying the individual. Somewhere within the legitimate company, perhaps even in his New York headquarters, someone else led a double life.

The information only added to my paranoia and distrust. I couldn't get too close to anyone at work. I had no idea if this person knew about me or whether he (I assumed a man; I'm not sure why) was in the dark about his alternate. More than thirty years later, I've given up on ever learning his identity.

It was another way Victor Kemp could remind me how short my leash really was.

I wish I'd known The Other Assassin. Maybe we could have hung out together, swapped stories. Who knows, perhaps there's an online support group for current and former assassins. Maybe members discuss developing work/life balance, the perils of bringing one's job home, the problem of achieving intimacy, or how to protect your loved ones without their knowing they may be in danger.

In most cases, assassins, spies, undercover cops, or soldiers probably compartmentalize. It's what I learned to do, before I had my own family. When your husband and son spend decades in hiding, when one is a member of British Intelligence and the other has been shot by one of your enemies, there is no point to keeping secrets.

"Victor Kemp might have had a few people who straddled both worlds. It would make sense. An accountant or a financial type. His lawyer, of course." I drum my fingers on the countertop. "I definitely remember that man. Weber, Frederick Weber. German-American. He came to work maybe half a dozen years after I did and flew to the top of the management heap. Clever man, good-looking, nice dresser. Maybe a couple years younger than me. Always willing to help. Very circumspect, though. That would be appropriate for someone who worked in the legal department."

"What about the mother of Kemp's illegitimate children? Luisa Guzman, right? All those years together, did she ever work with him?"

"If she did, it would have been as an outside contractor. Luisa was a very successful real estate broker, I believe. Her business was headquartered in Rio de Janeiro. As far as I know, she had little to do with the New York office."

"She's easy enough to find, isn't she?"

"I wonder if she is."

Brian has already considered a possible connection between Luisa and Daniel Guzman. No one else in his organization deems her a viable lead, so he's had to tread carefully. The official line is she's the one-time mistress of an international criminal whose power peaked in the nineties. Even before his presumed death, Interpol had been losing interest. Investigations related to Victor Kemp have been closed since the explosion.

In mid-January, Brian sent two trusted associates down to Brazil to talk with Luisa Guzman. I don't know if Grayson Carter knew, but he said nothing. The visitors learned from office staff that their boss had taken an extended holiday. In South America, that might mean six weeks or more. Moreover, she was supposed to be unreachable.

I can't help but wonder if her absence is related to Daniel Guzman's death or disappearance, or how she might be connected to Francesco Guzman. He, too, seems to have dropped off the face of the earth. It all sounds like something Kemp would engineer.

Damn it, I can't get free of the man.

"Mum?"

I chide myself. Sharing information with my son is one thing. Sharing my fears or anxieties is, to my mind, strictly off-limits.

"Sorry. Your dad is looking into her whereabouts. I never met her, never even saw a picture of her. I'm thinking I'd like to track down someone I already worked with."

"So, cherchons l'avocat?" Michael asks.

Like father, like son, I think. "By all means," I tell him. "Let's find the lawyer."

Chapter Twenty-Eight

Two days after Nancy Okorie saw Michael Foster, she left St. Mary's Hospital at 2:00 p.m. and walked over to Hyde Park. She'd just finished a backbreaking set of double shifts. Working for the Foster family meant she had to make up hours she owed to the hospital. She finally got two days off. She would spend them traveling instead of relaxing. No matter. The journey meant everything to her. Two years in the making, but soon she would see him again.

She'd been able to save every penny she'd earned over the past five weeks. The money from the Fosters proved a godsend. Nancy had been extraordinarily lucky to land the additional employment. She pushed her luck, asking to be paid in cash. Suzanne Foster didn't blink. In a startling display of trust, the woman even offered to pay up front. Nancy accepted with gratitude.

Today Nancy would betray that trust. She saw no other choice. Suzanne and Brian Foster went to great lengths to protect their family. She must do the same for hers.

Every day after work, she went through the same ritual. Even before she took off her coat, she sat on the edge of her neatly made bed in the tiny room of the boarding house she called home and pulled out a small tin box from underneath the mattress. She counted the pound notes. There was enough to settle her younger brother and float him a small loan while he looked for work.

She looked forward to taking him around to see the sights of London. What fun that would be! For all his book knowledge, Jonathon had little experience of the real world. She had no doubt the last week or so of traveling had been an education for him. And he hadn't even arrived at one of the world's grandest cities.

At Hyde Park, she picked up the tube to Piccadilly Station, transferred to the Jubilee Line, and exited across the Thames at Southwark Station. The trip took sixteen minutes. In some ways, she wished it had taken an eternity.

The area around Guy Hospital hummed with activity. South London was in the midst of a second wave of gentrification. The industrial plants, tanneries, and knitting mills of the nineteenth century had long ago disappeared; so did the filthy slums that inspired authors like Charles Dickens. Modestly priced flats and semidetached homes had taken their place, built to house an influx of early twentieth century immigrants. Now those were coming down to accommodate a slew of upmarket residential and commercial properties.

London, like so many other cities in Europe, was becoming unaffordable for most of the people who worked there.

Nancy turned away from the cranes and the bulldozers and walked toward Leathermarket Park. A bit of the early morning dampness had burned off. The soft winter sun made the stroll quite enjoyable. To take her mind off her task, she took note of the intricate walkways that crisscrossed the park. In late spring and early summer, strollers came upon a raised circular rose garden in the center as well as an array of flowerbeds.

Even in February's dim sun, the place provided a welcome respite from the sound of nonstop development. Already, progress intruded in the shape of the recently completed skyscraper known as the Shard. Many architects and others praised its innovative design. Nancy didn't much care for the way its sharpened point thrust skyward.

She took a seat on a relatively secluded park bench, one with a back she could lean against. She turned up the collar of her good tweed coat against the damp air and pulled her brown leather bag close. She found it difficult not to fidget. She glanced at her watch, patted her tightly pinned braids, and peered to each side, noting the absence of park visitors.

At 2:30 p.m. a man in a belted brown trench coat and a hat pulled low over his brow materialized out of nowhere, or so it seemed to Nancy. He sat down next to her and stared straight ahead. Had she not felt so afraid, she might have laughed. He looked like a character in a third-rate spy novel or a comedic film. She expected to hear him speak with an overripe British accent.

To her surprise, his voice was flat, the dialect American. A barely discernable emphasis suggested that English might not be the speaker's mother tongue.

"Thanks for meeting me on such short notice, Nancy. I know you have places to be."

Nancy didn't appreciate the tone, which managed to be both brusque and snide.

"I do. Shall we get on with it, then? Here is the address you requested."

The man turned to face her. He might be described as attractive, she supposed, with a straight nose, light olive skin, dark hair (what she could see of it under his hat), and a strong chin. Clean-shaven with wire-rim glasses. Somewhere between thirty and forty years old. His eyes caught her attention. They were a shade of blue that bordered on purple.

He reached for the piece of paper she offered and scanned it. Then he withdrew a lighter from his pocket and set the scrap on fire.

"Bloody hell! What have you done?"

"I've seen it and I've committed it to memory, Nancy. That's all that matters." The man stamped at the fallen embers, brushed the ashes neatly into his gloved hand, and pocketed them.

She tried to calm her thundering heart. "I've given you what you asked for," she said, her voice stern. "If you don't mind, I'll take my brother's papers now."

"Papers?"

"Don't play coy with me, you. I've done your bidding. Your end of the bargain was to get my brother out of jail and into France. Which you've apparently done. I received word yesterday he's waiting in Calais. I just need the proper UK documentation you promised me, and I'll be on my way. In fact,"—she made a show of looking at her watch— "I really need to move along."

Her fear emboldened her, allowing her to stare at this violet-eyed man who held her brother's fate in his hands. He smiled. He had a beautiful, chilling smile.

"Right, right, the papers. You see, I'm afraid we've run into a bit of a stumbling block. That phone call you got? A ruse. Your brother died in prison six weeks ago." He shrugged, as if apologizing for a reservation mix-up or an overdue library book. "Probably for the best. Given how they tortured him, I'm surprised he made it that long. The news pretty much broke your mother's heart, as you can well imagine. She passed away yesterday. Condolences to the family. Although you don't seem to have one, do you? Dear me."

Nancy felt as if she might shatter. All of the turmoil she'd repressed, the concern, excitement, the anticipation and yes, the guilt she felt over betraying the Fosters rushed to the surface in a tsunami of grief and anger.

"You knew. You lying piece of trash. You knew this whole time."

"I did. Although there's no need for name-calling."

She wanted to kill him. She at least ached to smash his teeth and pummel the life out of him. She didn't dare.

She rose to leave. The good-looking, violet-eyed man grabbed her by both arms and pulled her down to him. She struggled, but he tightened his grip and shook her so hard she felt as if her entire body might break.

"No more fun and games, Nancy. You will be quiet and stay still. We don't want a scene. This is hard to take, I know. Frankly, I wouldn't want to live with the kind of pain you must be feeling right about now. Fortunately, I won't have to, and neither will you."

He pinned her with one arm. He produced a syringe and jabbed it into the back of her neck before dropping it back into his pocket. In an oddly intimate gesture, he brushed a strand of hair off her shocked face and leaned her back against the bench.

Unable to speak or move, she watched the man dust himself off and straighten his hat.

"The serum won't take but a minute. It shouldn't even hurt too much, although I've never asked the others."

Nancy stared.

"It'll look like a heart attack," the man continued. "You're young for it, but you've led a difficult life." He stood and patted her on the shoulder. She couldn't feel it. "Good day and godspeed, Nancy Okorie."

The violet-eyed man pivoted and walked away.

A flock of starlings took flight from the oak tree across the walkway. She watched them rise into the afternoon sky. She let out one last sigh. The breath that escaped her lifted into the air and disappeared into the shadow of the Shard.

~

"It's done."

"You completed the task?"

"Yes. As you requested." He lit a cigarette and leaned against the stone facade of a café, out of the eye of any probing security cameras. He'd picked up the burner phone from a storefront five minutes ago. Holding it to his ear, he surveyed the crowds of retail-hungry and brand-savvy shoppers clogging Oxford Street. Commerce, meet acquisition. The same in every city and every country in every part of the world.

"How is the weather?"

He shifted his position, hunched his shoulders. "You know how it is," he said to his employer. "Damp and thoroughly unpleasant."

"You should be used to it after the winters you endured. You won't have to put up with it much longer. I'm sending you someplace warmer."

"Thank God. Where's Gabriel, by the way? Still in Florida romancing the crone?" He chuckled at his own joke.

"I've just sent him to New York on an errand."

"Not one like mine, I hope."

"Don't be difficult. You each have your strengths. Gabriel is going to see a man who has information vital to us. He can be extraordinarily persuasive. Besides, he has some leverage. Don't worry. He won't be involved with anything dangerous. I foresee a positive outcome."

The man with the violet eyes stubbed out his cigarette and pocketed the remains.

"I hope you're right. We don't need to contend with any more bodies."

"On the contrary, Lucas. I think we do."

Chapter Twenty-Nine

Privacy advocates have long complained that Great Britain is becoming a surveillance state. Possibilities for misuse exist. So does regulatory legislation. Much of the potential for abuse centers on data collection and retention. Technology has other ways to pry. Closed circuit cameras (CCTV) seem to be everywhere. Some estimates put the ratio of cameras to people at about one to eleven.

Most of the cameras belong or are leased to individuals and private companies rather than the government. The devices generally supplement security measures and are used primarily to identify shoplifters or intruders. Britain's Data Protection Act of 1998 allows the public access to footage from these cameras. In practice, obtaining the data is often difficult, even for the police.

The Met had already checked the Green Park images from 8:00 p.m. to 11:00 p.m. on the night of December twenty-first, as well as the private camera at Lord and Lady Edgerton's townhouse. The video from the Edgerton home showed a young man with his face turned away from the camera. The recording from the park caught a blurred running figure disappearing into the crowd moving up and down Piccadilly.

The cameras along the street belonged primarily to the various establishments on the block. The police were entitled to request to view those videotapes, but they had to go through channels. That might have stalled the investigation. Given the presence of so many government figures at the party, the CTC made a case for national security concerns, which speeded up the process somewhat.

Every bit of digital information provided by more than a dozen bars had been reviewed. Attractive men with dark hair weren't unusual. The streets were filled with them: alone, in couples or groups, dressed up or dressed casually. Many of the single male figures were, typically enough, glued to their phones. Heads down, they proved hard to identify. Most of them wore black.

Six weeks after the shooting, with no new bodies, no new leads, and no imminent threats to members of parliament, the case began to recede in importance. Except for the Fosters and their friends.

~

Once Michael showed signs of recovering, Simon went back to Brussels. It was the beginning of a new year, and he had work to do. He kept track of the search for Daniel Guzman, noting that other more pressing cases now occupied the attention of the authorities. He had his own deadlines to meet. A two-week assignment took him away from the continent altogether. Early in February, he arrived back home just long enough to claim a week's vacation, pack a bag, and head to London.

He was pleased to see how well his cousin was doing. Between his fiancée and his nurse, Michael had the best of help. His aunt and uncle seemed in better spirits, if still wary. They planned to move out of the luxury apartment hideaway in another week. No one, not even a member of the House of Lords, could find any more funding for security.

Though Suzanne and Brian offered to put him up, Simon took a room at the Ritz. It was decidedly lux, although by no means the hippest spot in town. He liked that.

Unfortunately, the venerable hotel offered no midwinter discounts. As generous as his employers could be, they weren't about to spring for a five-star hotel. Simon decided to treat himself for the three days he'd be in the city. Given the kind of work he did, he figured he deserved a bit of luxury whenever and wherever he could get it.

After a pleasant dinner with the Foster clan, he walked back along Piccadilly and stopped into a handsome bar near the Green Park Station. He ordered twelve-year-old Royal Lochnagar, neat. However much the fine Scotch whiskey cost, the drink wouldn't set him back nearly as much as it would at the Ritz. This place also seemed less stuffy.

"Here ya go, mate. Enjoy." The bartender set the drink down.

Simon looked around. Henry's Bar was one of the dozen or so pubs whose security recordings had been thoroughly reviewed right after the shooting. More an eatery than a nightspot, the place opened early and closed by 11:00 p.m. On a Tuesday evening in February, it was modestly busy but not at all crowded. He had plenty of elbowroom, and the man behind the bar seemed to have plenty of time.

"Slow night?" Simon asked.

"S'about average, I reckon." The bartender, a curly-haired, pudgy man of about thirty with a handlebar mustache, looked around to see if his other customer needed him. Satisfied he had his bar under control, he leaned his plump arms on the counter. Chatty sort, Simon reckoned. He didn't mind.

"February is quieter, though, isn't it?"

"True enough. We get some of the hotel overflow along with the regulars, though not the party types we get during the holidays and weekends. You visiting?"

"Working. Staying at the Ritz"

The bartender whistled. "Nice. Your company pays for that?"

"I wouldn't be there otherwise."

They both laughed.

"Well, we appreciate your gracing our humble abode with your grand presence."

"To tell the truth, I prefer the atmosphere here. It's a little more casual. The Ritz may have relaxed its dress codes, but I always feel like I should be wearing a coat and tie."

"We're more easy-going. I do have a very nice jacket in the back I can lend it to you, should you be wanting to impress anyone back at your hotel. Can you believe I found it in the trash over the holidays? Idiot must have been smashed to toss it like that. I've kept it all this time, thinking he'd surely come back for it. Who wouldn't? Black cashmere, soft as a baby's arse, pardon my French. Custom made, by the looks of it. Would set me back a month's worth of wages. I admit I might a nicked it if I could have buttoned the bloody thing. Not even close." He patted his waistline and grinned.

Simon had been slipping into a state of mellowness, thanks in part to the fine Scotch. All at once he came fully alert.

"As a matter of fact, there is a young lady staying close by I hope to meet later. A real looker. Classy, too. You know what I mean? It's obvious she comes from money. My clothes don't speak her language. Do you think I might I borrow the coat, assuming it fits?"

"I think it just might. Anyway, I don't see why you can't keep the damn thing. The nob's had plenty of time to get it, and I'm not running a storage unit. Let's put it to good use." The bartender went into the back and returned with the jacket, neatly folded. "Try it on, just in case."

"You know something? I bet it'll do just fine. Keep your fingers crossed."

"Wait, you're going already? What about your drink?"

"Have at it," Simon said. He slapped some money, including a generous tip, on the bar. With the coat carefully draped across one arm, he just managed to keep from bolting for the door. His phone was already out; all he needed to do was hit speed dial.

As he reached the door, he heard the bartender call out, "Good luck tonight."

~

The camera that kept a watchful eye over Leathermarket Park passed a few times over the solitary figure on the park bench. It was human observation and intervention—a late afternoon stroller with a curious dog—that brought Metro to the scene. The body was taken to the morgue on Sunday evening. A preliminary autopsy suggested the woman died of heart failure. The absence of a handbag or wallet slowed down identification and raised a few questions. Still, the detective leaned toward a natural death followed by a crime of opportunity by a purse-snatcher.

A clerk assigned to identify unknown victims got around to the Leathermarket case on Monday. Using facial recognition software, he found a Nancy Okorie, single, born in Sudan and here on a residence card she'd received in 2010. A registered nurse employed by St. Mary's Hospital, Ms. Okorie was thirty years old. The clerk called over to the hospital. The director of human services was out for the day, so the clerk left a message requesting a call to the police concerning an employee.

Southwark's regular coroner came in midday Monday. He immediately set about reviewing the work of his weekend substitute, an older man he respected for his long years of service and mistrusted for his lack of attention to detail. The case of the body in the park interested him. The idea that an otherwise healthy young woman would die of a heart attack puzzled him.

Upon reexamining the body, he found the tiny puncture mark at the base of the neck. He went back over the other doctor's findings more carefully, then called in the detective waiting (and hoping) to close the case.

"Sorry to tell you this, but you've snagged a homicide. Potassium chloride injected right here at the hairline." He indicated the location. "Smart choice. An overdose causes severe heart arrhythmias. Then large amounts of potassium get released into the bloodstream because the heart has been damaged. Who knows what came from where? No reason to suspect anything."

"Except the victim is young, otherwise healthy, and has a tiny puncture wound in the back of her neck."

"Except that."

"How the hell did Evans miss that? Never mind. Good catch."

Monday night, the detective stayed late to review footage from the cameras at the park. He watched Okorie meet an unidentified male. The man wore a brimmed hat and kept his head down. He saw the note passed and then set on fire, the ashes conscientiously swept up and pocketed, the victim's attempt to leave, and the way in which the man sat her back down.

By slowing down the recording and watching frame by frame, he could see how the man's hand went to the back of the victim's neck. He could just about make out a syringe.

The man left; the woman appeared to expire moments later. What he couldn't see was the perpetrator's face.

Cold, thought the detective. But very professional.

On Tuesday, the director of Human Services at St. Mary's learned that not only had a nurse at the hospital died, she was the victim of a homicide. The news spread throughout the day among members of the staff. A nurse's assistant remembered Nancy Okorie confiding she'd snagged work with one of her former patients. The practice was irregular but not unheard-of. The assistant shared the information with her supervisor, who then went back to Human Services.

The HS director knew Nurse Okorie had tended the gunshot patient with the high-level security clearance. Foster, his name was. She made a few calls and left a message with someone who promised to reach the young man's father.

~

The camera in front of the exclusive highrise where the Fosters stayed was operated by a private security company and reviewed daily. On Tuesday morning, February 5, it recorded a delivery by a young man working for a service called Complete Couriers. The guards at the door also noted the delivery because they were trained to do so, and because not that many people stopped by. The young man checked out; he worked as a messenger for the company. The parcel, addressed to Mr. Michael Foster, had no return address, which raised an appropriate level of concern.

Following instructions, the agents placed it inside a steel container and sent it over to New Scotland Yard. Then they notified Brian Foster.

Technicians there carefully examined the package for traces of inhalable or ingestible poison such as anthrax or ricin. Inside the mailing box was a smaller wooden container that held chocolates. The box appeared to be handcrafted and exquisitely etched. The lid attached with a set of hinges.

The lab examined the case for tripwires or latches that indicate an explosive device. Personnel ran tests on each piece of candy, on the paper in which they were wrapped, and on the note included with the box.

Brian decided to let them keep all of it. He requested that pictures of each of the elements be sent to his phone. Those arrived Wednesday morning in the middle of a class he taught on linguistic theory. He was studying them in his office when his mobile phone rang. After the brief call, he grabbed his coat, flipped the sign on his door indicating there would be no office hours, and ran out.

Chapter Thirty

Confluence, connectivity, happenstance, or luck. One of those has brought us to a moment when all the pieces of the puzzle have fallen into place. Answers don't bring relief—far from it—but they help bring the events surrounding the shooting into clearer focus.

Brian surprises us by showing up at the apartment at lunchtime. Kate is at work. Michael and I are expecting Nancy, who is an hour late. We put it down to her unpredictable schedule at the hospital. Michael has texted twice. I don't want him to become agitated, so I engage him in strategizing the best way for me to approach Frederick Weber. The lawyer still keeps an office and a secretary at the Manhattan headquarters.

Being private citizens, we haven't been able to check flight manifests or phone records to see where Weber has been or whom he might have seen over the last six weeks or two years, if it came to that. We know quite a bit, though. Michael has the ingenious idea of pretending to be the son of Weber's cousin and calling the New York office to "chat up the secretary," as he put it. I leave the room for fear I might burst out laughing.

My son deploys his considerable charm, entertaining the woman with tales of "cousin Fritz's" exploits; in the process, he learns valuable information. For instance, Weber made several business trips to London between December 23 and January 11 of this year.

"The spring before this last one, he went back and forth so often we thought he might move there," she tells Michael. "That was right after Mr. Kemp died, though, so it makes a lot of sense. I'm not sure what he has going on these days. Maybe he's seeing someone?"

Seeing his old boss, I think, but I don't say anything. In addition to being apprehensive, I'm also proud of my son.

"Maybe you ought to have a little sit-down with him, Mum," he says. "Fly to New York and have a drink for old time's sake. It's not like you'd be tipping your hand. You and Dad and I were splashed all over the news for a bit along with Kate's poor parents and the Westcotts."

I flinch at the memory. While Michael's welfare and my family's safety have been uppermost in my mind, I've experienced more than a little discomfort with being the subject of any discussion. After the shooting, I refused all interviews. So did Brian, Kate, and Annie. Tommy released a statement through his office. I couldn't keep people like Betsy Harrigan from commenting. The media is ruthless when pursuing a story. For most people, the attention is irresistible.

"He might wonder why I've suddenly decided to renew our acquaintance."

Michael cocks his head. "He might. Or he might be sitting around waiting for the ax to fall. Either way, what have you got to lose?"

As insane as this idea seems, I consider it. I'm searching online for direct flights to New York, and Michael is leaving yet another message for Nancy, when Brian throws open the door. He's not normally given to drama. The look on his face tells me we're not dealing with normal. I'm not certain if we ever will again.

I turn from the laptop. Michael disconnects his call. We look at Brian, who gets right to it.

"There's no good way to say this. Nancy Okorie is dead. Murdered."

"What?" Michael jumps to his feet. "When? How? Why, for God's sake?"

Brian orders him to sit down. He fills us in as to what he knows, including what the police have seen on the video. It's clearly a homicide.

Michael is beside himself. "I don't understand. Is it political? Someone from her country's government? Who would want to hurt Nancy?"

"What was on the paper?" I ask.

Father and son turn to look at me.

"What was so important the mystery man burned it and pocketed the ashes?"

Brian nods. He knows where I'm going.

"It's impossible to tell. That is the key, though. There's something else I need to tell you. When I got the call about Nancy, I was looking at photos of a package that arrived here yesterday addressed to Michael, no return address."

"A package? To me? But hardly anyone knows our address. Except—"

"Let's not jump to any conclusions just yet. Unexpected packages delivered here get special treatment. This one is still at the Met's lab. It hasn't been tampered with, at least as far as the technicians can determine. It's a handmade wooden box filled with candy. The box is artful, if peculiar. So is the note."

"Let me see." I stretch out my hand for the phone and notice it's shaking. I take a deep breath and catch Brian's eye.

"Michael, can you handle this?"

Relieved to have something to do, Michael transfers the images to the laptop. We huddle around, staring at a box carved out of a deep-brown wood with a distinctive natural grain.

"This particular box is made from olive wood. It is said to be excellent for carving. My grandmother had a figurine of a saint made from the same material. The wood gives off a distinctive smell. A bit too informative for boxing candy unless you're gifting chocolate-covered olives."

No one laughs.

I lean in, studying the object. The box looks like something you'd buy in an upscale store aimed at tourists. The etching is quite ornate. It depicts a beach scene, complete with a large body of water on which rides a distant ship. A sleek-looking seal poses on an adjacent sandy beach. I'm getting ready to look at the image of the note when the buzzer sounds.

Brian picks up the receiver and has a few words with the security guard.

"Simon's on his way up."

My usually self-possessed nephew enters the apartment in a state of high excitement. I consider that two of the most measured people I know have now burst through the front door in the space of a half hour. The thought is anything but comforting.

"You'll want to sit for this," he says without preamble.

When instead we move towards him, he holds up his arms in mock horror.

"Whoa, easy now. Don't sit, then, but at least stop coming at me. I'm feeling rather intimidated."

"I guess we're a bit anxious," I say by way of apology. "It's been quite the morning for news."

"I did rather throw myself into your apartment. Let's begin again. Tell me what's been going on, and then I'll fill you in on my news."

Brian catches him up on events to date. Simon listens, grim-faced.

"I don't know how my information is connected to everything you've just told me, but it sheds new light on Daniel Guzman."

We listen, thunderstruck, as Simon recounts his serendipitous visit to Henry's Bar. He's pulled strings to rush DNA testing and then matched it against a hairbrush one of Brian's associates pilfered from Luisa Guzman's office in Rio. Sure enough, there's a familial match. Daniel Guzman is Luisa Guzman's son.

Brian waits for Simon to take a breath, then says, "I assume we still don't know whether he's Victor Kemp's son."

Simon clears his throat. "About that. Remember the second son Luisa had with Victor Kemp? His full name was João Daniel Guzman."

I can't stifle my gasp. In unison, the three men swing their heads in my direction. Maybe they're worried I'll fall into a faint. It does feel as if I'm starring in a melodrama. All we need are a couple of ominous chords—dun dun DUH.

But I'm not about to lose consciousness.

"I'm fine, gentlemen. And frankly unsurprised. This simply confirms what I've suspected all along. What I can't figure out is why Daniel decided to kill me now. Did he act out of impulse or on orders? Whose orders? And what has happened to him?"

I sound calm. Am I calm? I wonder.

Brian and Simon exchange a look. Michael sees it.

"What, guys? Is there more? Come on, let's have it."

Simon looks at the floor, then back at me.

"As of this morning, Interpol is unofficially reactivating the file on Victor Kemp."

"Why? Because they have conclusive proof Daniel is his son?"

"Yes, but also because they suspect Kemp may still be alive."

"What makes them think that?" I turn to my husband. "Brian, have you suspected all along that Victor Kemp didn't die in Wales?" I'm trying to keep my voice level. It isn't easy.

"Kemp's remains weren't found at the scene. The explosion caused a lot of damage, as it was intended to. By the time a backup team came in to do a more thorough sweep of the area, the tides had done their work as well. There wasn't anything further to process. The office declared him dead and closed the case."

I breathe slowly in, slowly out. I don't know how else to keep from exploding.

"And now?"

"Daniel's likely relationship to Kemp is enough to raise questions. Informally, for now. We can only hope it offers the possibility of further resources."

I don't say anything, mainly because I have too much to say. I'm furious Brian didn't take me into his confidence and share with me his concerns that Kemp was still alive. I realize he didn't want to consider the likelihood any more than I did. But I deserved to have my apprehension taken seriously. I needed an ally. I didn't need to drive myself mad over these past few months.

On the other hand, what could Brian have done? He's at the mercy of his superiors as well as his own angst about our family. He needed to believe in Kemp's demise as much as I did. Or did I expect him to join me in this latest round of hell I've put myself through? What about what he's gone through? What about Michael? What would I have done in his place?

I don't look at my husband, but I reach out a hand. He grabs it as if it were a life preserver.

"According to your information, Simon—and Brian's—we know that Daniel Guzman is the son of Luisa Guzman and Victor Kemp. We don't know about Francesco Guzman, who may be a relative or a doppelgänger. At the moment, none of them can be found. They may be dead or in hiding. What's happens next?"

Brian exhales; he's been holding his breath waiting for me to go off on him. I remind myself that my moodiness affects the ones I love.

He waves his nephew over.

"Come look at these photographs of the mystery package. Another piece of the puzzle."

Simon peers at the screen. "Pretty box. What is that carved outline?"

"It's a sea animal. There's a note that wishes Michael a speedy recovery, signed from his 'friends' at Monachus. Which, by the way, is a biological subclass of seals on the verge of extinction. I looked it up."

I manage to smile at my diligent husband

"I don't get it," my son says.

"It's a message," I say.

Brian nods. "I think it is as well. Which is why I've got a staffer running an associative word search. I'd like to know who these so-called friends are and how they've located us."

"They're obviously the sort of people who were willing to kill Nancy to get to me."

We stare at Michael.

"What? It's not a big leap to suppose she gave the mystery killer our address, is it? Maybe he promised her something having to do with her family. Instead, she paid for that information with her life. I just hope—I know this sounds odd—but I hope she felt she had no other choice."

"I'm sure she didn't, Michael." What else could I say?

Brian's mobile rings again. He holds up a finger and answers.

"Hallo, Erin, whatcha got?"

He listens, offering only snippets on his end — "okay," "uh-huh," "you don't say" —before asking his assistant to text him the information. He hangs up and clears his throat.

"Alright, then. Most of the references to monachus concern the animal itself. The monk seal is a reclusive sort. It tends to hide away. Its isolation makes it endangered. Erin, smart girl that she is, also checked for theater pieces, movies, songs, last names, and new businesses using that name. Under the last category, she found something interesting." Brian pauses.

"And? Don't stop now." Simon is still staring at the screen.

"In late December, papers were filed on behalf of a new business entity called Monachus. The company is in the shipping business, and the logo is a silhouette of a seal."

Silence. Then Michael, my reliable treasure, speaks up.

"It seems we're looking for the elusive owner of a mysterious company named after a reclusive seal. What do we do now?"

It's meant to break the tension, and it does. Simon risks a small smile. But there is no laughter or joy, not with Nancy Okorie murdered and the rest of us once again at risk.

I face my son, my expression serious.

"Michael, if there's anything you can do to help, I promise to let you know. What I most need right now is for you to get strong."

"Without Nancy."

"For Nancy."

Simon throws an arm around his cousin. "I'm a poor substitute, mate, but your mother is right: you need to keep working out. What say we get you down to the gym, yes? You do the exercises. I'll be the cheering section."

The two of them head for the door. I hear bits of conversation.

"Guess I'm not getting outside for a while longer."

"All in good time, Mike."

Alone in the apartment, Brian and I slide into each other's arms. Then I lean away to ask, "Who owns this new shipping company?"

"An Afrikaner named Johan Krüger."

"And where do we find this Mr. Krüger?"

Brian doesn't answer; he doesn't need to. I already know.

The same place we find Francesco Guzman and Victor Kemp.

Chapter Thirty-One

At 11:00 p.m. the following Tuesday, Frederick Weber looked out from his floor-to-ceiling windows. His fifth-floor apartment afforded him a view of the traffic crawling up Third Avenue. The Macallan Scotch he sipped steadied his nerves some, although he noticed his hand still trembled. Drinking on an empty stomach was never a good idea. On the other hand, the earlier events had left him without an appetite.

Weber turned at the sound of his phone. A text. "thx for helping. dinner lovely, if all 2 brief. G"

He threw the phone on the chair.

Two hours earlier, he'd met his blackmailer at an Upper East Side establishment the lawyer favored. Quiet, well-appointed, and discreet, it catered to a wealthy clientele. The chef didn't bother to pursue the trend of the moment. Nor was the menu a monument to his creative genius. That's not what his patrons wanted or expected. Instead, the food consisted of a few reliably well-prepared dishes. Steak, chicken, a simple fish dish, a salad or two, a couple of familiar appetizers, and a vegetable dish. A gluten-free entree had been added, Weber noticed. Even popular establishments had to make concessions.

The attorney arrived fifteen minutes early and took his usual table in the restaurant's far corner. He ordered a glass of Chardonnay in place of his usual Scotch. He needed to keep a clear head.

The location provided maximum privacy along with an excellent view of the room, including the maître d's station. Weber's father, a devoté of American Westerns, always warned his son not to sit with his back to the door. Wild Bill

Hickok forgot just one time, he told the boy, and ended up with a bullet in the back. Frederick Weber never pictured himself the victim of an ambush during a card game in a saloon. He nevertheless found the advice practical. It was always best to keep an eye out for dangers both known and unknown.

At precisely 9:00 p.m., a man entered the restaurant. Weber judged him to be in his fifties, with silver-flecked hair combed back from a wide forehead and dark eyes. His skin was tanned, his manner relaxed. An urbane sort. Not the lawyer's type but undeniably good-looking. The man spotted Weber. He handed his overcoat to the maître d' and strolled over.

"Good evening, Mr. Weber. May I join you?"

The blackmailer spoke in a smooth baritone with a trace of an accent. He wore a well-tailored gray jacket and open-necked shirt. A lady's man, Weber decided. He looked familiar, like someone Weber knew, although the attorney couldn't say why.

The man sat without waiting for a reply. "I hope I'm not late," he began.

"You know you're not." Weber wasn't usually so short with his dinner guests, but this was no ordinary acquaintance.

The waiter came over with a glass of Malbec for Weber's companion. When had he ordered it, Weber wondered? When he came in? Or had he called ahead? The man sniffed, sipped, and nodded to the hovering waiter. Weber recognized the tactic; he'd used it in negotiations. Take one's time. Attend to the details. Set the tone, set the pace, set the agenda. It was a way to take control and unsettle one's opponents.

This man behaved as if he had all the time in the world. Weber forced himself not to squirm. He unclenched his hands and sat back, determined to steer the ship. "Since you called this meeting," he began, "I suggest we—"

"I applaud you on your selection of dining establishments, Mr. Weber. The restaurant has received very positive reviews. Is this one of your regular spots? I must ask you to make a dinner recommendation. I understand the dishes are simple but superb. I confess I prize a good cut of beef above all else. Not that we have to order right away. I'm sure there are many topics of conversation we could explore."

"I trust you won't mistake this for a social occasion."

The man pretended surprise.

"I see no reason we can't have a meal together. How enjoyable it is will depend on you."

"On me? How pleasant do you expect me to be when you're blackmailing me?"

"My goodness, who said anything about blackmail? I'm simply here to barter with you. I have something to offer, as do you. I understand negotiation is one of your many areas of expertise, is that not so?"

"If what you're offering is a ten-year-old picture of me with a dead friend,"—Weber swallowed— "I'm not in the least interested. Frankly, I don't know who would be. I can't imagine how you even got hold of that."

"We've been through this, Mr. Weber—Frederick. May I call you Frederick? You may call me Gabriel, by the way. Please don't call me Gabe, and I won't insult you by calling you Fred."

He took another sip of wine. "Our text communication was a model of precision, don't you think? You know what I have. You will soon know what I want. As to where the picture came from, the urge so many have to chronicle their lives predates cellphones. My friends used to show up at parties with Polaroid cameras. Do you remember those? Then there were the disposable cameras, which one took to the drugstore to develop, yes? Who knows what your friends brought to the bar that night or why this particular image survived? It's not important. What is important is how a viewer might interpret what he sees. A conversation between two friends or two men who are more than friends?"

Weber began to object, but the man shook his head.

"Don't waste your time or mine with protests, Frederick. I'm not the least bit interested. You wanted to get down to business. I'd prefer to enjoy my dinner first, but I will do that in any event and regardless of your apparent need to move things along.

"So, cards on the table. Your friend is dead. The issue should be as well, except his father, your employer is very much alive, as you know. He also has very particular views about his family members both living and not living.

"Now, you and I may not care about such things. We are cosmopolitan men of the world, yes? The Russians are less sophisticated, for all their clever business dealings. They are also far less forgiving. What would Victor Kemp say, even after all this time, if he suspected you'd been sleeping with his son? What do you think he would do?"

Weber experienced the pain of a long-buried and unfulfilled desire, along with a sharp stab of fear. This man seemed to know Weber. He also seemed to know the man who paid Weber's salary.

"I never—you can't believe we ever—" Weber stopped and began again. "Paul was straight."

Gabriel looked at the lawyer with a trace of pity. "You are a foolish man. What difference does it make what I believe?

Or even what is true? Surely your professional dealings have taught you that truth doesn't matter nearly as much as the appearance of truth."

Gabriel took a generous mouthful of wine, swallowed, and sighed. "Family is so complicated, don't you think? You're fortunate to have largely avoided entanglements, eh? I have a wife I love too little, a sister I love perhaps too much, and a son I fear. All of them impact my life and control my destiny."

Weber stared. "Who do you work for?" he asked. "Surely not Kemp."

"You ask questions whose answers are unimportant in the scheme of things. What you want is for this image to disappear, I would guess. We can assume no one remembers it; therefore, no one will notice its absence. I can destroy it, as near as anyone can destroy digital images."

"How do I know you'll keep it out of certain hands?"

"I think you may have to trust me."

"And what do you want in return?"

"I simply want to know the current whereabouts of one person."

"Victor Kemp?"

"Johan Krüger."

Chapter Thirty-Two

Back in his upscale hotel room, Gabriel looked at his watch. 11:00 p.m. Dinner had been as he expected, if brief and a bit strained. He'd at least had a chance to enjoy his steak and the Malbec was credible. Poor Mr. Weber left his dinner untouched, although he had ordered and downed a second glass of wine. He may have wanted to leave; he didn't dare. Gabriel found his terrified ambivalence amusing.

When they'd finished, the waiter arrived, not with a check—which Gabriel had already paid—but with a courtesy nightcap. That small ritual had completely unnerved the attorney. Gabriel imagined he was at this very moment in his apartment trembling either with fear or relief. Most likely both.

Weber really was most fortunate, Gabriel mused. Yes, he had perhaps lost his great love. And he had parted with a valuable piece of information that would earn him the everlasting enmity of his employer. At least he would continue to live, especially if he got out from under Kemp's shadow.

Gabriel surveyed the room with pleasure. He could not deny he appreciated the benefits that went along with his assignment. The hotel wasn't one he could have afforded on his teacher's salary. Back when he and his wife were more compatible, they took advantage of her family money. It never made him completely comfortable, although he didn't begrudge the luxuries it afforded.

This little project involved someone else's money as well. He'd committed to do his part and had been provided with nearly unlimited resources. He would have undertaken the work for nothing. Since he wasn't expected to, he intended to relish his present circumstances.

His nonstop flight didn't leave until midmorning tomorrow. Might as well take advantage of the Jacuzzi in the other room.

~

At 11:00 p.m. on the same evening, Lisette stalked through her walk-in closet, pulling items off hangers and out of cubbyholes and drawers. She tossed everything on the bed. The weather in the south of France was more unpredictable than in Florida. She had plenty of options from which to select, clothes that would allow her to be both stylish and warm. Besides, choosing what to pack kept her mind off the significance of her latest and more far-reaching choice.

She'd taken risks as a younger woman. She took up with and cast aside her heroin-loving partner, the father of her only child. She never regretted that decision. Mo was a danger to them both. She did regret the several desperate years that followed. She'd lowered her standards almost to the ground. She sought companionship as a way to stave off loneliness and the perils of aging. Her daughter had suffered. She'd never apologized to Suzanne. She'd only recently admitted to herself she'd been a terrible parent.

After she'd tossed out her only child, Lisette had slowly extricated herself from her dependency on men. Yes, there were a couple of opportunistic marriages. Those served to move her out of San Francisco and eventually into her own life.

Now she was about to travel abroad with a man about whom she knew little. Was this a late life slide into neediness or simply a much-deserved adventure? Without question, Gabriel was both attractive and attentive. As befits a stereotype, he was the younger suitor to her older wealthy woman. This was not uncommon in Europe. Fortune hunters came in all shapes and sizes.

He surprised her with his offer of an all-expense-paid getaway to Nice. Lisette found it curious that an unemployed teacher and part-time cabana boy had the resources to spring for such a trip. She couldn't help but wonder if this was part of a long con; pay now and reap substantial rewards later. He should expect to be disappointed.

She told herself to stop spinning out various scenarios. Gabriel was a skilled but not overly demanding lover. He seemed to enjoy her company. The affair had thus far been sweet and satisfactory. Some men appreciated mature women. Maybe there was nothing more to it than that.

She didn't fool herself into thinking love was involved. She didn't require love. If this February fling turned out to be a late autumn escapade, she still intended to enjoy every minute of it.

~

Several time zones to the east, Victor Kemp aka Johan Krüger looked out over the village of Èze Sur Mer from the back of a well-appointed hillside villa. He could just make out the jutting contours of Saint-Jean-Cap-Ferrat. A full moon hung low in a starless sky. Dawn wouldn't arrive for two more hours.

He inhaled deeply and picked up a faint aroma of mimosa. Spring came early to the Côte D'Azur. Kemp was used to being up long before the sun. He never slept well. Even in such a lovely spot, he couldn't entirely relax.

Just ten days earlier, he'd quit London for good and moved to this exclusive neighborhood. Arkady Dyukov was ordered to remain behind, though it clearly displeased the enforcer. Kemp arranged to install his personal physician and family close at hand, promising them a two-month vacation in return for which the doctor would remain on call.

His health needs covered, he contracted a local housekeeper/cook and a clever computer technician and offered them more money than they had ever dreamed possible. He also hired three men to provide security.

While Krüger listed a postbox in nearby Monaco, Kemp refused to live there. He found the place to be utterly sterile, drained of history and personality, and blatantly in service to conspicuous consumption. He rented in France because he could afford to, and because he liked the old buildings and the absence of anonymous highrises. There were plenty of occasions to spend lavishly. At least the galleries, restaurants, shops, and boutique hotels more or less blended in with the ancient walls.

Kemp's newest business venture didn't need a tax shelter. On paper the fledgling company operated in the red until investors could be satisfied. In reality his business had moved chiefly into gray and black markets. He didn't have time to work carefully or adopt the pretense of legitimacy. His ships carried eighty to ninety percent contraband. The stakes were higher. Consequently, the fleet was smaller, faster, and even further under the radar. The people he employed were merciless, willing to take on anyone. This wasn't a problem either at sea or at the docks, where bribes and threats still figured prominently in his plans.

THE FORMER ASSASSIN

He thought about the former assassin on the private flight from Gatwick. The flight attendant was a slender woman with light brown hair who might have been anywhere from twenty-five to forty-five. Attractive yet ordinary, with the kind of malleable face beloved of photographers and film directors.

Susan Smith had such a face. She could make herself unmemorable or beautiful. She could transform into someone else with very little effort. Kemp had made note of that very quality when he met her. He had assumed her personality might prove as pliable as her physique. He had been utterly mistaken, and it had cost him dearly.

They weren't done with each other yet. Her son lived, to be sure. Neither of his did. This alone suggested scores still to be settled and odds to be evened. A part of him engaged in working out exactly how that might happen. The rest focused on other tasks he had yet to complete.

Nearing seventy-two and with a permanent injury that constantly invited infection, Kemp nevertheless felt he had years left. He came from hardy stock. His mother had lived to be 104 years old. His father might have equaled or surpassed that achievement had he not run afoul of local gangsters. The shipping business was nothing more than a way back in. Kemp wanted to sit on top of the world, control its events, and feed its insatiable appetite—and his.

He couldn't help but feel the tug of mortality and regretted the absence of a family. Without blood heirs, he wasn't certain to whom he might bequeath his reconstituted empire. He respected Arkady Dyukov and admired the way in which he'd made something of himself. He certainly appreciated the man's singular devotion over the years. He simply felt the enforcer lacked the polish to head an international enterprise and move among the world's power brokers. As for Weber, he'd never considered the lawyer, a glib man with a big brain and, Kemp concluded, small balls.

He did know someone he thought worthy of the crown, someone whose amoral hunger matched his own. Luisa had a nephew, a handsome refined sort with impeccable credentials, including an MBA from Wharton. He lived in Chicago. Like his aunt, he worked in real estate, albeit in the commercial side. While Luisa never explicitly asked Kemp to leave her family out of his dealings, she indicated her brother was well situated and needed nothing from Kemp. The implication was that she preferred to keep it that way.

Kemp had no interest in the brother. The man was vain and weak. His son was another matter. Luisa might not realize her nephew already worked on behalf of some shady operators, including people with whom Kemp did business. Nor did she know those people had described to Kemp a cold-blooded man willing to say or do anything in service to a particular goal. He might or might not be a psychopath, but he was reportedly indifferent to the emotional consequences of any act, large or small.

Kemp decided to reach out to the nephew once he settled in France. He wasn't sure where the younger man's loyalties lay, but he believed he could offer a reasonable explanation for his actions. Kemp admitted he anticipated reconciling with Luisa at some future point. A nephew wasn't a son—no one could replace hers—but she might appreciate that he viewed her family as his. Such things were important, especially to South Americans. He would win her back and have her by his side many years in the future, before he decided how and when it was time to go.

~

The man with the violet eyes rose well before the sun. He pushed open the heavy curtains and opened the windows. The Hôtel Dieu afforded a decent view of Marseille's Vieux Port. This late at night, or rather early in the morning, the harbor was quiet, the pleasure crafts and sailboats pushed against one another by the relentless mistral. Marseille took the brunt of the icy wind that flowed from the Rhône Valley to the sea, especially in February. Locals claimed it caused depression and irritability. It was all nonsense, of course. People survived the dreary bitter winters back in the States and the oppressive damp of London.

As far as he was concerned, Marseille was still low-rent, lacking much in the way of world-class culture. Many neighborhoods reminded him of cities like Detroit or even Mumbai: run-down, over-crowded, filled with despair. On the other hand, things were looking up with the promise of a renovated waterfront and a new tram. The appearance of new eating spots forced the old ones to up their game. He'd paid dearly for his dinner at Le Ventre de l'Architecte, but the established old restaurant had offered impeccable service and a good enough meal. Not that the cost mattered; he wasn't paying.

He looked forward to heading up to Geneva for some real relaxation mixed with a bit of scouting. All before returning to the port city to complete another bit of business for his demanding boss. Then it was off to the Côte d'Azur for phase three.

He wondered how many bodies it would cost.

Chapter Thirty-Three

Arkady Dyukov stayed back in London like the good soldier he was. For the first time in his years with Victor Kemp, he chafed at his orders. From a purely practical standpoint, it made sense. He needed to clean up a few matters. He and Kemp stayed in touch, conducting business over a secure video feed.

He found himself disquieted. As Kemp's second, shouldn't he have seen to the move and hired the staff? No, Dyukov didn't need to idle away his time in some remote hilltop villa. He simply thought he ought to be stuck to the old man like glue, especially with this new shipping company. The model remained the same, but the execution required an enforcer who spoke with the authority given to him by his employer. In order to do that, Dyukov needed to know what Kemp was thinking. He couldn't tell from 1400 kilometers away.

He'd made two trips to Marseilles over the past two weeks. They expected to run more business through the Marseille-Fos port, one of Europe's largest in terms of tonnage. It divided between two sites, the struggling downtown location and a far larger and more active hub with aspirations of becoming the world's leading container entry point. Seventy-two percent of its cargo was crude oil. Despite assured employment in a high-growth market, workers at every level were always open to making more money.

A careful man, Dyukov nevertheless had a skewed perception of himself. He correctly valued his importance yet underestimated his visibility. He was indeed critical to the overall operation. He held more in his head about the business than anyone alive, including his employer. The deeper into the underworld the activities went, the more comfortably and skillfully he maneuvered.

At the same time, he didn't believe anyone really noticed him or tracked his movements. If he headed to a meeting with Kemp, he naturally took innumerable precautions. When he was out and about, he didn't always look over his shoulder. He figured he could take care of himself.

He never expected anyone to follow him to France.

Fourteen days after his boss left London, Dyukov landed in Marseille. He stayed in a cheap hotel a kilometer from the port. It suited him fine. He didn't plan to walk more than he had to. The gritty port area north of the city remained plagued by crime. Grinding poverty and the lure of drug money trapped residents in an endless cycle of violence. In this part of town, the risk of dying before the age of sixty-five was thirty percent above the national average. Dyukov had seen it all before.

After a surprisingly decent night's sleep, the enforcer cadged a cup of bitter coffee from the restaurant downstairs and walked over to Marseille-Fos. In contrast with the deserted streets, the docks were bustling, the workers an ethnic stew of sub-Saharan and Middle Eastern migrants. Not too many white faces appeared, but Dyukov figured the tattoos that covered his body offered a degree of protection, not to mention credibility. Indeed, several people gave him a wide berth.

He found his contact by Quai de la Pinède. Nassir Kateb was a sturdily built Algerian Dyukov had hired through recommendations. A one-time gang member, he was now married with a growing family. Though Kateb eschewed violence in favor of management, he welcomed money. He'd already moved from freight handler to supervisor. With a fourth child on the way, he didn't mind facilitating shipments of any kind where a cash stipend was involved.

"We have a problem. Two of your containers are missing." Kateb spoke English.

Dyukov couldn't believe it. In the nearly two years since they'd entered the business, no product had ever been mislaid, unless you counted the girl owned by the human trafficker, the one who jumped ship. Kemp prided himself on his near-perfect record. One container might go missing, but two?

"Are you sure?" he asked his contractor.

"Take a look." Kateb handed him a manifest. The Monachus ship looked to be carrying machine parts bound for Algiers. The real cargo involved weapons that would find their way to central Africa. A simple shipment, a well-traveled route, a well-documented lack of interest as to what went into and out of that part of the world, a reliable client. What happened?

"Show me the other cargo," Dyukov demanded.

"We need to drive over. Three minutes."

They climbed into Kateb's Toyota and drove the short distance to a small quay with a single warehouse. Dyukov noted the sleek new vessel with the outline of a seal docked adjacent. He nodded his approval. Kemp/Krüger still had the best-looking boats around.

The warehouse was dark and empty, save for for a pile of bags in one corner next to a small metal barrel and a single large cargo container in the center.

"What am I looking at?"

"Me." A figure stepped out of behind the box, a clean-shaven man with dark hair and a belted trench coat that might be worn by a character from the nineteen forties. As he stepped closer, the Russian noted the other man's peculiar eyes. More purple than blue, they glittered behind wire-rimmed glasses. The gun he held pointed straight at Dyukov.

"Nassir, what's going on?" Dyukov demanded.

"I'm sorry, Arkady. You seem like an honorable man, as much as any of us can be. You made me an excellent offer. This gentleman simply made a better one."

"Thank you, Mr. Kateb." The stranger spoke with an American dialect. "You've received your payment. You might wish to leave now. No need for you to witness further unpleasantness."

Nassir Kateb didn't wait to be told twice. He exited quickly without looking back.

Dyukov hadn't taken his eyes off the man with the gun. He couldn't see any way to disarm him, but he continued to calculate the odds. "May I know what this is about?" he asked.

The man chuckled. "What's it about? Let's see. Anger, injustice, revenge, love, and hate, to begin with. Or perhaps something else. I see it as a smart business move, long overdue. Then again, I'm simply taking orders. For now."

"Who is it you work for?"

"Let me ask you a question, Arkady Dyukov. How do you make someone disappear? I would guess in the course of your illustrious career you've had occasion to deal with that problem more than once. Given advances in forensic science, wiping out all evidence is challenging, isn't it? I'm no scientist, but I would opt for chemicals."

The man was a talker, Dyukov thought. That might turn into an opportunity.

"Walk over here. Now." The gunman gestured with his gun to a small freestanding set of stairs that led up to the open container. "Climb, please. It's easier if you go in over the top."

Dyukov mounted the stairs until he was level with the lip of the container. He glanced down. If he acted quickly, if the man kept talking, he could jump him. He risked a fatal gunshot, but it was better than standing here waiting to see what this crazy person had in mind.

Before he'd moved so much as a muscle, the man fired, hitting him in the ankle. Dyukov yowled and tumbled into the container. He lay there for a moment or two, trying to get his bearings and will away the pain. The man appeared above him.

"Hello again. Sorry about the fall. I figured it was the best way of getting you inside. By the way, I neglected to introduce myself. I'm Lucas."

He patted the inside of the container. "We've customized your new home. Look over in the lower corner behind you. You can turn around, can't you? It's just an ankle. Unless you hurt something else."

Dyukov struggled to prop himself on one arm and looked over his left shoulder. He saw an opening, perhaps eighteen centimeters round, into which some sort of tubing had been fitted. He wondered where it led. Then he remembered the metal barrel.

"Sodium hydroxide, also known as lye," Lucas said. "A high-volume industrial chemical, easily manufactured. Restricted, naturally, but readily available if you know where to look. Quite popular with the drug cartels, I understand. And Russian enforcers."

Lucas climbed back down the stairs and walked a few steps. Dyukov heard the man grunt, as if engaged in a difficult physical task. Something creaked, perhaps a door or a lid. Half a minute later, the man's face reappeared above the container, shiny and slightly flushed. Dyukov noticed an ominous gurgling sound.

"Had to use some muscle to turn the valve. The directions suggest I add a mixture of lye and water to a sealed chamber and then apply heat. I think hot water should do the trick, don't you?" Lucas laughed. "I'm kidding. I don't have any directions, just some pointers from a man whose services you've probably used.

"So. When everything cools down, we'll dump the bags of fertilizer on top. What the Americans might call a shit sandwich. Finally, we'll send the concoction out on one of Johan Krüger's ships. Perfect, yes? I'd like to stay and watch, but I don't want to risk getting hit by the backsplash. In fact, I should run. Flood's coming."

The gurgling became a roar as the lye-and-water mixture pushed through the tube and into the container. Dyukov had always known he might die violently. He had never envisioned such a hideous, ignoble death. He could barely think. "Wait, who is doing this?" he yelled.

"The answer may surprise you, Arkady." Lucas called out a name as he scrambled back down the stairs and ran for the door. No sense risking his life. He locked the warehouse behind him. Others would come to take care of the follow-through. His part was over.

As for Arkady, he didn't hear the man's reply over his own tortured screams.

~

After leaving Marseille and the mess that used to be Arkady Dyukov, Lucas made his way over to the lovely seaside town of Cassis. He enjoyed a meal of mussels and fresh bread, along with a decent local rosé. Then he went back to his enchanting hotel to relax on the balcony that overlooked the harbor and the cliffs beyond. In one hand he held a cigar, in the other a cell phone.

"I'm glad we've ended up here," he said to his caller. "I like this part of France. It's really quite charming. Almost makes up for my time in London."

"I'm delighted you can enjoy it, at least for tonight. You deserve some down time. Today must have been harrowing, not that I want you to share any details."

"None will be provided. Where to now? Are we all gathering in Nice?"

"We are."

"I assume that includes the former assassin?"

"Oh, yes. By this time, she's received her invitation."

Chapter Thirty-Four

After thoroughly examining the chocolates sent to Michael, the capable forensic technicians have given us the box, minus the candy. I'm at my favorite spot in the kitchen, turning it over in my hands. Michael is showering after his workout.

Our family has been granted a reprieve of sorts. Because of the latest threat, we're staying put until the end of February. Brian seems to think we'll get this all resolved one way or another by then. I can't see how.

Nor can we stay under lock and key. We've had enough of that to last a lifetime. My son has warned me that if he's not allowed outside in the near future, he will wreak all sorts of havoc. I believe him. We're all going stir-crazy.

Brian is at the office. Charlie is traveling, though I'm not sure where. Simon is back in Brussels. He's lobbied to be included as part of the newly reopened investigation into Kemp's whereabouts. No doubt he's off doing whatever secret things he does to get information. I'm the only one who lacks standing. I can't help; I can only brood.

My husband has bought me a white board and an easel.

"Sketch it all out, Suzie. You're trained at problem-solving. So is Michael. Maybe together you'll see connections we don't."

The board lays unwrapped next to the folded stand. Brian means well, but I'm not just an engineer. I'm also an aggrieved wife and mother. I need to talk and to be heard. Michael has volunteered to be my sounding board.

The package is from a shipping company named Monachus. The person answering the phone at the Melbourne office didn't recall sending it. She also claimed never to have met the boss. Charlie might well have gone to Australia posing as a potential client to see if he can shake loose more information. The thought brings me some comfort, but not enough.

Someone named Johan Krüger has bought the assets and debt of a shipping company formerly owned by Francesco Guzman. Who in turn seems to have disappeared following an incident involving a dead girl and human cargo on a ship that traveled along routes unique to his company. Since no one can find the vessel, the cargo, or Guzman, it's a dead-end.

Daniel Guzman, also missing and presumed dead, claimed to be the son of a shipping tycoon. We now know he's Victor Kemp's son. If Francesco doesn't exist, was he Daniel's invention or Kemp's? More likely the latter. Krüger is very possibly another doppelganger. It's too convenient that no one can find any pictures of either of those men.

My mind reluctantly considers the probability that Victor Kemp is behind everything that has happened, even the ill-conceived shootout. Did he survive the boat explosion with physical or intellectual injuries? The genius of using his underworld network to supply a specific and much-needed service points away from a mental defect. No one had the depth of contacts he did, not his mistress and probably not his second son. Kemp is the type who would try to reclaim whatever power he could, albeit secretly.

I run my finger lightly over the smooth olivewood box and across the raised logo. It's an exquisite piece, carved from a tree native to Southern Europe, Africa, and the Middle East. The Mediterranean monk seal, our Monachus, is on the critically endangered list and is rarely seen. Krüger has a residence in Monaco. If it's a message from Kemp, it seems extraordinarily heavy-handed. He might as well send a map with arrows pointing to his current hideout. Then again, the man was always fond of taunting his victims.

So: Kemp reinvents himself as Francesco Guzman and decides, perhaps with Luisa's prodding, to bring his second son Daniel into the new venture. The son then pushes the father to carry a different kind of cargo, one that Kemp has always avoided. Something goes terribly wrong, so wrong that Daniel can see no way to make his way back into his father's favor except to—

I nearly spill my coffee. It makes sense, given what I've sensed about Kemp's twisted family dynamics. I need to run this all by Brian. As I reach for the phone, it pings. Only four people text me: Michael, Kate, Brian, and Simon. I've invited Annie as well, but she is resolutely old-fashioned about using phones only for calls. I put my hand on the device and look around. My son is dressing. My husband is at work. The sun throws a golden patch on the rug. All we need is a cat to complete the illusion of domestic tranquility.

The number is blocked, the message brief.

"I did not kill D. I know who did. We must meet. Time/place 2 follow. VK"

I'm suffocating. The heaviness that pins me to my chair reminds me of my first encounter with Annie. My body burns hot and cold, as if I've come into contact with dried ice. You're not having a heart attack, my rational mind consoles, just another panic attack. The thought brings my breath back.

I drop the phone, which I've been gripping tightly enough to break, just as it pings again with a location and a time three days from now. For a long minute, I toy with the idea of leaving my son a note, leaving my husband a message, leaving London altogether to hunt down and destroy the demon who won't die. Never mind several of the world's most formidable agencies are once again interested in Victor Kemp. This is my fight, and he is my incubus.

You're not alone, Brian says in my head. I forgive him for reminding me so often. After all, I've made my own decisions without any guidance or support for much of my life. Only I'm not a fifteen-year-old on the street or a twenty-two-year-old determined to avenge her roommate. I'm an adult with responsibilities. My decisions affect other people. If I've learned anything over the course of my life, it had better be this.

I pick up the phone, text a quick answer, and call Brian.

~

We hold a meeting in the apartment that evening. Five of us are in attendance: Brian, me, Michael, Simon, and even Charlie. When I ask him where he's been, he raises an eyebrow at me but doesn't share details.

Kate enters the flat, takes one look at the assembled group, and turns back to the door with Michael trailing her.

"Katie, honey, you can stay."

"I think I'm better off going out for the evening. I'll text my cousin Amy. We'll grab a bite. Probably stay out until late. Not to worry. Dad's likely got me under surveillance."

She gives her fiancé a quick kiss on the cheek, waves at our group, and exits.

The rest of us are pretending to snack on the light spread I put out. We're talking. Actually, we're quarreling. How could we not be? We're five headstrong adults arguing about the best way to take down a long-sought-after criminal impresario who has negatively impacted all our lives to a greater or lesser degree. Two in the group have ties to a government entity to which they're expected—no, obligated—to report. One works for an organization that might well insert its own set of protocols for any imposed by New Scotland Yard, Interpol, or MI6. One is a young man whose knowledge of the workings of an operation I've proposed is limited. I'd like to keep it that way, but I can't ask him to leave.

And one is a former contract killer employed and then hunted by the man we're discussing.

"I don't care for myself, Charlie," Brian is saying. "I'm close enough to retirement. But you've already run what I'll call 'operation Foster' for years, sometimes with SIS backing and sometimes not. No reason for you to risk your career any further. I'm surprised they haven't already tossed you out on your can."

"They can't, man. I know where all the bodies are buried." Charlie laughs and claps a hand on Brian's shoulder. "I'm a field agent. I've also got a reputation as a loose cannon to preserve. Let me worry about what we share with our superiors and when, okay?"

Simon raises his hand. "I can handle my employers in Brussels. I just have to work it out so they somehow benefit. It's the price of doing business in the shadows."

"Don't suppose I've got a bloody chance in hell of going along." My son has joined our discussion.

"Not to the front lines, cousin, but there's a fair amount of recon involved. I imagine we can keep you busy."

Michael brightens.

"We'll need weapons." Brian has addressed this remark to Simon and Charlie. The Scotsman clears his throat.

"I don't know about the 'we' part, Brian, old boy. You're an analyst. You haven't fired a weapon in I don't know how long. Don't recall seeing you practicing in Wales, only Michael and Suzanne."

"I practiced plenty, Charlie. And let's not forget, I trained with the best. It's not as if I've lost my edge, what with twenty-five years on the run and ten before that in the thick of things."

"Hang on, boyo, I didn't mean—"

"Shut up, all of you." I manage to silence them from my cross-legged position on the rug. I fold my hands in front of my chest and go still. Simon looks puzzled. He's about to make a comment, but Brian shoots him a warning glance. Michael looks serious. Charlie studies his feet. I take a slow inhale and an even longer exhale, fifteen seconds at least. Then I focus on the men around me.

"I'll say this just once, gentlemen. Victor Kemp has summoned me. Only me. Never mind his other crimes over the years. This is personal. As such, it neither is nor needs to be officially sanctioned as far as I'm concerned. I contacted you because I love you, because I trust you to sort things out and back me up, and because I'm neither reckless nor foolish. Be that as it may, I'm going to France, with or without you. Preferably with at least some of you.

I take another breath and continue. "I imagine lines will be crossed once we arrive. If you can cross them, excellent. If you can't, I suspect I still can, even seven years out of the business. Especially when my family is at risk. And let's not forget; I'm not at all out of practice. Am I making myself clear?"

My voice is low and measured and perhaps all the more menacing because of it. I'm determined. I'm also human, and the look on my husband's face pierces my heart.

"Brian, please, you know I have to do this. I have to face down this man. For my sake. For all of our sakes."

"I know." His voice is tight.

"For this to work, I ought to have Charlie and Simon with me. I'd prefer you stayed back in London with Michael. We're going to need to utilize the services of your agency without anyone knowing we're doing so. That requires a man on the inside."

The silence is absolute, save for the muted sound of street traffic through the windows. Then Charlie says, "We'll keep her safe, Brian. I swear on my life."

Brian looks at each of us in turn. He waves a hand, as if shielding himself from further inquiry. "It's fine," he says.

Late into the night, we formulate a plan. Simon has the means to secure military-grade weapons on the Continent. I request a rifle and a handgun and a few other items. I don't know what I might need for a showdown with Victor, but I intend to be prepared. Simon and Charlie will leave early in the morning. Simon will meet me in two days in Geneva. He and I will drive to connect with Charlie in the small village outside Nice where Kemp is apparently living and waiting for me.

Meanwhile, Brian and Michael will stay behind. I ask Brian to monitor developments in the hunt for Nancy's killer. I'm hoping for any leads that will point to Victor or his man Dyukov.

We manage to go about our business for the next day and a half. Brian works from home. Kate does as well. She's unusually subdued. Who can blame her, poor girl? What a family she's marrying into.

I have one evening in the circle of my husband's arms. The afternoon of day two, I grab a cab for Heathrow and the flight to Geneva. Simon picks me up at the airport in a brand-new Audi. We may be heading into the unknown, but we're doing it in comfort and style. With a trunk full of guns.

The lobby of the Mövenpick near the airport is crowded with happy tourists itching to try their luck at the hotel casino. Alone in my room, I telephone my family, keeping it brief. Afterward, I have an urge to call Lisette. Her voicemail picks up.

"Hi, darlings. It's February. I'm somewhere exotic. Don't you wish you were? Leave a message."

"It's Suzanne, Mom. Just checking in." I have no idea what else to say, so I disconnect. At least someone is having fun, I think. I send off a hasty text to my son. The next call is to my traveling companion. The hotel voicemail picks up.

"Do you mind if I take a pass on dining out, Simon?" I say into the phone. "I'm exhausted. I'll use room service. See you tomorrow, bright and early."

I hang up, intending to order something to eat. Instead, I lay back on comfortable European down pillows and fall into a dreamless sleep.

Chapter Thirty-Five

Èze is a medieval city perched on a hillside above the Mediterranean Sea. Built around a twelfth-century castle, it remains remarkably well preserved, although marred by rampant commercialism. Tourists throng its narrow streets, which are crammed with shops, galleries, restaurants, and one or two hotels vying for attention with the spectacular views. I visited here once before with an international group that met in nearby Monaco.

Just south and west, Èze Sur Mer caters to the rich and reclusive. Five-and-a-half hours after our dawn departure, we're sitting with Charlie at a beachside cafe near the town's train station. It's a beautiful day: cloudless sky, soft breeze, dazzling seascape. I'm surprised I can notice such things.

The address I have is for a residence on the upper end of a treacherous switchback on a street of villas. Charlie has confirmed via the local realtor that the house has been rented to an old man whose name no one can remember. A nosy neighbor confirms the man pays his staff handsomely and has also retained three armed guards. No one thinks twice about it. Along the Côte d'Azur, many of the wealthy take such precautions. Although no one has seen the man, rumor has it he is either very ill or horribly disfigured.

Simon drops me off two blocks away just before noon. The villa is well set back from the narrow street behind a low wall covered with flowering vines. It's also partially hidden by an eclectic mix of palm, pine, and eucalyptus trees. I walk up the path as if I'm expected. I've dressed in dark green slacks, a beige sweater, oversized sunglasses, and a scarf worn over my head. Very Jackie-O. I don't carry a handbag. Two men gently examine me for weapons and ask

279

me in French if I'm alone. I stifle the urge to tell them the cavalry is right behind me. All the while, I'm trying to spot the third guard.

I hear the voice before I see its owner.

"Welcome to the South of France. What a pleasant surprise."

The guards step aside. I follow the sound into a small sitting room, dark but cozy. To my right, the house opens to a light-filled dining room and then to a canopied porch with comfortable chairs. Beyond is a swimming pool and beyond that, a glorious vista. Typical people would find much to celebrate in that view, but we're not typical and neither is this visit.

Victor Kemp steps out of the shadows. His appearance shocks me. He's much smaller than I remember, not just thinner but somehow diminished. He wears loose-fitting navy slacks. His beige sweater seems two sizes too big for him. He's stooped, almost frail. The ghastly injury to his face is both repellant and captivating, like a science experiment gone wrong. He's missing every finger but one on his right hand. My revulsion is replaced by something more devastating: pity. I almost feel sorry for this wreck of a man.

"Not so pretty, is it? Although I've grown rather used to these changes. I've even learned to use my left hand. Eating is still difficult, though. Of course, I have you and your family and friends to thank for this, along with the loss of everything else I cared about." His smile is awful.

I shake my head. "No, Victor. You don't get to play the victim with me. Your condition is a result of your obsession. You never cared about anything except control. You didn't have to try to kill my family. You didn't have to try to find us when you discovered they hadn't died."

"But I did, and you know why. Control isn't something I worship. It's something my business model requires. Control and obedience. And vigilance. You knew that coming in."

"I never had a say in the matter."

"We all have choices, Susan. No, it's Suzanne. You chose not to thoroughly consider yours. Come, though, let's not immediately delve into such unpleasantness. Where are my manners? Would you like something to eat? Perhaps some lunch? I don't eat it, but I'm sure we can come up with something, although the housekeeper is away at the moment."

How like him to take charge by changing the subject. I never could argue with this man. His unshakeable convictions and his twisted logic did not permit it. His approach always infuriated me, even as it tapped into my insecurities. Nothing has changed. I tremble with the effort of controlling my temper. I want to lash out and pummel his horrible face. Breathe, Suzanne, I tell myself. I inhale and exhale. He will not get to me.

"Why did you really summon me, Victor? Comeuppance?"

"Comeuppance? I've already forfeited everything: my business, my sons, my mistress, my fingers, even a part of my face. Why would I want another confrontation with you at this point?"

"Didn't you invite me here to tell me something about Daniel's death?"

"I didn't invite you here at all. As for Daniel's death, the thought of it stings, if you must know. I simply had no choice."

I step back, confused. "Wait, you're saying you did kill him?"

"I had him killed. The distinction is merely a technicality. What could I do? First the incident with the human trafficking—"

"The dead girl from the ship that belonged to Francesco Guzman. Your second identity."

He flashed his disagreeable smile again. "You're up to date. Daniel was responsible for the debacle with the girl. Then the fool tried to get back into my good graces by attempting to kill you. An idiotic move."

The puzzle pieces fall into place, all but one.

"Then why did you send the box of chocolates to Michael? The text to me, claiming you hadn't killed Daniel but you knew who had? The invitation to meet?"

"I didn't send those things."

"Who did?"

"I did."

We turn to look at the woman standing in the foyer. I judge her to be perhaps sixty. She is, in a word, stunning: tall, slender, and thoroughly elegant. Her dark, shoulder-length hair falls around a face barely touched by time. She could pass for a model with her blue-black eyes, white skin, straight nose, full lips, and high cheekbones. She's even dressed like one. Her charcoal slacks are complimented by a lightweight poncho in gray and red worn over a white silk turtleneck. A thin silver bracelet encircles one wrist; simple earrings twinkle at her lobes.

She's perfectly put together, right down to the .22 LR NAA Sidewinder she points at us. The gun is small, relatively lightweight, and almost old-fashioned in appearance. Not the most accurate weapon at a distance, but she's moved closer.

Luisa Guzman.

"How did you get in, Luisa? Where are my men?"

"Disabled, Victor. Or dead. No one feels threatened by an old woman, do they? And no one expects a Taser. I may have set it too high, though." She shrugs and turns to me. "You must be Susan Smith. No, it's Suzanne Foster. Excuse me for eavesdropping. I simply wanted confirmation that he killed Daniel. And I have it."

She seems too composed for a person who's learned the father of her son had him killed. Her voice is smooth, her accent light. It produces an almost heady sensation, like a fine wine drunk too quickly.

"I assume you came by yourself," she says, nodding at me. "Victor always said you were inclined to work alone. If not, I would guess you've kept your people at a distance. Just in case, I have your mother as collateral."

"My mother?"

"Luisa, I'm so glad—"

"Don't say a word, Victor. I am here to kill you. She is here to watch. I can grant her that bit of satisfaction before I end her life as well."

Luisa walks all the way into the room and looks around the corner. The light makes more apparent both her beauty and her pain. This woman has suffered greatly.

"Stand together, please. By the fireplace."

Neither of us moves.

"Where do you have my mother?" I ask.

"You are just like him, aren't you? Obstinate, unyielding, demanding. Your mother is fine, Suzanne. My brother Gabriel is entertaining her. If all goes as planned, she will have a nice vacation before returning home to news of her daughter's death."

"Luisa, you can't do this."

"Please, Victor, stop. I can do anything. Put up with years of neglect and disrespect. Love a man without a heart.

Live with the death of my eldest because, like you, I blamed her. Although it appears I should have blamed your preoccupation with her."

She swings the gun back and forth between me and Kemp.

"What I can't live with is the death of my remaining son at your hands, Victor. Or perhaps you had your man Dyukov do it. I think that is what happened. Which is why I had Lucas take care of him. I believe he chose the punishment to fit the crime." She giggles.

"Your nephew? That psychopath? What did he do to Arkady? Answer me."

Kemp is so deeply flushed, I wonder if he might have a heart attack and die before she has a chance to shoot him.

"I see you have some feelings to spare for at least one of your employees. As well you should. He was, after all, your dedicated servant to the end. What did Lucas do? The kind of job you've no doubt asked of Arkady Dyukov many times. My nephew has his peculiarities and his predilections, I'll grant you. But he knows the meaning of loyalty."

The hand holding the gun wavers. Luisa is nervous. Despite Kemp's frailty, he frightens her. She looks away from his murderous gaze and addresses me.

"This is what we put up with all these years, didn't we? This monster who turned you and me into collaborators and my sons into pawns."

Her arm is definitely wobbling. It's not just fear. She's not used to holding a gun, even a light one.

"Luisa, listen to me." I want to reason with her, presuming she isn't beyond all reason.

Her mouth opens to reply. It's open when Kemp shoots her with a handgun he's pulled from under a table. Before

284

she's hit the floor, he's trained it on me. He kicks the small weapon out of Luisa's lifeless hand without looking down.

"Damn it. Arkady was one of my best men. Lucas will pay dearly for this." He narrows his eyes at me. "Why do you look so disapproving?"

"She gave you most of her adult life. Yet you just stepped over her as if she were a spot on the floor."

"Please, spare me. Luisa meant a great deal to me. She fathered my sons. She may have loved me. She also betrayed me. This was her choice. Nevertheless, I will mourn her."

He peers at me with surprise. "You're shocked," he notes. "Yes, you are. There are many ways to express passion. Luisa wore her heart on her sleeve. But you? I couldn't believe you'd fallen in love with your teacher. Or that you were even capable of such feelings. You hide everything. Well, almost everything. You traffic in a sort of moral outrage you put on display when it suits you. A bit hypocritical, considering how many lives you've taken."

He walks closer to me. His amusement shifts to anger.

"You've always displayed a sort of priggishness, Suzanne. Do you realize that? You sit in judgment of others as well as yourself. You pretend detachment. You imagine yourself removed. As if you were above the sordid business of death. As if you're better than the rest of us. That was always one of your shortcomings. It's why you could never look your victims in the face. Why you preferred long-distance killing."

I want to shut my ears against the torrent of words. "Did you bring me here to lecture me, Victor?"

"As I told you, I didn't bring you here at all. This was Luisa's doing from the beginning. The scheme had merit, I admit. Locate you in your safe house. Locate me in the south of France. Bring us together for the dramatic finale. Use her brother and nephew for support and backup. Use your mother as collateral."

"You knew all along?"

"Every plan has holes in it. I found out about the text Frederick Weber received threatening him with blackmail. Not because he told me, which he should have done, but because I monitor the phones of my employees. The lawyer will be punished accordingly." His face grows momentarily dark. "There's also the matter of his relationship with my older son. Well, never mind. I shall deal with it." He sounds almost cheerful.

"Victor, do you know where my mother is?" I try not to plead.

"The box was a nice touch, I must admit. So was the text. No one ever thinks to verify such things. Et voilà. Here we are. As for your mother, she is, as Luisa told you, close by. They've rented a lovely villa just outside Nice. Gabriel may be waiting for his sister's call. Perhaps Lucas has gone to help. How I would love to take them all out. Maybe I still can."

The pale eyes are ice and fire now.

"You're still wondering how Luisa found your mother, how she connected a writer of lowbrow fiction to the former assassin. The answer is simple; I told her long ago. We even shared a laugh about it. You see, I've always known who you are, Suzanne Brooks, unloved daughter of the untalented Morris Greenbaum and the unstoppable Betty Brooks. Mo and Lisette. Two faux San Francisco artistes bent on reinvention. Did you think I wouldn't make it my business to learn everything I could about the lonely sharpshooter with the missing past and made-up name?"

He steps so close I inhale the foul odor coming off him. I see images of rot and decay. Hell must smell like this.

He shoves the gun under my chin and whispers in my ear, "You vex me, Suzanne. I can't decide whether to kill you here or take you to where Gabriel holds your mother. Are you two close these days? Do you care if she dies in front of you?"

I let my eyes flick over his right shoulder as if tracking a movement. It's the oldest trick in the book, yet he allows it to distract him. I drive both fists straight up between us, forcing his gun hand to the ceiling. The barrel just misses the side of my face. My luck holds; it doesn't discharge as it falls to the floor. I drop my hand to his chest to stab him with a tiny syringe I've had tucked inside my wide fabric bracelet the entire time. When I first got to Kemp's door, I lifted my hands into the air like a cooperative guest. The careless guards who searched my body failed to check my extremities. Rookie mistake.

The poison takes effect almost immediately. His body sags. I grab his arms as his body goes limp and pull him close, ignoring the odor of imminent death. I shake him; I force those dimming ice eyes to focus. Then I deliver my message.

"You never thought I could handle close killing, did you, Victor? You were wrong. I will look into your eyes, and I will watch you die."

Chapter Thirty-Six

Charlie burst in through the front door to find Suzanne standing quietly above the lifeless bodies of Victor Kemp and Luisa Guzman.

"Are you okay?" he demanded. "I couldn't get off a clean shot. I heard everything, though. I feel as if I'd been listening to a damned soap opera."

Suzanne removed her earring, which held a tiny microphone. Yet another device the doomed guards overlooked. She looked around.

"Where's Simon?"

"Here." Brian's nephew walked in from the dining room, his rifle at his side. "Thank God you're all right," he continued. "I wasn't sure what was going on in here."

"Where are the guards?"

"Luisa used her Taser on two of them. I found the third man by the pool, knifed in the back."

"Lucas did that. Luisa's nephew." Suzanne grabbed Charlie's arm. "Someone has my mother. Luisa's brother. Gabriel. We have to find her, Charlie."

"I know where she is. We're about twenty kilometers away. Simon will drive."

"How do you know? Forget it, tell me on the way." She swayed on her feet.

Charlie took her arm. "First, I need you to slow down for a minute. Do that breathing thing you do. Come on."

She did as he asked. Some of the tension seemed to drain away. "What about the bodies?" she asked

"I called in some favors. It's covered. Let's go."

The Audi was parked in a nearby driveway that conveniently lacked a security camera. They tossed their weapons in the car and jumped in. Suzanne angled her body so she could see Charlie in the back seat. He noticed her color was returning along with her characteristic calm demeanor.

"Do you think Lucas called Gabriel with instructions to kill my mother?" she asked him.

"Unlikely. Gabriel Guzman's not cut out to be a killer, although he has a deep attachment to his sister. How deep, I can't say, nor can I vouch for what he's willing to do. He's devoted to her. And to his own son, the nephew, who is supposed to be a borderline psychopath. Delightful family, that one."

"But what if Lucas told his father about Luisa's death? That might set Gabriel off."

Charlie leaned forward and put a hand on her shoulder. "They want you, Suzanne. That's always been the plan. Your mother is more valuable alive. As bait." He nodded for emphasis.

"How much of a head start does Lucas have?"

"It won't matter. Simon knows a shortcut that doesn't show up on the maps. That should get us there before or at the same time. There's something else, though."

"What?"

Simon looked at Charlie in the rear-view mirror. "You might as well tell her."

"Tell me what?"

Charlie cleared his throat. "Ah, well, it seems Brian is also in the area."

~

After Michael received his mother's instructions, he set about locating Lisette. According to her personal representative, his grandmother had gone off with a mysterious Latin lover she'd met poolside. The representative recommended he call Lisette's travel agency. There, Michael had more luck. Although they didn't arrange the vacation, they followed their client's request to do some follow-up to ensure the accommodations her "friend" booked were satisfactory. They had an address.

Michael called Lisette's condominium on a hunch to inquire about visitors and staff. The gossipy concierge recalled the man who worked at the pool in January as "unusually attentive" to Ms. Brooks.

"She didn't seem to mind. He was older but good-looking."

"I don't suppose he still works there?"

"No, he left. Just about the time Ms. Brooks went on vacation, come to think of it. You can draw your own conclusions."

Before disconnecting, Michael got a name. Gabriel Silva.

He prepared to text the information to his mother. Something made him hesitate before pressing "send." Great, he thought. Now I'm infected with spidey sense.

Instead, he called his father and filled him in on his research activities.

"Well done, son. I can understand why your mother might be concerned, what with all the strain she's under."

"Should I go ahead and text her?"

"Why don't you hold off for now? It's entirely likely Lisette is simply off having a good time. We'll let your mother know tomorrow night."

Brian disconnected with his son and immediately called his chief. He filled Tenant in on his fears about Lisette. He held back that his wife was on her way to the south of France for a personal confrontation with Kemp.

"Does Suzanne know Kemp has her mother?" Tenant asked.

"No."

How easy it was to shade the truth, he thought. His wife doesn't know this; his son doesn't know that; he denies his boss another piece of information. Brian put those thoughts aside and pushed ahead.

"Look, Chief, what I'm about to ask will put you in a difficult position."

"What do you need from me?"

"Your private plane."

At 8:00 a.m. the following morning, Brian boarded a Cessna 172s Skyhawk out of Heathrow. He carried a small locked case. He'd hoped to leave Heathrow hours earlier, but a horrific accident on the M4 had put him behind. Then he had to jump through hoops at the airport because of the absence of a flight plan.

Though a licensed pilot, he hadn't flown in ten years, a fact he hadn't mentioned to Tenant when he asked to borrow his superior's plane. He guessed the man knew that, just as he probably knew Brian wouldn't be filing a flight plan. Fortunately, not much had changed with the Cessna in a decade. It really was like riding a bicycle.

He landed at Nice at 11:00 a.m. local time, picked up a rental car, and drove out of the city. Along a quiet road, he pulled over. He removed his Walther and holster from the case, checked and sighted the pistol, then placed it on the seat next to him. Locked and loaded, as the Americans said.

He lifted a slightly flattened sandwich out of the case and wolfed it down. He'd found it on his gun case with a note that said simply "safe travels." Kate, he reckoned. The girl knew more than she let on.

The villa he sought was listed in Gairaut, a suburb of Nice north of the city. Like most of the homes in the area, it was behind an old wall and off a private road. Considering how densely populated the area was, it seemed quite isolated. Brian stood two streets away and lifted a pair of high-powered binoculars. From what he could tell, the place was quite modern with so many windows the structure seemed to be made entirely of glass. That might be an advantage, providing both ingress and a view into the house.

Rather than navigate the narrow roads, he decided to leave his car down the hill and hike the two kilometers back to the house on the hill. He expected to encounter security guards, police, or even dogs as he walked along roads marked "privée," but he arrived at the address without incident just at noon. He entered, staying close to the low wall, took up a position behind a shrub, and texted Charlie.

~

Gabriel paced nervously. Luisa had promised to call by 12:30. He kept watching his phone while trying to appear happy in the old woman's company. He had to promise an afternoon of lovemaking to keep her in the house. She wanted to see an exhibit or go shopping or parade around Nice with a younger man. He didn't care about any of it. He was sick of her, sick of pretending to enjoy her company. He wanted to leave. He wanted his beloved Luisa.

The phone rang at 12:45.

"We've had a change of plans, Gabriel. You must do exactly as I say."

"Lucas? Where are you? Where is Luisa?"

"I'll be there shortly, *Papà*. I'll explain everything to you then. Meanwhile, you must continue to behave as if all is well. Do you understand?"

"Let me talk with Luisa. I need to talk with her."

"Stay calm, Father. Do you hear me? And stay away from the windows."

He hung up.

~

We make good time. Then the Audi breaks down outside a modern-looking hospital called Clinical St. Georges in the hills north of Nice. Charlie has brought us as promised to within two kilometers of the villa via an unmarked road that has lead us to the highway and then this exit. We pull up, forced by pedestrian traffic to actually stop at the stop sign. The car returns the favor by shutting itself off. Nothing Simon tries can persuade it to start again.

"Shit," he yells. "I think it's the fuel line!"

Charlie adds several other creative curses. "We can't wait for help. We need to—"

Before he finishes speaking, I grab the rifle case and jump out of the passenger side. "Simon, Charlie," I call out, "go on foot. I'll track you from here."

Simon sprints away, fast as a jackrabbit. I know he will cover the distance in a few minutes. Charlie sends off a text to Brian, plants a quick kiss on my cheek, and whispers, "Good hunting, lassie." Then he takes off, slower than Simon but steady.

I look for a structure with some height to it.

Across from the clinic sits a nondescript apartment building with an open roof. I race over and press every buzzer. It's so common as to be almost a prank. It works, though. Someone buzzes me in. I ignore the lift and take five flights two stairs at a time. I don't hear any alarms go off when I push open the door to the roof.

I drop and crawl to the side of the building that faces away from the clinic to the north and west. From this position, I can see up the boulevard to the back of the white mansion whose picture Charlie showed me in the car. It sits higher than the others and is exactly as he described, an odd mix of Southern France and Southern California.

I assemble the L115 Simon brought for me along with an adjustable bipod. At least I know the weapon. I fiddle briefly with the knobs on the scope to tweak for the uphill shot angle and wind speed, which seems to vary from moment to moment. I still have to factor in ground temperature, humidity, and even the curve of the earth. I don't have time for fine-tuning. I don't even know if the rifle has been properly zeroed.

I can't recall ever working under so much pressure, even during my years with Victor Kemp. Then again, I never had so much at stake as I do at this moment.

Through the scope, I look at the back of the house. Good God, it seems to be made of glass. The many windows reveal little. Nothing moves except a palm frond. I focus on a tree by the pool. Using the scope's optics, I run some quick calculations in my head and my breath catches in my throat.

The house, the tree, and whichever humans come into view in the next few minutes have at least one thing in common. They are all about 2,050 meters away. More than a mile and a quarter.

~

Brian's position at the side of the property gave him a decent vantage point. He'd been observing Lisette and Gabriel for the better part of an hour. At first, they seemed companionable, even affectionate. Two mature people on vacation along the Côte d'Azure. He had his first look at Suzanne's mother. A slender woman, she seemed as light as air with her gauzy blouse, her flowing skirt, and her pale hair. Brian sensed she was far less fragile than her appearance suggested.

He knew Luisa Guzman's brother from surveillance photos. Gabriel Guzman was movie-star handsome. He wasn't relaxed, at least not today. He glanced at his watch; he looked out the window. He kept picking up and putting down his phone. Then it rang.

There was no disguising the man's agitation after he disconnected. He walked out of the kitchen and paced the patio. Lisette came out to join him, lightly touching his arm. He pulled away angrily. Trouble in paradise, Brian thought.

Twenty minutes later, a small gray Nissan pulled up the driveway. No security barred the way, possibly because the house was essentially a full-time rental. The driver jumped out and strode around to the back to the pool area. Tall, broad-shouldered, black-haired, mid-thirties: Luisa's nephew and Gabriel's son. Lucas.

Gabriel caught sight of the younger man and immediately began to talk, a voluble outpouring of pent-up emotions. They spoke in Portuguese, a language Brian understood. He edged forward, realizing he'd be able to hear just fine. Gabriel was yelling. Lucas had to raise his voice to match his father's.

"What the hell is going on, Lucas? Where is she? Where is Luisa?"

"Has anyone shown up here? Or called?" The younger man swiveled his head this way and that, his eyes narrowed. Brian flattened himself against the grass.

"Lucas! Goddammit, answer me."

Lisette came out on the porch. She looked confused and nervous.

"Gabriel, what's wrong? Who is this?"

The men ignored her.

"She's dead, Gabriel," Lucas said. "There was nothing I could do. Kemp killed her. The son of a bitch shot her in cold blood."

Gabriel began to wail. Lucas slapped him across the face. Lisette gasped. Even Brian flinched.

"Shut up, damn it. She's gone. We can't bring her back."

Lucas looked around again, grabbed Lisette by the elbow, and shoved her at his father.

"Take her. Others are coming. I'll deal with as many as I can. For now, think of this woman as your hostage. Keeping her alive is our way out." He handed his father a revolver and pulled a second weapon from his waistband. Then he crept around to the front, just passing but not noticing Brian. He crouched, facing the street, and pointed his gun in the direction of the driveway.

Gabriel pulled Lisette back into the house. Brian had a decision to make.

~

Simon got to his destination in under five minutes. He imagined Charlie would take another three or four, but he wasn't sure they had that much time. The gray Nissan that tore past him, forcing him off the road, had been heading for the house on the hill. He'd caught a glimpse of a hard-faced man behind the wheel. Lucas Guzman.

As he approached, Simon heard yelling. Then it ceased altogether. He paused to catch his breath and assess the situation. Lucas might be expecting a carload of people or individuals on foot. Dropping to his knees, he risked a peek over the low wall. The Nissan was haphazardly abandoned almost at the front door. No sign of Lucas, his father, or Suzanne's mother. Or Brian.

He backed away and followed the stone barrier. It extended a few meters before joining a much higher barbed-wire fence obscured by greenery. Clever. He'd have to go in the front.

From his position near the driveway, Lucas rose into a half crouch. If they were arriving one at a time on foot, he thought, his job would be that much simpler. He raised his arm to shoot the intruder. The cold barrel at his right temple stopped him.

"Don't move."

He did move, as Brian anticipated. Lucas swung away and to the right, expecting to knock a gun out of his adversary's hand as he shot the man. The object Lucas knocked aside was a steel cylinder, a simple piece of metal connected to nothing. The shot that killed him came from the gun in Brian's left hand. The violet eyes opened wide. Otherwise, Lucas barely had time to register that he'd been duped before he died.

Brian signaled to Simon, and they ran to the back of the house just as Gabriel began yelling hysterically in Portuguese and English. Rounding the corner, they saw him at the edge of the pool, a pistol to Lisette's head.

"Gabriel, wait." Brian spoke in Portuguese. "We can talk. Look, I'll put my gun down." He made as if to lower his weapon. Simon tried to edge out of the gunman's line of sight.

"Stop. Get back. You've killed them, haven't you? All of them. All of you."

The man sounded half out of his mind. He kept his gun on his hostage. His finger rested on the trigger.

Suddenly, Lisette's hand went to her chest. She slumped in Gabriel's arms, her head lolling. She seemed to lose consciousness.

Good Christ, Brian thought. Was she having a heart attack?

Gabriel continued to rant, even as he struggled with Lisette's limp body. "I will not die before I make sure you all go to hell," he screamed. "All of you. I will see to it—"

All at once, he came to a dead stop. His face registered an interested sort of surprise. He dropped Lisette to the ground and followed her down, a neat round hole in his forehead. Simon and Brian looked at each other, astonished, just as Charlie puffed his way into the yard.

"Lisette!" Brian yelled. He ran towards the older woman, expecting to see blood or worse. Blood would at least mean she was alive. For the moment.

She was already back on her feet, not a scratch on her. She stared not at the body of the man who betrayed her but at a point in the distance, down the hill and toward the sea.

She smiled, raised her hand, and waved.

Epilogue

The latter part of May carries a risk of thunderstorms along the Welsh coastline. This month has, in fact, been unusually wet and cold. Fortunately, today graces us with a hint of warmth. A strong sun beams down from a dazzling cobalt sky, clear but for a few billowy gray clouds glued to the horizon. Even the wind has died down. The Bristol Channel sparkles as if dressed for a party.

Wrapped in a voluminous wool shawl, I'm enjoying the view. Two years earlier, on this very spot, I sat with a gun pressed to the side of my head. Today is quite the improvement.

Nearly three months have passed since I killed the man I hated and feared more than anyone else in the world. Those last moments still replay on a loop in my brain but less frequently every day. I regret many actions and many deaths but not that one. I am grateful I managed to do what my enemy believed until his last breath I would never be able to do.

That same day, I also got off a shot that would probably smash quite a few records if it were ever made public. It never will be. When Simon, Brian, Charlie, and Lisette came back down the hill to pick me up—an ordinary, middle-aged woman standing at the curb with an odd-shaped bag over one shoulder—they couldn't stop talking. Until Lisette shushed them all by stating the obvious.

"I don't know what you're all going on about. She was never going to miss. She's my daughter."

I enveloped her in a hug. The gesture surprised us both; I dropped my arms. Nothing comes easy, I thought. Not a life or death calculation nor a relationship with one's mother.

"Your faked faint was exquisitely timed," I told her.

My mother laughed, which got the rest of them going. How we must have looked, five foreigners laughing on a street corner. Passersby smiled, imagining our vacation was going well. They had no idea.

I feel a hand on my shoulder. I don't flinch, though. I know that hand.

"What are you doing out here, Suzie? Don't you need to get ready?"

"I'm dressed," I reassure my husband, opening my shawl to show him the Aegean blue silk sheath I'm wearing. "Just have to change shoes." I point to my Wellies with a laugh.

Brian comes around to sit beside me and takes my hand. "I hope you're not nervous."

"With current and former spies swarming the place? Brian, I've never felt safer."

"That's not what I mean, Suzanne. Are you having mother of the bride jitters?"

I turn to my handsome husband. He's dressed in a pearl gray suit. It brings out the silver in his hair, which is more pronounced, I realize. Time marches on. We're getting older.

"But we're alive," Brian says aloud, as if he could read my mind. "And our son is getting married today."

Michael caught us by surprise when he asked if he and Kate might marry here.

"So soon, Michael?" I asked. "And here?"

"We don't see the point in waiting. Life is for the living, right? Don't worry about pulling it together. Kate's mum is made for this kind of planning. As for having a separate ceremony here, it seems fitting. It's where we came together as a family. I love it here."

He looks directly into my eyes, a purposeful young man. I see in his handsome face the generations that went before and those yet to come.

"Think of it as coming full circle, Mum. Or maybe it's closure. Either way; take your pick. Kate approves."

Kate approves. I've accepted the idea that my almost daughter-in-law understands a great deal about the family she's joining. I don't know where she stores that knowledge, or where my son does. I'm still struggling with reconciling my past with my present and my future. As a concession to today, I've stuffed all of it into a mental box labeled "unpleasantries." I will visit it again; of that I have no doubt.

Full circle. Closure. Either one.

We've invited perhaps twenty-five people, including Brian's sister Juliette and nephew Jules, whose brood numbers five. Simon will also be present, as will Grayson Tenant, Charlie Campbell, and Annie Westcott, along with their respective spouses. Kate and Michael's closest friends make up the balance. We've brought everyone up by bus.

Later in the day, we'll all return to London. There's a larger church service and reception this evening. Black and white, very sophisticated. Everyone seems perfectly fine with the arrangements. These days, two ceremonies are all the rage for those who can manage the logistics, not to mention the finances. We've decided we will manage.

"Is everything all right?" Maggie Edgerton calls to us from the top of the stone steps. The young designer who created my outfit has also created Maggie's dress, a subtle shade of sapphire that perfectly suits her shapely figure and still-red hair. On her head is a small head piece, a fancy, as the British like to call them. She's wearing sensible heels; we'll be on damp grass when Michael and Kate take their vows out of doors. Once again, I throw out my thanks to whatever forces brought us this sublime weather.

"We're fine. Just coming up."

My mother appears at Maggie's side. Her white-blonde hair is cut short, flattering her remarkably unlined face. She wears a vivid shade of royal blue. There's nothing subtle about the color choice or about her dress. The fitted crepe dress has a deeply asymmetrical neckline. The material gathers at one hip and falls in gentle folds. I've never seen a woman over twenty-five in heels as high as the ones she wears. Like Maggie, she is wearing a fancy. Hers is exceptionally ornate and adds another two inches to her height. Somehow, she pulls it off.

"She looks as if she's about to set sail," Brian whispers. I choke back my laughter.

"Suzanne, what on earth are you doing?" my mother yells. "Come up here and change your shoes. The guests are starting to arrive." Lisette speaks like the mother of a young child rather than a middle-aged woman who is about to see her own grown son wed. She's the mother I never had. The mother I now have.

I stand and face the bay. In just half an hour, we will gather at the bottom of the ancient steps that lead up the steep hill to the stone cottage, the sea at our backs. The wedding party will descend: Kate's cousin Amy as maid of honor, Widgy escorting his mother, and my son, who not six months ago lay near death. Then the glorious bride, dressed in a pale blue confection of silk organza and seed pearls, will appear on the arm of her father. These people will be part of my family going forward. The very idea swells my heart.

We'll do it all again in London, but this ceremony is the one I will hold close to my heart. I will mark every detail and note every moment of joy. The bad memories, when they escape from their temporary prison, will at least have competition.

I take Brian's hand and move to the stairs. "Let's go marry our son, shall we?"

~ End ~

About the Author

Nikki Stern is the author of two non-fiction books, *Because I Say So* and *Hope in Small Doses*, an Eric Hoffer medal finalist for books that "provoke, inspire, or redirect thought." Eight of her short stories have been published in various online literary journals. Her essays have appeared in *The New York Times*, *USA Today*, *Newsweek,* and *Humanist Magazine,* as well as three anthologies.

Nikki has just completed the first in a series of mystery/science fiction novels about an unorthodox crime fighter named Samantha Tate.

For more, please visit nikkistern.com

Made in the USA
Columbia, SC
16 April 2018